IN HER
SIGHTS

IN HER SIGHTS

ROBIN PERINI

The characters and events portrayed in this book are fictitious. Any similarity to real persons, living or dead, is coincidental and not intended by the author.

Published by Montlake Romance
P.O. Box 400818
Las Vegas, NV 89140

ISBN-13: 9781612181523
ISBN-10: 161218152X

Dedication

In loving memory of my grandmothers, Gennie Carder and Hazel Perini Brown—to fulfill a very special promise. Their belief in me never faltered; their confidence in me never faded; their faith in me never wavered. My love and gratitude for them is never-ending.

Prologue

Seventeen Years Ago

She hurt too much to cry.

At the slam of the screen door, Jane burrowed her head under her lanky arms. Her ten-year-old body shrank beneath the lopsided kitchen table, its cheap pine scarred and rotten with age. Her heart pounded as she swallowed down the sobs. Quiet. She must be quiet. Mama said so.

Slowly she closed her eyes and let her mind drift to another place, the safe place she visited when things got too bad. Her body floated on the cool water in her dreams. Protected, safe.

For a fleeting moment, the pain went away.

Please, don't let him come back.

As if in answer to her prayer, the heavy footsteps didn't cross the scuffed linoleum toward her. Instead, they lumbered down the front porch. A loud tumble followed by a sharp curse echoed through the rickety shack she and her mother called home.

When the diesel engine cranked to life, Jane gulped back the relief.

He'd left. For now.

"Mama?" She barely recognized the muffled whisper through her bruised and swollen lips. With a groan she tried to sit up, but the second she raised her head, sharp pain scissored through her arms and legs. She fell back with a whimper and fought to stop a scream from escaping her. Mama would cry, and he'd hurt them enough tonight.

"I'm sorry...I tried to stop him, Mama. I tried to do my job."

The wind beat against the gray wood walls, and she could almost feel the house sway around her. She waited for the soft shuffle of her mother's footsteps to pad down the hallway. Tonight would be better than most. The whiskey bottles were empty. *He* was gone.

She shoved her hair out of her face and blinked against the darkening of the room. The aches had settled to a dull throb. Gingerly Jane straightened and rose, her eyes squinting as she eased down the hallway. "Mama?"

One step, then another, then another.

Her feet slipped on something wet and cold and dark. She stumbled forward. Her mother lay at a strange angle on the floor, her blond hair plastered against her head, stained red with blood.

"Mama!" Jane fell to her knees. "Mama?"

She barely recognized her mother's face, one eye nearly swollen closed, her cheek multi-colored black and purple.

Her mother's eyelids flickered. "Jane?"

She tugged at her nightgown, using the thin cotton to wipe away the blood oozing from her mother's injuries, but they kept bleeding. "What can I do, Mama? What?"

A gurgling sound echoed from her mother's chest. "Too late."

"No!"

"Shh." Her mother's voice was a bare whisper, and Jane leaned forward, her ear right next to her mother's lips.

"It's okay. Better this way." She tugged in another shallow breath. "Leave. Do what we planned. Change who you are."

Jane fell against her mother's breast, the red blood soaking the polyester that her mother had pretended was silk. "I can't."

"You will." The words were so quiet. Her mother raised a hand and gripped Jane's chin. "Don't be like me. Be strong, like the jasmine growing in the windowsill. Never count on anyone."

A gasp for air shook her mother's broken body. The deathly cold fingers tightened, hurting Jane's bruised jaw. "Never let them inside...your heart."

Her mother shuddered. Her hand dropped, and the wheezing from her chest went silent.

Her eyes stayed open.

Trembling, Jane hauled her mother's hand back to her chin.

"Mama, please. Wake up," she whispered.

But tug after tug wouldn't wake her. And Jane knew.

She scooted away, huddling in the corner of her mother's bedroom, splinters digging into her heels, until the final rays of sun sliced through the window's blinds. "I'm sorry, Mama. I tried to protect you. I tried. But he was too strong."

She buried her face in her arms. She didn't move. Didn't weep. A chill wrapped around her heart.

She hurt too much to cry.

Chapter One

The trigger felt right.

The sight was zeroed in, the balance perfect. The Remington 700/40 fit her body and her mind like an old friend she could trust, and Jasmine "Jazz" Parker didn't trust easily. But she and this rifle were connected in a way a lover, friend, or family could never be. The Remington would never let her down.

The only hitch—she didn't have an ideal shot at the kidnapper. Not yet, anyway.

Sweat beaded her brow in the Colorado midmorning sun. Without taking her gaze from her target, she wiped away the perspiration. Every second counted, and she had to stay ready. Negotiations had fallen apart hours ago and the ending seemed inevitable. To save the governor's daughter, Jazz would excise the five-year-old girl's captor.

Jazz shifted, relieving the pressure against her knees, the stiffness in her hips, but the rifle remained steady. She centered her sight on the small break in the window.

Having focused through the high-powered Leupold scope for hours, she waited for an opportunity for the scumbag's blond head to move into range. They all made a mistake sooner or later. His face or the back of his head, she didn't care, but she needed a clear shot through to

1

the medulla oblongata. The kill had to be clean; the man had to crumple with no time to think and no reflex to pull the trigger.

"Blue Four, have you acquired the target?"

The question came through her earpiece loud and clear, but she spoke quietly into the microphone. "Negative."

"Blue Two, what is target's position?"

"Zone Two, pacing. He's carrying the girl, a gun at her head, a Bowie on the southeast corner table. He's nervous, unpredictable."

Jazz could trust Gabe Montgomery's assessment of the situation. He, unlike his brother, Luke, she could count on. And what was Luke doing in her head anyway? Now was *not* the time to be thinking about the one guy she should never have let near her.

"Blue Two to Blue Leader." Gabe's voice filtered through the communications system. "He's on the move again. Going toward Zone One. I repeat. He's headed to Zone One."

Jazz's body froze in readiness. He was coming her way. If Blue Leader ordered the guys to rush the house, she had to be on her game. She *would* protect them. She wouldn't fail.

The blinds fluttered. Jazz forced her breathing into a comfortable, familiar pattern. "Blue Leader, this is Blue Four. I see movement."

A blond head peered out, face straight on front, the area between nose and teeth in clear view.

"Target acquired. It's a good shot."

"Can you see the girl?"

"He's got a gun to her head."

Only a second passed before the expected order came through.

"Take the shot, Blue Four."

"Ten-four, Blue Leader."

Slowly, deliberately, Jazz exhaled and, between heartbeats, squeezed the trigger.

Luke Montgomery ducked through the door of the bar, closing out the last hints of sunset behind him. He hated not knowing his enemy's identity, but hc would adapt. His Army Ranger unit had always been ready for an ambush. Five years in special ops had made him suspicious of most. On that last mission, though…even Luke had been taken in.

Not again. Never again.

He shifted his shoulder, the stiffness and scarring a permanent reminder of how close a bullet had come to sending him home from Afghanistan in a body bag. Lesson learned. Except for his family, Luke assumed everyone was lying. Tonight would be no different.

He kept to the shadows, studying the surroundings for potential threats and quick exits. He preferred covert operations, but stealth wasn't an option here. Even he couldn't blend his six-feet-four-inch frame in this cracker box. Though he hadn't set foot in the joint in a couple of years, too many people would recognize him.

A sharp rap of the cue ball hitting its target echoed like a gunshot over the raucous laughter. Nope, Sammy's Bar hadn't changed. Neither had the clientele.

Cops. And some of them were on the take. How many guns would turn on him if they knew he was after one of their own? It didn't matter. His informant had risked her life coming to him. She didn't want her son forced into the world of organized crime. Luke understood the need to protect a child all too well. He'd get Grace and her son out, and bring down the bastards. Not only the criminals who threatened her, but also the cops who enabled them.

He searched the room as if he were casing the streets of Kabul for concealed insurgents. Colorado wasn't Afghanistan, but his mission was almost identical. Ferret out the liars. As an investigative journalist, he just did it with a pen these days instead of an assault rifle.

Acutely focused on his surroundings, he stepped into the light and waited, patience something he'd learned the hard way in the field. The hum of whispers started soft then grew louder. Most everyone in the bar turned toward him. Excellent. He scanned the new faces and recognized one that definitely interested him. Sheriff Tower's son, Brian. Luke's intel hinted that the corruption went all the way to the top. How ironic if he ended up using an Internal Affairs cop in the sheriff's office to get to the rotten core. And what better way to get at the father than through the son.

Luke stalked his target at the far end of the bar and slid onto the stool next to him, adjusting his position to create a clear view of the entrance while minimizing his blind side. "Cola," he said to the bartender. "Straight."

Tower snorted and sipped amber liquid from his shot glass. "Sure you don't need some ice to water it down?"

"You got a problem?" Luke said. Tower's eyes were bloodshot and glazed over. Good. Lowered inhibitions made Luke's job that much easier.

"What are you doing here, Montgomery? Slumming with the boys in blue? Don't you military types stay to yourselves?"

"Ex-military. I'm a civilian, and it's a free country. Thought I'd catch a game of pool. Join me?" Luke nodded to the table that had just come open.

"Nah." Tower swirled his glass. "I'm having a party of my own right here."

"Celebrating?"

"You could say that."

A shout blasted through the bar's door, and a group of men shoved into the room led by none other than Luke's brother. "The blue team beat the bad guys this morning. We've been waiting all day for this." Gabe's exclamation boomed over the bar's chatter. A hearty cheer sounded. "Line 'em up, barkeep."

Great. His brother wouldn't be happy Luke had infiltrated Gabe's favorite bar. Luke stroked his jaw. Might as well prepare for the punch that would come later.

Tower lowered his head, a sly smile tilting the corners of his mouth. A tingle vibrated in Luke's temple, an alarm he'd learned the hard way not to ignore. Something was definitely up with the guy. Maybe his source had been right after all.

Glasses clinked as the SWAT team members piled into the bar. "Wait a minute," Gabe said. "Where's Jazz?"

The second Luke heard her name, he couldn't fight the urge to watch for her. He surveyed the room then lasered on the bar's entrance. A flash of blond glinted in the dim light and a tall, lithe frame filled the doorway. He knew that silhouette well, from the generous curve of her breasts, to the narrow waist, to the slim but strong legs that could hold him...Damn, if he let his mind travel any farther he'd need a cold shower. She did look good, though. Better than the academy photo he'd stared at all day on CNN.

He'd spent too much time thinking about her today after avoiding her for the past two years. They'd replayed the story of her precision shot and the rescue of the governor's daughter over and over. His editor, sucked into the idea of a female sniper as much as the rest of the country, had tacked on the human interest assignment to Luke's already full investigative plate. Just because he knew Jasmine. Now she was here. Much too close for his own sanity.

He'd have to talk to her. Soon. He forced his attention back to Tower, who'd gone rigid in his chair.

"Let's hear it for Jazz!" Gabe called out.

A roar of applause rocked the bar.

"Yeah, right," Tower muttered into his drink.

"You got a problem with her too?"

Tower slanted a disgusted look toward the doorway. "Parker's got female quota written all over her. She doesn't belong."

The swarm of SWAT bodies concealed Luke's presence, so he took the opportunity to study Jasmine. With stiff movements, she strode to the bar and nodded as Gabe handed her a drink. She squirmed under his brother's toast, edging away from the group as soon as she could.

The laughter and conversation rose, but she pulled away. Tower was right on one count. She didn't fit into SWAT's easy camaraderie. She stood apart from the group, solitary and watchful, just like the first time they'd met in this same bar, when he couldn't resist introducing himself to a lone goddess. He'd wanted to know if the full lower lip that didn't smile hid untapped passion. He hadn't been disappointed.

"What are you doing here, Luke?" Gabe's voice came out of nowhere.

Luke had to admire the stealth flank. His little brother really could've been a Ranger. He shook off the memories. "Just having a drink with my friend here. Join us?"

"Looks to me like you're consorting with the enemy," Gabe said.

"Internal Affairs keeps the riffraff out of the sheriff's office, Montgomery." Tower stared at Jasmine. "Most of it, anyway."

Gabe let out a low curse and nodded toward the bar's entrance. "Outside, Luke. Now."

He tossed down a couple of bills and called the bartender over. "I'm buying this round," Luke said. He'd made initial contact. It was a start.

He slid off the barstool and followed his brother. His gaze swept the room one last time for Jasmine, but she'd vanished. Probably for the best. One investigation at a time. He had an article on her coming out in tomorrow's paper. He wasn't looking forward to telling her about it or requesting an interview for the follow-up.

At least he wouldn't have to go searching for her hangouts when he needed to talk to her. Jasmine was a creature of habit, and Luke knew her patterns. Hell, he knew much more than that. He knew she loved her sex hot and her whiskey straight. He knew she couldn't stand cantaloupe or cauliflower but was addicted to butter rum Life Savers. He knew she liked her showers scorching, her kisses gentle, and that she purred in the middle of the night when he splayed his hand along her hip and nuzzled her neck.

Whoa. Where had all this rehashing the past come from? He'd been burned with Jasmine's brand once too often, and he still had the scars as evidence. He had to remember that. *She'd* been the one to walk out. With a soft shake of his head, he shoved out of the bar and stepped into the cool night breeze. Instinctively he gave the dusk-lit parking lot a quick scan.

Before he could finish, Gabe turned on him. "You just had to bring the investigation here, didn't you? And who do you start on? Tower?"

Calmly Luke removed Gabe's hand from his clothes. "You don't care if there's a dirty cop working beside you?"

"Of course I do, but Tower's on a power trip. He thinks his old man's position as sheriff gets him a free ride, and he hasn't been far from wrong. When Jazz beat him out of the sniper slot, he moved to Internal Affairs for a reason. He plays a good game with the brass, but he's got more than an eye on SWAT. He'd like to bring us all down."

"Then you should be glad he's on my radar. I won't stop until I get to the truth."

"Life's not all black and white, Luke. You've never tolerated the gray, and if you get this wrong, good cops could lose everything." Gabe poked Luke's chest. "You have one source. No corroboration."

"That's where you're wrong. I've been on this story a few weeks, and I'm already receiving threats to lay off or be sorry. I don't like threats, little brother."

Gabe's expression hardened, but not before Luke caught the flash of hurt behind his brother's eyes. Luke understood all too well. He knew from experience how much it sucked knowing the "supposed" good guys could let you down.

"Are you carrying?" Gabe asked.

"What do you think?" Luke lifted his jacket, revealing the HK in his shoulder holster.

"There're a bunch of good cops in there, putting their lives on the line, Luke. Don't screw them over."

"I'm only going after the dirty ones. The ones with something to hide. They deserve what they'll get."

"This isn't Afghanistan. You go Rambo, I'll throw you in jail myself."

Luke nodded, knowing his brother didn't really understand. He hadn't watched an entire unit massacred because of deliberate deceit. Good men dead because of a lie.

"Just be sure," Gabe said quietly. He turned back to the bar, his posture stiff, then looked over his shoulder with a grin. "See you Sunday at Mom's? I'm bringing chips. I can't take another veggie tray."

"I'll be there."

Speaking of his mother...Luke checked his watch. He had a few more minutes before she arrived to meet him. He could make some more inroads with Tower.

"You haven't changed at all. Asking too many questions. Ruining people's lives."

He stilled. *Jasmine.*

The familiar voice wafted over the August breeze from a darkened nook. Those husky tones sent shivers through him even though it'd been two years since they'd spoken.

She stepped into the light only feet away. Oh boy. No one else sported hair that particular color—like honey kissed with sunlight. She'd pinned the silky strands tightly to her head. What a crime. He'd loved taking it down, studying the way the color changed as the soft strands slipped through his fingers and feathered the smooth skin of her arms and back, all the way down to the lush curve of her hips.

His best intentions evaporated. Every memory of every night they'd shared rushed through him, one after the other. His body responded, going heavy with desire. Man, he was toast.

He clutched at a light post in an attempt to steady his reaction. She'd always been magnificent, an Amazon beauty, and the way she'd fit him when they'd made love had rocked his soul. Obviously she still did.

"Doing a little recon of your own?" he asked, trying to sound normal when she made him feel anything but. "Why aren't you partying with the team? You're the hero of the hour."

"An innocent girl's alive, but a man is dead. I did that. Celebrating would feel…wrong."

Her words as much as her flat tone sobered him quickly. Taking a life was never easy. "I checked out the kidnapper. The guy had ties to organized crime and a record. A long one. He was a criminal almost from the time he was born."

Jasmine shrugged, as if hoping he'd drop the subject. He studied her closely beneath the flickering light. He'd seen that haunted look on the snipers in his unit—the acknowledgement that they'd ended a life. The weight could smother the soul.

"You saved a child. He would've killed her."

"I know." A shiver went through Jasmine and the shadows left her face, like a curtain being drawn. He'd seen this before as well. In battle. When a warrior pushed aside the reality so they could live with what they'd done.

The sniper was back. She crossed her arms and faced him. "From what I overheard you're after cops these days instead of criminals? Are you out for a story or justice?"

"You *did* hear a lot. I just want the truth."

"The truth doesn't always lead to justice," she said.

"Justice will come. My informant knows details. Enough for me to believe some cops *are* criminals. You know anything about that...Jasmine?" Deliberately he let her name roll off his tongue for the first time since she'd walked out two years earlier.

She clenched her jaw in irritation as he'd known she would. *Jazz* was the sheriff's deputy, the sniper. *Jasmine* was the woman she revealed only in rare, unguarded moments. He'd always called her Jasmine when they made love; he still thought of her that way. She hated that about him.

"Do you know anyone with secrets they're trying to hide?" he pressed.

Her eyes flashed with panic for a split second. Well hell. She *did* know something. Why did it have to be Jasmine? And why wasn't he surprised?

She'd always been closed mouthed about her past, but he'd spent all day working on the supposed fluff piece about the woman behind the sniper. After hours searching her background he hadn't found anything on Jasmine before she played basketball at Metro State. The lack of information pinged his instincts and made him wonder just what he'd stumbled onto. No one popped out of nowhere as an eighteen-year-old woman.

Damn her. If she was involved in anything illegal, he'd expose her. No matter what their relationship had been. No matter how much he still wanted her.

Before he could push for information, a beam of headlights bounced into the parking lot pulling into an empty space near him. He recognized his mother's vehicle. So did Jasmine. Her mask fell into place. Any chance of talking was over. For now.

A small girl's shining face peered through the glass. After his mother released the car seat's latch, the bundle of energy leapt out of the vehicle and raced toward him. He grinned and knelt down, holding out his arms as his daughter ran to him, a stuffed orange clown fish clutched in her hand.

"Grandma said Hero and me could have ice cream for dinner." Her words rushed out as she thrust the toy into his hands.

"Hi, munchkin." Luke wrapped his daughter's warm body in his arms and buried his face in the baby shampoo smell of her hair. His child, his Joy. The only truly honest human being he'd ever met. "Do you know how much I love you?"

Her arms spanned wide. "This much, Daddy?" she beamed.

"Oh my God." A whisper erupted from Jasmine's lips, and she stumbled back several paces.

Luke's shoulders tightened at the shock in her voice. He forced himself to relax for his daughter's sake and handed his mother the keys. "Take Joy and put her in the SUV. I'll be right there."

Anna Montgomery grabbed Joy's hand and her curious gaze shifted from Luke to Jasmine. "Jazz. It's good to see you. Really."

Jasmine swallowed, her face strained. "Mrs. Montgomery."

His daughter's curious expression sent a chill of foreboding through Luke. Joy wasn't one to hold her tongue about anything, and Jasmine looked astonished enough to ask a question he didn't want to answer. "Mom?" he urged. "Please."

His mother bundled Joy off to his car, though his daughter kept looking back, staring at Jasmine and whispering to his mother.

The SUV door slammed shut, and Joy's face pressed against the glass, peering at Luke. A cool night breeze batted a tin wind chime hanging near the bar's entrance, its awkward tones oddly appropriate.

Luke faced Jasmine. "She's my daughter. Joy."

"Who...How...?"

The world spun around Jazz as she struggled to right her balance against the ache erupting inside her.

Luke, a father. He'd said he couldn't do commitment; that his life was constantly in danger, especially when he'd been in Afghanistan. She'd understood. As a cop, so was hers. For just that reason, she'd succumbed to his seduction. Then, like a fool, she'd let herself start to believe in happily-ever-afters—at least in that still, small place inside her soul. And all the time he'd had a child and a family of his own.

"You're one to talk about honesty and not keeping big secrets," she said. "You should've told me about your daughter while we were dating. Oh. Wait. Maybe you didn't think having a child was important enough to mention to the woman you were sleeping with. It's a good thing I walked when I did, isn't it? I've never been one to stay where I wasn't wanted."

"You were wanted, and you know it. I didn't tell you about her existence because I didn't know. Not until she ended up on a plane to Denver after her mom died in a car accident."

Joy had lost her mother too? The words sucked all the anger out of Jazz. She'd never been able to depend on anyone, especially her family. Unlike Jazz, Joy could count on Luke and the rest of the Montgomerys to love and protect her. What would that have been like? To have someone care enough about Jazz to defend her? She'd never know.

"Don't expect me to apologize for Joy," Luke said. "I won't. She's a gift." His gaze shifted to the SUV where his daughter waited, and he sighed. "Look, it's been two years. Maybe it's time we talked instead of avoiding each other."

His hand reached out and clasped hers. The electricity crackling between them erupted, and her traitorous heart quickened. Her fingers itched to push back the lick of mahogany hair that had fallen onto his forehead. Between that errant lock and the long lashes framing molten chocolate eyes, her breath still caught at the sight of him. She longed to touch him; his hot gaze still melted her insides. She was a fool to think she was over him. Lord, what kind of Pandora's box had she opened? She should've stayed hidden. Being invisible was the only way to protect herself.

She'd been right to leave two years ago, before he'd gotten any closer to her heart, before he'd learned the truth. She had to get out now, before passion drew her back in, before unthinkable possibilities seduced her again.

"There's nothing left to say, Luke. Nothing."

Their gazes locked, and a trembling began inside her. She turned and raced into the bar. Anything to distract her from these crazy feelings. Like a reflex, she dug into her pocket searching for a butter rum Life Saver. Nothing but an empty wrapper. She needed a refill.

She paused and watched through the window as he went to his daughter, careful to check the girl's car seat before giving her a tender kiss on the forehead. As he slid behind the wheel he glanced back at Jazz through the small window in the bar's door. She recognized the speculative gleam that lit his eyes.

Nothing had changed in two years. She had only one choice. Stay away from Luke Montgomery before he focused his quest for the truth on her.

"What do you mean I'm under investigation?"

Jazz watched as Sarge, with measured control, clicked shut the utilitarian door, offering a rare bit of privacy from the rowdy antics in the SWAT team's den. He sank into the leather chair behind his desk and leveled a serious look at her.

She'd entered the office this morning expecting a promotion, not this. "I saved the life of the governor's daughter, and now I'm being investigated by Internal Affairs?" She met her commanding officer's gaze. "How does that happen?"

Sarge's square jaw clenched.

Oh, boy. Only rarely had Jazz witnessed even a hint of emotion in her boss. She admired the trait. That she recognized his anger worried her.

"Tower happened. He convinced his commander in Internal Affairs to reopen the post-incident investigations into your terminations. It's a witch hunt, Jazz. He wants to see you burn."

Stunned, she backed away from the desk. First Luke and now this. She shoved a hand in her pocket and fingered the familiar roll of Life Savers. She wished she could pop one right now. She could use the comfort of a sugar fix. "I *knew* he was pissed when I beat him out of the opening on the SWAT team. I haven't done anything wrong. Every action was a result of direct orders. Every shot deemed justified."

"You think that matters to Tower? He's used to getting what he wants. In his eyes you humiliated him, and he wants to bring you down."

Sarge tossed down her folder on a desk so pristine the dust didn't dare settle there. "Be careful, Jazz. This file doesn't go into a lot of detail, but Tower claims he can prove you're not fit to be a cop."

She clutched the candy in her pocket and squeezed the frisson of disquiet into submission. Emotions were weak, and she could never reveal even the smallest crack in her armor. "He's bluffing."

Sarge leaned forward in his chair. "A smart cop doesn't make a move like this without an ace in his hand. Do you have any idea what Tower's latched onto? What he can use against you?"

Her mind flashed to the angry runaway she'd been, a child forced to do anything to survive. Twelve years had passed since then. Her juvenile records had been expunged, erased as if they never existed. She pushed away the thoughts. It was impossible. Tower couldn't know.

"He's grasping at straws. I've done nothing to dishonor my badge." She met Sarge's look and forced her face into a calm mask. He nodded as if reassured, but she could detect the underlying concern.

"He'll fight dirty. He's got a lot to lose."

"I can stand up for myself." She was good at her job. She protected her team. She never failed. She was Jazz Parker, one of the boys in blue who could thread a needle with a bullet.

"Just be smart about what you say—and what you do. He'll be looking to trip you up." Her commander drummed his fingers over the file. "I want you as lead sniper, Jazz, but this situation has to be cleared up."

"I hear you."

"Good." Sarge gifted her with a supportive smile. "I made the right decision when I chose you over Tower."

He lowered his gaze to a razor-edge stack of paperwork. "Dismissed, Deputy."

Jazz snapped to attention and turned on her heel, burying her unease deep inside. She pulled out the butter rum she'd been craving and popped it in her mouth. The smooth sweetness exploded on her tongue. Yes. Much better. She could deal with this. She had Sarge's confidence.

She also had one very large vulnerability.

Jazz steadied herself as she reached for the doorknob. She'd covered her bases. The past she'd taken such great pains to hide *would* stay buried six hundred miles south. It had to.

She marched out of Sarge's office, shut the door behind her, and then froze at the unbelievable sight greeting her—Brian Tower, holding court, surrounded by her teammates. He leaned against the metal lockers lining the equipment room, smirking while a half-naked, red-headed bimbo fawned over Gabe.

Tower's smile oozed with triumph. "Why don't you wait in the car for me, darlin'. I have one last piece of business."

Swinging her hips like a working girl, she sashayed toward the door. Gabe's eyes were glazed as he stared after the swaying figure. Half the team's jaws were hanging on the floor. Jazz chomped down on the candy in her mouth and swallowed. Men. It would be funny if it weren't Tower's woman they were gawking at.

He slapped her lycra-covered assets as she waltzed past him and exited the room. "Keep the motor running." Tower turned around and grinned at his audience. "Takes a lot to keep her happy, but I've got her covered."

A few sniggers filtered among her teammates.

Jazz gathered her temper. She strode toward the workbench, but Tower cut her off. He flopped down in *her* chair, next to *her* rifle, and crossed his legs as if he owned the place.

"You're in my seat, Deputy Tower."

He didn't respond, just unrolled the newspaper he held and shifted in the chair. His ash-blond hair was perfectly groomed, his tailored charcoal pinstripe immaculate. Her entire wardrobe didn't measure up to that suit.

With a smirk, Tower threw down the afternoon paper and looked at her. "Well, if it isn't my favorite media suck-up. I thought I'd congratulate you on making the front page. You're a hero, Parker. Looks like you saved the governor's daughter all by yourself." He rose from the chair. "Sorry, guys. You barely got a mention. Guess you just don't have her star power."

Tower straightened his jacket, and his confidence gave Jazz a chill of apprehension. What was he up to?

"I need to catch up with my lovely goddess. She's got my day off planned, and I don't intend to miss a minute of...fun." He flashed a grin and sauntered out of the room.

Jazz watched him with growing frustration until the door shut behind him. "Jerk."

Gabe chuckled at her barb, but Steve Paretti whistled under his breath. "How'd Tower get his mitts on that luscious babe?"

"God only knows," Carl Redmond said.

"She sure found your lap interesting, buddy boy," Paretti said, turning to Gabe. "Practically slid off the table onto you."

"Hey," Gabe protested. "I was just looking after Jazz's gun."

"Yeah, that's what you were thinking about," Paretti shot back. "Jazz's gun."

Gabe winked at her, but she couldn't rustle a smile. She stared at the Remington near his elbow and studied the rifle intently. It looked okay. No smudges on the barrel, no fingerprints, and the settings looked right.

"See if I leave her in your care anytime soon, Montgomery. Some bozo brings a woman in here and your brains slide south."

"We're only human," Gabe muttered.

A wave of laughter followed, but Jazz didn't join in, her attention caught by the front page of the newspaper Tower had left on the table. An academy photo of herself stared back just below the fold. She leaned closer even as her teammates crowded around her. "What's my picture doing on the front page?"

The caption below the image made her squirm.

Jasmine Parker, Jefferson County Sheriff's Office's first female SWAT team member, and Colorado's only female sniper, shot and killed the man who kidnapped the governor's five-year-old daughter.

"They've got you as some kind of cross between the Archangel Michael and Joan of Arc," Gabe murmured as he read a few lines of the story.

What was going on? Between the media coverage and IA's investigation—not to mention Luke—her entire world was under attack. Someone might just recognize the girl she had been from the photo of the woman she had become. She didn't need this.

She slammed her hand on the table. "Dammit."

Silence blanketed the room. Finally Gabe leaned back against the oak workbench. "Okay, I'll be brave and ask. Why are you wound tighter than Sarge right before a mission?"

"IA's investigating my record," she said dully.

"You gotta be kidding?" An awkward pause settled over the room. Finally Gabe patted her shoulder. "Look, nothing makes people happier than tearing down a hero. Especially a hero who got her picture in the paper. They'll see him for what he is."

"Gee, thanks. Trusting the brass. That makes me feel better." Jazz grimaced and skimmed her fingers across the print, sweeping past the headline, *Female SWAT Sniper Rescues Governor's Daughter, Kills Kidnapper.* The byline screamed through her head.

Luke Montgomery.

She skewered Gabe with a glare. "Your brother wrote this."

Gabe raised his hands in surrender. "I swear to God, Jazz. I didn't know."

She found that hard to believe. The Montgomerys were in each other's pockets all the time.

She glanced once more at the paper, and a small, italicized phrase below the article filled her with apprehension. *First in a series?* She clutched the paper in her fist. She couldn't allow that to happen. Not now. Not with Tower on a mission to bring her down. One bullet she could probably dodge, but she couldn't count on luck a second time. She'd never been that fortunate.

As much as she hated it, she had only one option. She had to talk to Luke. She couldn't control Tower's actions, but somehow she had to find a way to stop Luke Montgomery from making things worse.

Jazz Parker would pay for what she'd done.

The Desert Inn's neon sign flashed red, the last three letters winking on and off as if sharing in the joke—and the success.

Everything had gone like clockwork. The bitch had stood only feet away, and she knew nothing. Face to face with her past, and she was just as ignorant now as she had been then. Low-class, unworthy whore who'd ruined everything.

The television and newspaper had made her out to be some kind of hero. Lies. All lies. They didn't know the truth, but they would.

Wearing a badge she didn't deserve, Jazz Parker mocked from the front page. Killing her quick was too easy. She needed to suffer.

Just the thought sent shivers of excitement prickling through every nerve. Yes. Make her *suffer.* Make her lose *everything.* Everything she cared about, everything she loved.

An old Truth or Consequences board game balanced on the rickety nightstand in the dilapidated hotel room. Jazz Parker's past would rise again. The truth would destroy her.

A smile tugged at determined lips. The plan was set. The end was near. The newspaper crumpled in eager hands, destroying the face of the traitor. After all these years living with the pain, justice would finally be done.

Jazz Parker would pay inch by inch. Then she would forfeit the ultimate price—her life.

Chapter Two

She'd made a huge mistake. Jazz never should've called Luke about the article yesterday. Just leaving the message had flooded her with too many memories, and they'd followed her—even into sleep. Which was why she'd insisted to Gabe and everyone else on the team not to mention Luke. Ever. She should have listened to her own advice. Too late she'd recognized she'd probably whetted his curiosity even more. Fool. What had she been thinking, reaching out to him?

He hadn't bothered to answer, and she'd tossed and turned all night, fighting the erotic dreams that left her body hungry for a man. Not just any man, unfortunately. Only Luke made her tremble with longing that way. His body was the stuff of pure fantasy—washboard abs, muscular biceps, and a charming grin when he wanted something. Not to mention a butt that any woman on the planet would like to watch walking the other way. But his mouth, that's what set Luke apart. He knew what to do with his lips, knew when they should be soft and coaxing or hard and demanding. He could find every erogenous zone on her body…he'd discovered some she didn't even know existed.

By the time dawn's overcast light parted her bedroom curtains, she punched her pillow. He was trouble. She had to get him out of her head, and she knew of only one way.

After rolling out from beneath the blankets, she brushed her teeth, threw on her sweats, grabbed her car keys, and rushed out the door. When she reached the parking lot, the sky had opened up with a downpour. No way could she go for a run in Apex Park now. At least the gym would be open.

The sparse, Saturday-morning traffic let her keep her pace, leaving the dreams behind. She hoped. Within minutes she'd pulled into a crowded parking lot not far from the sheriff's office.

The clang of metal and the smell of sweat drifted over Jazz as she strode into the gym shaking off the rain from her jacket. Familiar faces and figures greeted her. Grunts of exertion merged with a cacophony of male voices in a testosterone-laden sea of bodies. She breathed in the sounds and scents of the physical challenge. Yes, this was where she belonged. In this place, in this morning ritual, she could erase thoughts of the investigation—not to mention Luke. She needed to be here, needed to push past her body's betrayal.

After a stiff wave of acknowledgement to several team-mates, Jazz stretched and warmed up on the versa-climber before working her way to the bench press. The weights tallied two-fifty, and she pulled forty off of each side. Dusting her hands with talc, she positioned herself below the barbell and regulated her breathing.

"Need a spotter?"

Gabe's face peered at her from overhead. She usually turned his offer down, but today a dozen questions rushed through her mind. Jazz closed her eyes against the swirling thoughts. She didn't need a Montgomery standing over her while she tried to pound her libido back into submission with a hard workout, but there were things she needed to know.

"I guess so."

After Gabe positioned himself, she pressed the heavy barbell up until her arms straightened then lowered the weight to her chest. Muscles straining, she pushed through three sets of eight. As she exhaled through the last rep, Gabe guided the bar back to its rest.

"Not bad. For a girl."

She quirked an eyebrow at him, and he lifted his hands in submission.

"Okay, okay, I'll stop." Gabe added several weights to the bar. "Seriously, you've taken on twenty pounds of iron since the last time I spotted you."

"Keeping track?" Jazz waited at the head of the bench.

He shrugged and slid beneath the bar. "Not really. You passed the SWAT physical. That's good enough for me." He grinned. "But as a guy, it's a bit scary to know that an attractive woman can almost bench press you."

They moved through the stations, their conversation sparse, their bodies focused. Jazz couldn't figure out how to ask what she really wanted to know. When Gabe finished the last set and walked across to her, she knew she'd run out of time. With a pause of apprehension, she dove in. Business first, then personal. "What are the guys saying about IA's investigation?"

He snagged the towel she handed him and dried the sweat dripping from his forehead. "Not much."

She sipped at her water bottle. The tepid liquid slid down her throat. "We both know most of the team wasn't exactly excited when I beat out Tower three years ago. They must be happy IA is sniffing around."

"No one is happy when IA noses into our business."

"Point taken."

Gabe settled on a wooden bench and chugged some water. "Look, we have a few Neanderthals on the team, but all you have to do is let people in a bit, Jazz. You'll have their support. You proved yourself as an Arvada police officer before joining the team. You're a hell of a marksman. They've seen what you can do. And yesterday, that shot was a thing of beauty." He rolled the cool bottle across his forehead. "Not to mention, you've got one other thing in your favor."

Jazz sat down beside him. "What's that?"

"They all hate IA more than they dislike having you on the team."

Slumping back against the concrete wall, she tried to grin. "You sure know how to make a girl feel loved and appreciated."

Gabe's face grew serious, and he leaned toward her. "If you're tired of the struggle, Jazz, tell me now. You knew what you were getting into when you applied for SWAT. You need to meet them halfway."

"I know. I appreciate what you're trying to do."

A few gutter curses punched through the rhythmic ringing of bars and low grunts.

"That's what teammates are for," he said.

When Gabe rested his hand on Jasmine's knee, Luke's first instinct was to bench press his brother through the front window. His second thought was why in hell he was reacting like he had a right to care.

He strode toward them, his muscles tense and poised for battle. He took in the warm glow on Jasmine's skin and the firm shape of her curves outlined by the soaking T-shirt. The transparent cotton outlined her bra and showed off the firm planes of her belly and the strong lines of her arms. The view left nothing to his imagination—or anyone else's. He could just envision peeling off that wet material and tasting the saltiness of her skin, bringing to life the responsive nipples starting to pebble as if teasing him.

Luke dragged his gaze away from temptation and surveyed the room, striving to rein his body under control. Incredibly, none of the men seemed aware of the raw sexual energy emanating from her. Good thing. He'd have had to knock some heads together.

"Cozy, aren't we?"

Jasmine started then glanced down at her damp T. Her face bloomed red as she quickly slipped a thick sweatshirt from her bag and jerked it down over the clingy cotton. She planted herself in front of him. "What are you doing here, Luke?"

"You called me."

"Yesterday."

"Some of us have a life to live and a job to do."

"Is that what you call this?" Jazz reached into her exercise bag and threw the newspaper at him. "Doing your job?"

The tail of her sleek French braid whipped over her shoulder. Her hazel eyes, which shifted in color depending on her mood, blazed a brilliant green to match her fury. "Going out of your way to screw with people's lives?" She leaned toward him, using her body language in an attempt to intimidate him.

She failed. The up-close view of her apricot-soft skin, the fullness of her lips, and the pulse beating at her neck only served to tempt him more. Lord, she was sexy like this.

"What are you trying to do to me, Luke?"

"Uh, guys, I'm gonna do a little stretching," Gabe said, scooting down the bench.

"Keep it down to a low roar, okay? You've got an audience."

Several cops had paused in their workout to stare. Luke met the curiosity with a glare that'd made more than one Ranger in his unit back off. Within seconds, the voyeurs ducked their heads and returned to their workout.

"Let's take this private." Luke grasped Jasmine's arm and tugged her into a small alcove. She jerked away and faced him toe-to-toe.

"What—"

"I get it. You have a problem with the article," he interrupted. He didn't mention that he'd sent out queries on her, looking into a past that didn't seem to exist.

"Cut the crap," Jasmine said. "You didn't think I had a right to know last night that you'd plastered me on the front page?"

"We were…distracted. Why are you so upset about that article? I made you into a hero. Most people would be happy."

"Do I look happy to you? The article should never have happened, and I intend to make sure the so-called follow-up dies a quick death."

She vibrated with a tension he didn't understand. Her intensity, her…he couldn't call it anything but desperation. Most wouldn't see it. Jasmine had a wall around her so thick few could get through, but Luke recognized the anxiety. This was about more than the article. An uneasy feeling settled in the pit of his stomach. The more he dug into her past, the more he had to wonder what Jasmine had to hide.

Leaning back, he settled his body into a position of casual indifference. "Is there some reason you don't want anyone to know who you are and what you do?"

The green flecks in her eyes blazed even brighter. Breathing hard, she jammed her fists against her hips. "You know better than anyone SWAT is a team. Why did you single me out? I've had a tough enough time fitting in as it is."

"*You're* the one who took the shot. You killed the bad guy, so you're the story my editor wants. He likes to sell papers."

"I just do my job, Luke. I don't want to stand out from my team. I don't need that kind of attention right now."

"Why is *right now* different?"

He rubbed the spot tingling at his temple. She eyed the movement, her expression guarded, and slowly Luke forced his hand down. Did she remember the quirk as clearly as he recalled every time they'd set fire to the sheets?

He shook his head. He had to stop thinking about sex, but standing near her made that difficult. She captivated him with every word, every gesture.

She exhaled sharply. "I just want to be left alone."

"Well, we can't always have what we want, Jasmine. You told me that once. I learned it in spades after you left."

He'd never forget that last night. He'd been hurting. Had thought they had the potential for something...special after six months of dating. He'd been wrong. He'd needed her support, and she'd walked out without a second look. His life had changed profoundly soon after—when he'd learned about Joy. He'd put Jasmine out of his mind and out of his life. Until now. He had a job to do. He wouldn't let their history stop him.

Luke pulled a notebook from his pocket. "How about some background information for the next article? Where did you learn to shoot? Did your father teach you?"

Her jaw tightened and she shivered, just slightly. He'd shaken her with his question.

"I didn't know my father, Luke. He wasn't a hero like yours."

The words escaped as if she couldn't stop them. That small statement was more than she'd revealed the entire time they'd dated.

She stared at him, her expression troubled, almost vulnerable. "Don't write another article about me, Luke. Please."

Jasmine Parker? Vulnerable? Armadillos had less armor, and yet he'd seen something today in her he'd never seen before. Fear. Why did she want to stay under the radar so desperately?

A shadow fell across them. "Well, well, well." Tower's sarcastic voice rose above the noise of the gym. "Colorado's newest celebrity and the reporter who made her. More interviews? I would've thought you'd had enough, Parker."

Jasmine's countenance went flat and cold. She folded her arms across her chest. "I'm surprised to see you here, Deputy Tower. I didn't think you liked to sweat."

Tower smiled. "It's true. I prefer to make others do it."

The tension in the gym rose sharply as the team gathered around the alcove, watching, waiting. Jasmine's stance was ready, like a panther waiting to pounce.

"Gentlemen, a word of caution." Tower addressed the suddenly quiet room. "Steer clear of Parker, unless you want to get dragged into her mess."

Luke had heard enough. He stepped forward, but before he could intercede, Jasmine's clipped words sliced through the air.

"Don't threaten me, Tower. I won't forget it."

"Your fans think they know you," he sneered and sent a sidelong glance to Luke. "Don't you, Montgomery? The truth needs to come out. We all know she didn't get the job because she deserved it."

To hell with becoming drinking buddies with this jerk to get an in with his old man. Luke would bring them down another way. "Back off. Now."

"Or what? You'll take me out with your pen? I'm real scared."

"Would you like to step outside?" The idea had appeal. He *could* take the guy out twenty different ways in less than ten seconds—with or without the pen.

Jasmine's shoulders flexed, as if she were ready for battle. "Cool it, Luke. I don't need you to fight for me."

So she thought she could get him to back down with a few words…and yet he watched as she faced Tower. She was amazing

"I earned my spot. Unlike you…" she turned to Tower, "who's been trading on *Daddy's* position his entire life."

Tower's countenance twisted in anger, but he didn't retreat. Was the man an idiot?

"If you're accusing Jazz of being unqualified," Gabe said, stepping forward, "you'd better have proof."

Tower's face turned snide. "I have confirmation she's a liar." He paused, letting his words settle around him. "Ask your illustrious sniper what her real name is. Because it sure as hell's not Jazz Parker."

Luke's attention snapped to Jasmine. He waited for the explosion, for the rebuttal, but she said nothing. She seemed frozen in place.

"No comment, Parker?" Tower taunted. "Didn't think so. Like I said, only the beginning."

Silence blanketed the gym. No one breathed.

Tower turned, and the sea of men parted as he swaggered out of the gym.

Unlike the others, Luke didn't turn to watch the troublemaker leave. Instead he studied Jasmine. No fire or anger burned in her eyes. Her face had gone milk-white, and her stricken look sickened his soul.

Without a word, the men mumbled and shuffled back to their exercise equipment, unable to meet her gaze.

"My name is Jazz Parker," she whispered, too softly for anyone but him to hear.

Her words were too late. Tower had left her flayed open and vulnerable. Luke had to uncover the truth now. He just prayed Tower or his father were the ones guilty of corruption and that Jasmine's secrets weren't as bad as he feared.

The aroma of fresh-baked bread and oatmeal cookies permeated the Montgomery house in an unchanging Sunday lunch ritual. Even after the family had lost their father, Patrick, to a wayward bullet during a convenience store robbery, the comforting tradition lived on. Since Patrick's other four sons were out of town, though, Luke and Gabe had the living room to themselves.

"I've talked to everyone, called in favors. I even contacted an old-fashioned clipping service to search the surrounding states," Luke muttered. "It's like she didn't exist before coming to college in the Denver metro area." He fingered the all-too-short stack of clippings littering the coffee table. "She's lived in the same apartment in Arvada since then. I found a few sports articles, a mention of a few arrests she made while at the Arvada Police Department, and then a blurb about her being named sniper to the Jefferson County SWAT Team. Other than that, nothing."

"That's crazy, Luke. I know she hates publicity, and being singled out put her in a tough spot with the team, but we've known her for almost three years. You dated her for six months. You can't say we don't know anything about her."

"She avoided talking about herself. Turned around every question I asked into a quiz on our family." Luke cursed under his breath, irritated at the unanswered inquiries burning inside him. "You're one to talk," he countered. "How much do you know about her past, other than she's blown away every cop's score on the target range, including your own, little brother?"

A tense silence stretched before Gabe answered, his voice quiet, "She still gets to you. More than Joy's mother, more than anyone. You two could've spontaneously combusted at the gym yesterday, and I wouldn't have been surprised."

"Tower doused that heat pretty quickly with his accusation. What gets me is she didn't fight back."

Gabe grabbed the contraband bag of chips and paced the living room, his unchanneled frustration obvious in every step. "Tower gives cops a bad name. Even IA. You should've seen him ragging on her in the den yesterday. Arrogant, nosy piece of scum. I can't believe I'm saying this, but I don't think I'd mind too much if you found out he was on the take."

Messing with the fins of Joy's favorite toy, Hero, Luke resisted the urge to rub the ache at his temple. He'd listened to Gabe's tirade and, coupled with Tower's attitude in the bar, he'd figured out more than his brother intended.

"How long has Tower been using IA to scrounge for evidence on Jasmine?"

Gabe came to an abrupt halt. "How do you know about the IA investigation?"

Satisfaction tugged at the corners of Luke's mouth, but when he leaned back in his chair the implications for Jasmine weighed on him. "I didn't. Until you just confirmed it."

"Anyone ever tell you being a human radar detector is downright annoying?"

"Got it from Mom."

"Yeah, well, it's just as irritating now as when Mom discovered we'd sneaked out with Steve Paretti and Derek Mason to meet up with the Smithson sisters for a little touch football in high school."

"Quit trying to change the subject. A few weeks ago I received a reliable tip about cops on the take. Now Tower is using IA to build a case against Jasmine. The timing makes me wonder if there's a connection." Luke shifted in his chair. The instincts that had kept him alive in the Middle East thrummed in warning. He knew not to ignore the feelings. "So, little brother, do *you* think there's anything to his allegations? Is Jasmine Parker her real name, and if not, what's she hiding?"

His brother didn't speak for a moment, then his jaw tightened. "She was admitted to the police academy. They do background checks on all the applicants. If there was something serious to find, she wouldn't be a cop."

"Maybe Tower's twisting the facts to make her look bad."

"Joy Marie Montgomery! Don't you move!" A frantic yell came from the kitchen. "Luke!"

He bounded out of his chair and raced into the room, Gabe pounding behind him. Luke's heart stopped as he caught sight of his three-year-old daughter perched on top of the china closet, an impish grin splitting her face. He'd face down the Taliban without a qualm, but the sight of his baby girl nearly eight feet off the ground brought him to his knees.

"I don't know how..." his mother said, her hands shaking.

Luke lowered his voice, searching for a calm he didn't feel. "Joy, you stay very still. Daddy will get you down, okay?"

His daughter stuck out her bottom lip and shook her head with ferocity. Luke froze.

"Want Uncle Gabe to catch me. I want to fly like Uncle Zach."

Luke sent his brother a pleading glance.

"She's your kid all right," Gabe muttered under his breath and positioned himself, his hands only a few inches beneath his niece. "All right, you little daredevil, come to Uncle Gabe."

Joy launched herself into the air, giggling, and Gabe caught her midair.

Luke's heart beat again. He grabbed his daughter from his brother's arms and settled her on his knee. "Joy Montgomery, don't ever do that again. Do you hear me?"

She simply smiled, her eyes lit with excitement. "Did you see me? I flew, Daddy. Just like Uncle Zach in his movie."

Gabe leaned over Luke's shoulder. "I vote to cage our miniature superhero. With no movie privileges."

"You know the rules, Joy," Luke said. "No climbing on the furniture. And you know the consequences."

Limpid eyes pooled with tears, and Joy bowed her head. Luke felt himself waver, but the love for his daughter strengthened his resolve.

"Three minutes in 'time out,'" he said.

Joy gave her father, then her uncle, and finally her grandmother a longing look, but finding no weakness in them, she moped off to a corner stool.

Luke shook his head at his mother, whose starched apron and left cheek were dusted with flour. "My darling daughter is going to be the death of me," he mused. "I'm supposed to protect her, and her fearlessness terrifies me more than anything I faced overseas."

Now that Joy was out of danger, his mother seemed to have recovered her nerves. She pushed the cinnamon-and-sugar-colored hair away from her face. "You were worse."

"That I don't believe. I think Joy gets her independence from a certain Irish grandmother."

"I don't know what you're talking about, dear," she said. "And Gabe, if I see any crumbs from those chips… no oatmeal cookies for you."

A cell phone's ring cut off Luke's bark of laughter and Gabe's stammering reply.

They each rummaged through their pockets. With a rueful grimace at his mother, Luke pulled out the ringing phone. "Sorry."

His mother waved him away and turned back to the kitchen as he scanned the screen for a number. Blocked call. Interesting. His informant? Would Grace block her calls? "Montgomery."

"I didn't expect you to lie to get your name on the front page," a mechanical voice said, the tinny tones chilling in their anonymity. "That pissy little sniper doesn't deserve anyone's praise."

What? The call was about Jasmine? He forced his tone to remain calm. "How'd you get this number?"

He motioned Gabe to follow him and headed to the living room for privacy. Luke punched the speakerphone button. Odd, electronic laughter floated through the line. "Journalists aren't the only ones who know where to find information, Mr. Montgomery. The web is a wonderful equalizer. I've been reading your past articles. 'The Plight of Europe's Lost: Bosnian Refugees and Their Battle to Survive' and 'The Truth from the Battlefield: Afghanistan Uncovered.' I had high hopes for you, but you disappointed me. That's not good. People get hurt when they let me down."

Gabe's expression turned dangerous, mirroring Luke's instincts. He wanted to climb through the phone and shut the coward up.

"Are you there, Mr. Montgomery?"

"I'm here." He forced the fury from his voice. He needed an ID. "Why don't we start over? What's your name?"

"Don't patronize me. I'm giving you a chance to make things right, to tell the truth for a change. I'll even give you a hint, if you think you can follow a real lead."

"I'm listening," Luke said as he struggled for control.

Silence echoed through the line.

"Hello?" Luke asked. "Are you still there?"

"You may not be the right man for the job," the voice mused. "You defended her already. So has your brother. Not smart. It could get the people you care about in trouble."

"Who the hell is this?"

"No need to fear. Not if you write the truth this time. I know you're investigating the sheriff's office, so here's a riddle for you. 'Which member of SWAT is hiding her past because she's a murderer?'"

Chapter Three

Jazz pulled her truck into the darkened parking lot of her apartment building and yanked the keys from the ignition. The gloomy night matched her mood. Luke Montgomery had been back in her life for two days, and he'd already wreaked havoc. Yesterday's confrontation at the gym sure hadn't dissuaded his interest in her past, and it certainly hadn't helped her equilibrium. She couldn't deny her body's reaction to him or her desire to feel those broad shoulder muscles ripple under her hands. She missed touching and being touched, but her head knew she couldn't let herself want him. She had too much to lose.

The temperature outside had dropped, so Jazz tugged her Arvada Police Academy sweatshirt on, then slung her exercise bag over her shoulder and exited the pickup. Her muscles ached with fatigue. In the past twenty-four hours, she'd clocked more than her share of miles on the Apex jogging trail near her apartment, and she'd spent more than her share of time in the gym pummeling the punching bag.

One question still pounded in her head. How had Tower known about her name?

He'd enjoyed spouting off the information in front of the team—and Luke. She'd seen the guys' uncertainty spike at the accusations, and Luke's gaze had turned suspicious, his focus intent.

Lord, she'd seen that same look in his eyes when he'd received the first tip about his close friend, Derek Mason's, involvement in that city works scam. Hundreds of thousands of dollars changing hands, all the rumors pointing Derek's way. It hadn't mattered that he'd been Luke's childhood friend. Luke had started to dig, ferreting out the truth. When it came out that Derek had lied to Luke, he'd torn Derek apart in print.

She shivered. His fury over his old friend's deceit had been as terrifying to watch as the tenacity with which Luke had followed every lead. He'd acted like Derek's activities and the secrets he'd kept had been personal betrayals.

She'd almost let herself trust him, but she couldn't deal with Luke coming after her like that. She'd realized then he'd never forgive the things she'd done in the past. She'd had no choice. She'd left him before he could mount an investigation on her. If he found out her birth name, he might learn it all. Jazz gripped the strap of the canvas duffel. Her past was no one else's business. Her *legal* name was Jasmine Parker. It had been for twelve years.

She fingered the plastic nametag attached to the bag. She'd spent a long time getting the name on that tag. After five years in foster care, seeing the distrustful looks and listening to the whispers of each new foster family upon recognizing her name from all those sordid newspaper articles, she'd finally been old enough to request the change in a New Mexico court.

As Jazz, for the first time in her life, she'd been free. A new name, a new town, a new state, a new life.

Jasmine Parker *was* her real name. She hadn't lied at the gym, but she hadn't revealed the whole truth either. She'd learned the hard way: sometimes it made sense to give up and start over. That's what she'd done. So why couldn't Luke just leave her alone? Why couldn't Tower?

She rounded the corner of her apartment building and headed toward the back entrance. A faint shuffling came from the shadowy stairwell, just audible over the sounds of faraway traffic. She peered into the darkness. Silence billowed around her; her muscles flexed in readiness. Listening, waiting.

Could it have been a cat or a squirrel? She squinted along the hedge bordering the sidewalk, but she couldn't see the stairs leading down into the building, much less a scurrying animal. She cursed her landlord for not fixing the bulb in the entryway yet. The nearest light was down the street, barely illuminating a beat-up VW and a rusty red Pinto a half-block away.

Both seemed empty, but she couldn't banish the sense of being watched.

She slid deeper into the shadows, then slowly shifted the duffel off her shoulder and worked the side pocket zipper to reveal the holstered gun inside. Sweat trickled down her back as she grasped the Glock, the extractor flush with the slide. The chamber was empty of bullets.

Jazz eased the duffel onto the ground beside her then pulled the slide back until the comforting click echoed in the night.

An owl hooted. Slices of moonlight bounced off a figure slouched in the shadows next to the cave-like stairwell entrance, hands thrust out of sight in his jacket. Was he hiding a weapon?

She tightened her fingers around the butt then stepped forward. "You there. This is the police. Come into the light, hands where I can see them."

A throat cleared. "There is no light, Jasmine. Not unless you count the moon."

Luke's velvet baritone sent shivers through her. She hadn't forgotten what his whisper sounded like in the dark. She wished to God she had. Her fingers relaxed against the trigger even as nervous anticipation throbbed at the base of her neck.

A slight breeze rustled the trees nearby. She searched the darkness for his features, and he stepped into the moonlight, his footsteps silent on the concrete despite his size. That solid, muscular build had made her feel small when he held her against him. The beam illuminated the square jaw she'd caressed many a morning, and his eyes still mesmerized her. Brown pools of chocolate that could see straight into her soul, and when they turned dark with passion...

She shivered. He could melt her with a look. But seeing him didn't get any easier. "What are you doing skulking out here, Luke? If I'd been more paranoid, I could have shot you and asked questions later."

"In your dreams, honey. I could've disarmed you in seconds, and you know it. Besides, you're too good at your job to shoot first."

"Lucky for you." With a few deft motions, she unloaded the weapon and replaced the bullets in a small leather case.

"Not bad. You know your way around that gun."

"I'm a sniper. I'm good at a lot of things, including detecting bull when I hear it." She tucked her gun in the duffel then straightened. "We've said all we need to say."

Luke took in the fierce expression meant to terrify mere mortals, and damn if he didn't get hard, because he also saw the translucent glow of her skin and the heightened flush of her cheeks as the moonlight bathed her face. His body didn't know how to be cautious with her. His heartbeat quickened and tension worked its way through him. The damp tendrils framed Jasmine's face, begging his hand to push them out of the way. How easy it would be to walk over, yank her against him, and kiss the hell out of her. Get it out of his system. Maybe her lips wouldn't taste as exotic as his body remembered.

He wished he still had the right to steal her very breath then kiss her lips to softness.

"Old man Peterson should fix that light," he said to distract himself.

"Mr. Peterson died a year ago. His son takes care of the place now." She shifted the bag to her other arm. "What do you want, Luke?"

You. Naked in my bed two years ago, explaining what really caused you to walk out on me. "I need more information for the next article."

"Use what's in the press releases. No way am I giving you an interview."

"If I don't get it, my editor will send someone else. Might as well admit you can't get out of the discussion. Just start with something simple. Where'd you grow up?"

Her eyes flickered and shifted left. The back of his neck bristled and the tingle in his temple returned. *Don't lie to me, Jasmine.* He knew from experience that lies begat lies, and secrets led to blackmail and bad choices. Things that could corrupt cops.

In his jacket he held the true answer to his question: a twelve-year-old notice from the *Sierra County Sentinel* in New Mexico, a small weekly press with fewer than five thousand subscribers and no database. Only the old-fashioned clipping service had discovered the truth misplaced in its archives.

She swallowed and met his stare before pulling away from him. "Fine. I grew up in Idaho. Now will you leave?"

"You're lying...Jane." He closed in on her, cornering her against the hard concrete of her apartment building. "Truth or Consequences, New Mexico, is a long way from Idaho. Imagine my surprise when my investigator tracked down the legal notice. Jane Sanford, ex-ward of the state of New Mexico, legally became Jasmine Parker on her fifteenth birthday."

Her face drained of color. Her shock gave him no pleasure, no satisfaction, but she couldn't know how seeing that fax come in through his office had sent him reeling in disbelief. Her life was a fabrication. He'd given her a chance to tell the truth, and she'd lied anyway. Now he wanted to know why, and he would find out...one way or another.

A car door slammed in the parking lot. Luke lowered his voice. "I don't think we want to have this conversation in a stairwell, do you?"

"I don't want to talk to you at all."

"Not an option anymore and you know it."

She scanned the area, and the chatter of a family coming toward them seemed to make up her mind. "Fine. Come on."

Jasmine resettled the duffel on her shoulder, unlocked the door at the base of the stairwell, and hurried into the apartment building. Luke followed in silence.

As he strode into the apartment he hadn't entered in two years, he studied the tidy room and for the first time noticed how little of Jasmine he saw here: no photos, only a few knickknacks, nothing on the bookshelf but official-looking training manuals, nothing to give him a hint of who she was or used to be. The scene was in stark contrast to his own house, with its wall of memories and photographs of each and every family member at nearly every important event in their lives.

Perhaps he hadn't wanted to look beyond the passion between them in the past, but as she faced him in the center of the room, hazel eyes darkened, flashing green as she glared, memories assailed him. A touch football game at his mother's house, a touchdown, an illegal tackle in the end zone culminating in a kiss. Jasmine sitting on the porch swing in the backyard, watching him and his brothers battle it out in volleyball, her expression surprisingly wistful. The longing on her face had been so deep he'd asked her later if she missed her family, but she'd shut him out—again. It had been the beginning of the end of their relationship. A few days later, she'd walked out.

"Why are you doing this?" she challenged. "My past, and my future for that matter, are none of your business."

"As a journalist, the truth is my business. Why are you lying to me?"

She shifted and the tension emanating from her rose. "I haven't lied. I *am* Jazz Parker."

"You *were* Jane Sanford." Luke leaned forward. "What happened to you? Why would a fifteen-year-old change her name? What's so scandalous that Brian Tower thinks he can use it to bring you down? Or maybe there's more to this than just your past? Like something going on in the sheriff's office right now?"

"You think I'm corrupt? I would never dishonor my badge. My job is what I live for."

"Would you do anything to protect your career? Like Derek did anything to protect himself and his father?" He grasped her shoulders and forced her to face him. "Trust me. Tell me the truth."

Scorn colored her expression. "Why should I? So you can do to me what you did to Derek? Expose my life to the world? He pleaded with you to drop that investigation, but no, you had to keep pushing. Too bad you didn't find out he wasn't guilty until after he put a gun in his mouth and blew his brains out."

He winced at the dead-center hit. Did she think he hadn't wondered if he could have done things differently? "He covered up his father's activities. If Derek hadn't asked *me* to lie for them both, maybe we could've worked together to bring down the organization. *He's* the one who betrayed our friendship. He knew what happened to my unit in Afghanistan, and he lied to me anyway."

"He was protecting his family. Don't tell me you wouldn't do anything for your brothers, or your daughter."

"Hell yes, I'd kill for them if they were in trouble. But they'd never put the innocent at risk. They'd never put me in a position to lie for them."

She swallowed, and her breath hitched. "Then you're lucky."

A vulnerability Luke had never seen before washed over her before she pushed it back with palpable force. She shoved her hand into her pocket. He recognized the instinct. Had seen it more times than he cared to remember, and he'd never clued in on the real vulnerability the small act revealed. Going for a comfort fix, Luke realized. Her hand shook as she pulled out the roll of butter rum Life Savers. In her nervousness, the candy dropped to the floor.

"Great." She knelt down to pick it up, but Luke hunkered beside her and reached for the sweet. Their hands touched.

Luke's nerves tingled with awareness. He knew she was hiding something more than her name, but her secrets didn't smother his desire for her. The scent of the herbal shampoo he remembered so well curled its tentacles around him. His body hardened, his heart pounded. The first time he'd met her he'd wanted her then and there. Nothing had changed. He knew the strength of her—and the accompanying softness. All this enticement he could have handled, but when her breath caught in an answering pull to his nearness, his treacherous body couldn't deny the attraction.

A flash of panic crossed her face, but Luke had seen enough.

"Why don't you just leave?" The slight quiver in her voice revealed more than she would ever admit.

"I don't want to leave."

He gripped her fingers, entwining his with hers, and squeezed. He saw the moment she recognized his desire. Her breath caught and she drew her hand from him.

She rose, shaking her head. "No, Luke. It's a bad idea. We're better off leaving the past alone. I've moved on and so have you."

"It's a very bad idea." As if pulled by an invisible rope, he closed the remaining distance between them and grasped her arms, tugging her against him, her body fragile and defenseless against his strength.

If she'd resisted he would've let her go. But she didn't. Something stronger than logic drew them together. They fit together. In so many ways it was like coming home.

His mouth hovered over hers and the emerald green of her eyes flared hot, smoldering with promise. "If you really don't want this, Jasmine, tell me now. Tell me you don't remember how good it was between us."

She didn't pull away. The pulse at the base of her throat pounded, and her tongue peeked out to moisten her lips. Her cheeks flushed and her voice came as no more than a whisper. "I remember. Even when I don't want to."

With a groan, he let his desires take over. He cupped her face in his hands. Slowly, savoring the sweet anticipation, he lowered his mouth to hers. At the first touch of her softness, his heart slammed against his chest. He felt too much of the past, but at this moment, he didn't care. He ground his lips against hers like this wasn't their first kiss in two years, but as if they'd never parted.

He held her head still so his mouth could explore the sweetness of hers. Moments later, she yielded, pressing her body even closer. A flash of heat surged through him, and he let himself sink into the passion.

Her tongue parried thrust for thrust, the mating ritual reminiscent of an age-old, erotic dance. His hips strained forward and she cradled him, nestling against him, welcoming him. He wrapped his arms around her and held her even tighter, eliciting a soft series of sighs. She would be ready for him. He knew that.

He knew her.

He moved his mouth to her ear and nipped the lobe. A throaty purr whispered from her. He smiled with satisfaction. Yes, he knew her.

In answer to his every wish, Jasmine groaned in surrender to the passion and leaned against him, backing him toward the sofa, shoving his jacket from his shoulders to the floor. His foot tangled in the cloth, and he kicked it aside. With a crackling paper sound the wrinkled fax documenting her name change fell from his pocket and landed face up beside his coat.

Luke froze as Jasmine glanced down. With excruciating deliberation, she bent down to pick up the fax and stilled.

"What was I thinking, letting you touch me again, when I know what you really want. A story."

Her accusing gaze flew to his. Hurt and betrayal burned in her eyes—replaced in seconds with pure fury.

"So, Luke," she bit through clenched teeth. "Just how far were you willing to prostitute yourself to learn about Jane Sanford and land on the front page again?"

Jazz wiped the stain of stupidity from her mouth. Her lips still tasted of Luke. She felt branded, and that really ticked her off. "I *won't* be used by anyone." She stalked to the door and opened it wide. "You know your way out."

His expression closed down as he shrugged his jacket over his shoulder holster. "You could've trusted me, but that's not in your makeup, is it? You haven't changed at all."

"Why should I?"

He stalked past her. She slammed the door after him, shutting his presence out of her life once again.

Damn him. For a few moments she'd been swept away. He knew exactly how to touch her, to melt all her defenses. It'd been so long since a man had held her, made her body tingle, made her want to be close. Why was he the only one she wanted, when he was out to use her?

She gripped the fax in her hand and stared at the legal notice of her name change. Stupid. She'd witnessed the obliteration of every article in the *Sierra County Sentinel*'s archives referring to Jane. Somehow, though, this obscure notification had slipped through—probably because it was buried in a long list of legal mumbo jumbo. Leave it to Luke to find hard evidence linking her to Jane. She ground the paper into a small ball and leaned back against the worn oak doorframe to rest her throbbing head. If he found out the truth behind her name, he'd destroy the life she'd fought so hard to create.

The cell phone rang and she grabbed it as a shield more than anything. "Parker."

"We've got a hostage situation. Maybe a copycat of our kidnapper. Blue Team is up."

"I'm there in ten, Sarge." She hung up the phone, grabbed the keys from the table, and caught her determined reflection in the mirror. She was a sniper. Nothing more, nothing less. She had to remember that. Jane Sanford was gone, irrelevant now. Only Jazz Parker's ability to protect the hostages and her team mattered.

She took the stairs two at a time as pounding steps rose to meet her. Suddenly Luke blocked her on the first floor landing. She lurched to a stop when she saw the HK gripped in his right hand. "What—?"

"You've got a problem," he said.

"Yeah, you," she snapped, but he moved to block her. "I don't have time for guessing games. I got called in. We're done, Luke."

She moved to sidestep him, but in one efficient motion he shoved her against the wall and pinned her, his hard body pressed intimately to hers. The square line of his jaw throbbed and his dark brown eyes had gone black with intent. It might've been sexy if he hadn't gone mission critical.

"Listen for once in your life. Someone knifed your truck. Tires. Seats. Everything. It's not going anywhere."

She pushed past him. "But we were just outside—"

"Which means someone was watching and waiting for an opportunity. I heard footsteps running from the parking lot. Big guy by the sound of him."

"If you're lying, I'll kick you across the asphalt."

"I'm not, and you know it."

She yanked free, pulled out her own weapon, and maneuvered past him down the last flight of stairs. "Fine, but *I'll* catch him. You aren't in the army anymore. *I'm* the law."

She grabbed the doorknob. He slammed his hands on either side of her and leaned forward, his weight preventing her from opening the door.

"I don't care if you're Wonder Woman. You're not going out there alone. Got it?"

She turned in the cage of his arms and faced him. "I have to get to the station. I have a duty."

"We go together. Slowly. Back each other up." He punched 911 into his cell and handed it off to her. "Report in. You'll get a quicker response."

Jazz spoke to the dispatcher then tossed Luke his phone. "I've got to be in the SWAT den ASAP. There's a situation."

"Then let's do this," he said.

"Stay behind me."

"Right." He slid into lead position and headed out.

God, he infuriated her.

They slid quietly into the enveloping darkness then stopped. Jazz tensed. The night held a discordant edge. Even though the street noise seemed louder and grittier, the normal night sounds in the surrounding trees were eerily silent. Was the vandal still out there?

They scoured each area for anything out of place, quickly working their way around the parking lot, back to back, allowing for maximum visibility.

Many snipers worked alone. She did. How different yet how reassuring would it be to work *with* someone—with

Luke—that closely? He literally had her blind side. No one had ever done that. Not even the man who taught her cops were the good guys.

She scanned the nearby trees and along the street, the dim lamppost casting only shadows. Nothing. "Seems safe enough," Jazz said. "Looks like he's gone."

"He left a hell of a present."

They made their way to her truck, but Jazz skidded to a standstill when she saw the mess. Luke clicked on a small flashlight and pointed the beam on the vehicle interior. The passenger door hung open and the upholstery was flayed in shreds.

Her hands white-knuckled her Glock. Someone had violated *her* property, in front of *her* home. Someone had attacked her where she lived.

Then her trained eyes noticed an odd pattern of gouges on the hood. As she moved closer, the marks collided into familiar shapes of letters. A message left by the vandal.

Killer Cop.

The truth in the words made her shudder.

Luke crouched down and swept the outer edge of the truck's undercarriage with his flashlight. He could still move like a mountain lion—silent and stealthy. A warrior to the core. A man she wanted at her side in battle.

"Anything?" she whispered.

"Without the right equipment, I can't verify there isn't a bomb." He thrust her away from the truck. "No point taking chances. Perimeter seems clear."

From a distance, she studied the shredded leather seats, the vicious slices. Her stomach burned. "Bastard. I've still got two years of payments."

He faced her, and the intense expression in his eyes worried her: concern, curiosity, and determination—a deadly combination within Luke Montgomery. He rested his hands on her shoulders. "So, Jasmine, who'd you piss off?"

"I—"

Suddenly his gaze shifted. In one seamless motion he smashed her to the pavement, his arms wrapped around her head, his body shielding her.

A sharp crack echoed into the night.

Chapter Four

Ten seconds, fifteen seconds. No second shot. Yet. Luke had to get them to safety. They were exposed and vulnerable.

He shifted his weight, angling his body so Jasmine remained protected. His entire being in combat mode, he raised his head and scanned the area around them. "The red laser sight vanished after the shot. See anything from your vantage point?"

With a steady hand, she aimed her Glock toward a group of oaks and peered into the night. "Nothing."

"He's playing with us," Luke muttered.

"If he wanted a hit, he had the shot," she said, her voice certain. "Clean line of sight from those trees."

"And we're lying in the middle of a parking lot with no cover. On three, make for your truck, north side behind the tire. Ready?"

Jasmine nodded. "One. Two." Her muscles tensed beneath him. "Three!"

Luke rolled off her and to his feet. She sprang up, crouched, and serpentined toward the vehicle. Keeping himself between her and the sniper's location, he maneuvered behind her, weaving and following quickly. They hunkered down behind the vehicle, weapons ready.

"No more shots," she said. "You think he bailed or do we have a chance at him?"

Luke studied the layout. "In Kabul, they'd play us like this. Wait until we relaxed a bit and start shooting again. Not this guy, though. He's delivering a message."

"A sniper pinned by a sniper. Unbelievable," Jasmine said.

A black and white screamed into the parking lot. Two patrol officers jumped out. Seconds later another backup, lights flashing, followed suit.

"Shooter," Jasmine called out. "Last known position, south of our location, in those trees."

The men took off toward the oaks, weapons drawn. Luke kept his HK steady, covering the cops. Jasmine paralleled his actions.

"He's gone, isn't he?" she said as the cops swarmed in a search pattern.

"Yeah. This was no ambush. Otherwise we'd be dead."

"A warning."

"Or a distraction," he said. "It worked."

"Clear," one of the officers shouted.

She was safe. Luke slipped his HK into his shoulder holster. He tugged Jasmine aside and cupped her face, his thumb lingering on the scrape on her otherwise alabaster skin. "You're okay? I didn't hurt you?"

She leaned into his touch, and for a moment the world around them faded. He wanted to wrap her in his arms and let the heat between them ignite again. It would be so easy to scoop her up, climb those apartment stairs, and finish what they'd started.

He pressed closer, but the crime scene van rumbling into the parking lot shattered the moment. Jasmine shifted away from him.

"I can handle a little tumble," she said.

He lowered his lips to her ear. "I'm not letting this go. We need to talk. About more than the shot."

Her cell phone rang. She scowled at the screen and turned from him to answer the call. The message was one-sided.

"On my way," she said. "That was Sarge. They called my backup when I reported the vandalism, but he's... indisposed. They'll wait ten minutes, or I have to meet them at the site." Jasmine turned to him, her face a professional mask once more. "I have no right to ask anything of you after what just happened, but would you drive me to the cop shop?"

"Unless you can get us clear of these guys," he said, nodding toward the slew of investigators roaming the perimeter of her apartment building, "I have a feeling we're in for a long night here."

"Leave it to me." She stepped away from Luke and motioned to an officer. He couldn't make out the quick dialogue between her and the cop, but she nodded in his direction and headed back to him.

"They'll interview us later. Let's move out."

"Mount up."

He grabbed her bag before she could heave it over her shoulder and, with a quick move, pressed a button on the keychain to unlock the doors of his SUV. She slid into the leather interior, and he slammed her door shut and rounded the vehicle. He slung her duffel in the back seat where it landed next to Joy's second favorite toy, Sparkles. The pink elephant bounced to the floor.

Jasmine's gaze latched onto the stuffed animal. "Now that's not something I imagined Luke Montgomery would have in his big black SUV."

He picked up the toy and arranged it on Joy's car seat. "Things change. People change. Priorities change. Mine are family these days."

She squirmed in her seat and laid her hand on his thigh. "I'm sorry," she said quietly.

His muscles tensed under her touch and he gripped the steering wheel. She could set him off with the smallest stroke, but he couldn't afford to give in to the urge to take her home and keep her in bed for a week. Not if he wanted to keep her safe. He had to keep his mind clear.

"I didn't believe you when you warned me, and my job put you at risk," she said. "You should stay away from me, Luke, until we catch this guy. For your daughter's sake if nothing else."

She was apologizing to *him*? "I appreciate the sentiment, Jasmine, but you don't have the whole picture."

"It's simple. Someone took offense when I eliminated the kidnapper and wanted to let me know. The cops'll find him."

"You don't get it." Luke shifted the car into gear. "I received a call earlier today. Untraceable. About you."

"That doesn't make sense."

"He'd read my article and didn't like my portrayal of you as a hero." She didn't need to know how much of an understatement that had been. "He implied your secrets have something to do with my corruption investigation."

"That's crazy."

"Maybe. Could be someone's wanting me to focus on you. Or maybe they're setting you up to be the fall guy for the whole investigation. I don't know. Yet."

"You're looking for conspiracies where they don't exist."

The light changed and Luke gunned the car forward. "Whoever called me accused you of hiding your identity because you're a murderer. *Killer Cop* was scratched into your car on the same day. That's *not* a coincidence. They want me to expose everything about you."

Even in the darkened vehicle, he could see her face pale as they sped under a streetlight.

"I'm a sniper. That's it. I'm no murderer. I do what I have to do to save lives, but all my terminations were justified. You should know that since you've been poking into my life." She rapped her fist against the window glass. "Can we just drop it?"

She could've been killed tonight, and she'd never flinched, but one mention of her past and she lost her cool like a rookie? Why?

"I'll lay off for now, but there are a lot of blank spots in your history. The person on the phone knows *something*," Luke insisted. "He's trying to make you look suspicious, and thanks to your evasiveness, he's succeeding."

"You suspect *me?*"

Interesting question. She was an expert at diverting questions from her past, even when their relationship had been at its best. He'd been so enamored with her beauty, with the amazing sexual energy between them, and with her sheer determination and guts, he hadn't recognized the thickness of the wall she'd built around herself. Not until he'd tried to get closer, to bring her more fully into his life. Not until he'd wondered if they couldn't have something permanent.

He'd asked questions.

She'd pushed him away. No communication, no conversation. One day, she just picked up her toothbrush from his house and didn't come back.

"You have a lot of secrets," he said finally. Luke didn't mention his suspicions concerning Tower. The guy had to be involved somehow. He was a sniper. He had access to Jasmine's private employee records, and his father was on Luke's suspect list. A convergence of convenience.

"And you're a son-of-a-bitch." She reached into her pocket—for her Life Savers, no doubt. A sure sign she was shaken, no matter how strong a mask she wore.

"Maybe, but I won't lie to you either. Can you promise the same?"

"Get me to the sheriff's office. This conversation is over." She stared out the side window, but he could see the hurt on her face.

He sighed and pulled into the parking lot at the precinct. "Look, I've been burned by trusting people who've lied. Men died because of it. You know that. Better than most."

He'd bared his soul to Jasmine. Like a fool. And not just about Derek. He'd revealed his biggest failure, hoping she would return his trust. He'd told her how his long-time translator in Afghanistan had given his unit faulty intel on a stash of weapons. Luke's wounded shoulder seized at the memory of his decision to capture the arms cache. He'd made the call and led his men into an ambush. It was a blood bath. Nobody walked away. Not even the idealistic embedded journalist standing right beside him.

"I couldn't save my men. Not any of them. I don't take anything at face value anymore, Jasmine. I can't."

"Never trust anyone. I get that. We're in one hundred percent agreement."

As he stopped the vehicle, Jasmine jumped out. Luke cursed, threw the car into park, and leaped out after her. He grasped her arm and turned her toward him. "One last thing—I watched you tonight. Your head isn't all there. If you were in my unit, I'd pull you off. Let someone else do the job tonight."

"There's no one else." She jerked away from his touch and his hand closed on air, empty and cold. He studied her fierce expression, but she couldn't hide the strain. She *hadn't* let go of what happened.

"I'm a sniper." She slung her duffel over her shoulder and it slammed against her body. "I have a responsibility to my team and to the victims. I won't let some idiot who doesn't have the courage to face me stop me from doing my job and protecting my team. I won't fail. I can't."

She turned her back on him and, with a determined stride, charged into the sheriff's office.

Luke stared after her. He'd really screwed up this time. Jasmine was vulnerable whether she admitted it or not. She needed someone to watch her back. He bypassed the front desk and headed to the SWAT team's den. As he opened the door, Luke soaked up the flurry of activity.

Gabe rushed over to him, glancing furtively side-to-side. "What are you doing here?"

"Montgomery," Sergeant Carder bellowed from his office. "Get your snooping brother out of here before I write you up and throw him in jail."

Gabe winced and pushed Luke out of Sarge's sight. "I don't know why you're here, but now is *not* the time."

Luke stopped him with a sharp tug. "I came with Jasmine."

Gabe's jaw dropped. "You're kidding. Is that why she whipped through here? What'd you do to tick her off?"

"What didn't I do? But that's the least of her problems. Someone shot at us. After they vandalized her truck," he whispered.

"What's going on?" Gabe said.

"I don't know. The shot could be retribution for one of her terminations. Could be about my investigation. I'll figure it out, but I'm worried about her. She handled the truck and getting shot at pretty well, but when I told her about the phone call, she started to crack. She's trying to act like she's fine, but I don't think she is. Can't you tap someone else for this mission?"

"Collins was at a wedding and had a few too many. She's our only available sniper. No other backup. No choice."

"Look out for her, Gabe."

They watched Jasmine, who was checking her tactical rifle and night optics. Her adroit movements seemed so in control, Luke wondered if he'd been too quick to judge. Then she fumbled with the keys to her locker, dropping them with a clang on the floor, her expression shocked, her discomfort clear. Within seconds she scooped up the keys before double and triple checking the items in her gear bag.

Gabe blew out a stream of air as he pushed Luke clear of the SWAT team den. "Don't worry, bro. She's got ice for blood. Once she gets to the site, she'll be fine. *She's the one who watches out for us.*"

"Okay, Blue Team, move out." Sarge's voice shot into the room.

The sound of a final few zippers closing echoed through the room. Jazz checked her gear a fourth time and fell in line with her nine teammates. She longed to sneak a butter rum, but on the ride, the close quarters of the SWAT van would give her away. One last time she looked over her shoulder at her locker and the bench in front of it. She hadn't forgotten anything, yet even after ensuring the state of her equipment multiple times, uneasiness gnawed under her skin like a splinter. She shifted the bag on her shoulder, confirming the weight of her gear.

She tried to shake off the disquiet as she walked toward the parking lot outside. A quick glance told her Luke's car had left.

Good. She couldn't afford to dwell on what he'd said or how he'd made her feel. The latter she'd forget. The former, well, after the mission, she'd consider the unwelcome possibilities of what had happened tonight. For now, she had a job to do.

Her vision adjusted to the darkness, and the distinct black SWAT vehicle loomed before her. She didn't consider asking for help as she jumped in the back. When she was with the team, she wasn't a woman; she didn't need or want special consideration. She was *their* protector, not the other way around.

Jazz slid onto the last seat available in the back of the van next to Gabe, only to find him studying her with disconcerting intensity. The van's motor roared to life and they sped to the outskirts of the city. Finally she couldn't take the silence. "Out with it, Gabe. What do you want to know?"

"Heard you had a close call."

"I got through it."

"Like a pro." He leaned toward her, his voice low so no one else could hear him. "I also know there's a lot more than shots fired going on with you. I need to understand. About Jane. About you."

A shudder skittered down her spine. He'd said *her* name. For twelve years Jane Sanford had been dead. Jazz had fought long and hard to bury the past, and now Luke had resurrected Jane.

She'd thought she'd escaped—but could she ever really be free? The girl from the wrong side of the tracks in T or C, the girl who'd walked the streets to put food in her belly, that girl no longer existed. Jazz Parker had emerged from the rubble. Why couldn't everyone just leave her alone?

"Does it matter, Gabe? I'm still the person I was a week ago."

He shook his head, and Jazz's stomach rolled with nausea. She'd known this would happen. That's why she'd changed her name. That's why she'd never trusted anyone with the truth.

"You're not the person I thought you were," he said. "You haven't been honest, and that changes things. Somehow, this," he motioned between them, "feels...off."

"Nothing in my past affects today. It shouldn't matter that I changed my name."

"I know you must've had a good reason, but I don't get why you hid it from us. We're supposed to be family, Jazz. The whole team. Families don't hide secrets from each other. Not about important things."

Family. She hadn't thought he could surprise her, but his statement did more than that. He'd shocked her. She had no family. She couldn't afford to care that much. Sure the team depended on her, but that wasn't the same thing.

Her gaze slid from man to man. There were a few tentative nods, but mostly doubts. She could see them. After what Tower had said, how could the team not wonder? When they discovered the truth would they trust her to protect them? Had Tower destroyed everything already?

Old fears bubbled up inside her from a dark place, a dark time, when she'd let down the only family she had—her mother. Jasmine could feel the child's, Jane's, presence here in this van—Jane's limitations, Jane's insecurity, Jane's failure.

Jazz couldn't afford any qualms right now. Every instinct screamed to protect herself from her own weakness—from *Jane's* weakness. *Jazz* had a hostage crisis to deal with.

A small farmhouse and family waited, terrorized by a group of gang members. She had to be confident for their sake. She had to save them, like she hadn't saved…No. She wouldn't let the memories intrude. Not now.

"Gabe, this isn't the place for this discussion."

He leveled a knowing look at her. "Then after. Because we will talk, Jazz. We have to."

Carl Redmond's voice rose above the sound of the van's speeding tires on the narrow road. "Sarge said these guys are Four Corners Hustlers. That's not good."

"You got that right," Steve Paretti bit out. "The psychos think they're hot stuff because they swing weapons around."

"Kill someone and you're a full-fledged member. Kill enough and you're a bloody leader," Carl muttered.

"I'll bet these yahoos were watching the news about the governor's daughter and decided to make headlines for themselves. I overheard Sarge say they want a million dollars. Idiots. It's gonna be tough to back them down," Gabe added.

A grumble of agreement filtered through the van. No one wanted this standoff to end with a dead hostage.

Gabe leaned toward Jazz, his voice dropping just above a whisper. "Forget I said anything. I shouldn't have brought it up. I can see you're antsy, and neither one of us can afford to be preoccupied."

He sent a pointed stare to her leg bouncing nervously. She reined in the movement.

"We'll talk later," he said. "Once we've taken care of business."

He'd never shown this kind of deference before tonight, before Luke had pulled him aside. "Why the kid gloves all of a sudden? What did Luke say?"

Her voice rose in anger, and she caught a few quizzical glances thrown her way. Deliberately she lowered her tone. "He implied I couldn't handle myself tonight, didn't he? Well, he doesn't know what he's talking about. He doesn't *know* me."

Gabe couldn't hide the concern on his face, which annoyed her even more.

"He still cares about you, and he knows what distractions can do. He's been through a hell we've never imagined. He's worried, Jazz."

"Luke thinks the sniper attack and vandalism's got me spooked," she cursed under her breath. "I'm pissed, but I'm not rattled."

Gabe clicked his tongue. "I'm not so sure about that. I don't see the 'Ice Queen' sitting next to me, Jazz. Can you push it all aside?"

The nickname she'd long been proud of fired her fury. He wouldn't have dared suggest such a thing to one of the guys. Her gut burned. Somewhere in the last few days he'd stopped seeing her as a teammate and started seeing her as weak.

"I'm fine."

"Seriously, nobody would blame you if you didn't want to be primary tonight. If the situation is getting to you at all, you should turn it over."

"When I have to, I can pull it together, Gabe."

"Are you sure?"

"Watch me."

She closed her eyes and took a few slow, deep breaths. Her imagination dipped her into a lake of tranquility, washing away the worries and memories as if she'd escaped into peace.

She'd learned the technique early in life, to divorce herself from the worry, the pain. Back then, she'd needed the control to find enough to eat, to outwit the dark side of her mother's world, to help her bear what was happening to her. Now she used the skill to prepare for battle.

As if she'd cleansed herself in hot springs, the night's events, the conversation with Luke slid to the corner of her mind. Moments later she opened her eyes to Gabe's fascinated expression.

"Wow," he said. "That's freakin' cool, Jazz. A little scary, but definitely cool."

"Okay, you two, break it up." Paretti leered at them. "Or is there something you'd like to share?"

Gabe rested his arm on Jazz's shoulder. "I just want her looking out for me, boys. I was reminding her who's the quarterback of this team."

The van burst into laughter, and Steve Paretti howled over the rest of them, "You wish."

"Hey, Paretti, I heard Tower was nosing around today."

"Did you get a whiff of him? The guy reeked of perfume. And that smile on his face, no doubt he'd been doing the horizontal mambo with that redheaded angel." Carl wiggled his eyebrows.

"She's a hottie all right," Steve added. "I'd love to take a peek to see if those curves are real or silicone. Gabe could probably tell us. They were up close and personal."

Gabe cleared his throat. "A gentleman never tells tales."

"Then you must have lots to say, Montgomery," Paretti said.

A fresh bout of laughter erupted, filling the van until the vehicle stopped. At the final squeak of brakes, the antics ceased. Each team member turned his focus toward the job.

Two by two they jumped out into the dark night, ready to work, steady in purpose.

They formed a close-knit circle around Sarge. He pulled out an aerial photograph and a map of the surrounding area and shined a narrow beam of light on the layout. The farmhouse stood amidst several barns, a water pump station, a vegetable garden, and clusters of piñon trees.

Immediately Jazz's attention turned to a small hill about a hundred yards to the west of the farmhouse.

Sarge followed her line of sight. "Good eye, Parker. Take Zone One."

Jazz ticked through the procedures. She was ready; she would protect them. "I'm there."

"Okay, people, take position," Sarge said. "Let's just hope the negotiators can pull this one out and we can get home before dawn."

Jazz strode away from the group and climbed the hill. She pulled on her camouflage cloak and made her shadow invisible on the crest, the netting and threads blending into the grass profile as if nature had engineered them both. As she estimated the distance to the farmhouse and to the windows within her sight, she clicked the night optics in place then double-checked the windage and elevation of her Leupold Mark V scope. She adjusted the windage knob two clicks, moving the scope to a perfect position for the distance then did the same with the elevation knob.

As she lined up her sight, a flash of color sailed past the window. Then she saw them. A family of four cowered in the corner. She could barely make out two small pairs of legs as a man and woman tried to shield their children, but they couldn't hide the fear. She had a bad feeling about this one.

"Blue One ready, Blue Leader."

"Roger, Blue One."

"Blue Two in position," Gabe's voice whispered over the intercom system.

A car's headlights sped up the road, and she heard a vicious curse from Sarge. She recognized the SUV immediately. Luke.

"Great. Just what we need. Michaels, set up a perimeter. Keep the press away from here."

A couple of uniforms manned their positions, and even from her vantage she recognized Luke arguing with them. His tall, muscular frame towered over the men. He was a lethal weapon. He could've thrown the cops aside with a few quick moves, but he didn't. She shook her head to regain her focus. He wasn't here because of her. He was here because of the story.

"Secure, sir." Michaels' voice crackled through the intercom.

"Let's make it happen, children."

The team deployed, following Sarge's attack plan. They were good. Gabe and his entry team moved into position to storm the building; the perimeter guards strategically positioned themselves to shoot tear gas or lob a flashbang into the farmhouse. She prayed they wouldn't need either distraction. She didn't want to have to take another shot. Some snipers went years without neutralizing a target. Jazz had taken down more than her share.

As the team moved in perfect precision around the farmhouse, she surveyed the movements from above. It was like watching a ballet. Pure art.

The negotiator's calming voice as he tried to talk the gangbangers down echoed through her earpiece.

"Get the pigs out of here, or the woman's dead. I ain't kidding!"

The kid was strung out. That made him dangerous. Jazz caught a rustle in the window visible from her vantage point.

"Movement at the window, Blue Leader."

"Hold position, Blue One."

A shot fired inside the house. The window shattered. One of the gang members—he looked to be almost thirty—brandished his weapon. Jazz stared through her scope. The perp's eyes were wild, his pupils dilated, and his hand was shaking around the butt of the gun. He dragged the woman out of the corner, shoving her husband to the floor. Not good.

"Adult female. Guy's got a .357, Blue Leader. Itchy trigger finger. He looks strung out."

The guy whispered something into the woman's ear. She tried to shake her head, and he dragged the barrel down her cheek. "Gun moved. He's got the barrel under her jaw."

A sharp curse echoed through the microphone. "Look for a shot, Blue One. We may have to move in. Get ready, but watch that weapon."

Blocking out the woman's tears and fear, Jazz lasered her focus on the kidnapper through the scope. She needed that shot. Her muscles tensed, waiting for his mistake.

The perp didn't disappoint.

"Blue One to Blue Leader. Subject One is not moving. I can eliminate him, but Subject Two is three meters to the east. Too high of a risk to take them both."

Silence bellowed through her earpiece until Sarge's voice cut through the quiet.

"We have a go, people. We'll take out Subject Two once we're in. Make the timing work. Blue One, you terminate Subject One. I want a flashbang at the same moment as the entry team batters the door. Eliminate Subject Two. Everyone got it?"

The team members checked in. Jazz breathed in and out slowly, focusing, waiting for the order. Once she downed Subject One, the woman would be in less danger, and the team could safely restrain Subject Two. The strategy would work if he'd just stay in her sights. *Don't move, don't move.*

"Stand by, Blue One." Sarge's voice had gone clipped and tense.

"Ready, Blue Leader." Jazz willed the man not to blow the woman's head apart before she received her orders.

She heard a slow inhale over the microphone. "Fire."

Jazz exhaled and squeezed the trigger. The flashbang exploded. The entry team burst in.

Her target didn't drop.

She went numb. Impossible. He should've gone down.

One second lasted forever. When the team realized the plan had gone south, curses erupted in her ear.

"Move, move, move. Get that woman safe."

All hell broke loose, and Jazz could do nothing but watch the green-tinted images through her scope. Too many bodies, too much movement for her to risk a second try. Powerless, she watched as Gabe blazed past her line of view. He grabbed the woman, swinging her aside, his weapon drawn.

Out of nowhere, Subject One raced past, a flash of metal glinting at the edge of her field of vision. She recognized the jagged blade of a Buck hunting knife. "Blue Two. Knife. Behind you."

Gabe whirled around, and Jazz lost her view in the struggle.

Steve's voice yelled through the microphone. "Officer down! Get an ambulance here. Now. He got Gabe."

Jazz froze at the words. No.

She closed her eyes and had to remind herself to breathe. Oh, God. Luke. She couldn't risk even a glance away, but she knew he was standing there, behind the tape, not knowing his brother had gone down.

For the first time she cursed her job. She needed to get off the top of this hill and take out the bastard who'd sliced Gabe. But she couldn't leave her post, not until Blue Leader gave the all clear.

"Come on, guys," she whispered as her thumb tapped against the stock.

She watched through the powerful Leupold as the team herded the suspects. Finally they clamped the last one in cuffs and shoved him in the back of a black and white.

She scanned the windows with the scope but detected no movement. Where were they? Why hadn't Sarge called the all clear?

An air ambulance roared in from the east, its rotor wash stinging Jazz's face. Gabe was bad, or they wouldn't have called the chopper.

Once it landed, the EMTs rushed in. Within minutes they carried a stretcher out of the house. Gabe's black uniform had been cut away, revealing a body that had paled to the color of milk. An IV dripped into his arm, and his face was hidden by an oxygen mask.

Her mind receded to a distant nightmare: a death-gray face and a blood-soaked body. Her mother's body. So very still, just like Gabe.

Alice Sanford had never awakened again.

Gabe couldn't die.

A sharp yell caught her attention. Luke shoved the perimeter guard aside, ducked under the tape, and out-maneuvered another uniform to rush to Gabe.

As they loaded him into the chopper, Luke lifted his head and searched the hill where she lay. She couldn't read his expression, but she knew what he was thinking. This was her fault. She'd said she could protect the team, and she'd lied. He'd been right not to trust her.

Somehow, she'd missed, and now Gabe might forfeit his life.

Chapter Five

In the cramped space of the helicopter cabin, Luke crouched beside the stretcher, ignoring the vibration and urgency in the pilot's voice as the helicopter took off. He hated medevacs. He'd flown in a lot of choppers with a lot of injured soldiers over the years. Too many hadn't made it home. Luke refused to consider the possibility this time. His brother wouldn't be a fatality statistic. He couldn't be.

Luke gripped Gabe's hand tight. "Man, little bro. You know how to work the situation. First-class ticket to the hospital and all this drama for a little scratch."

Gabe tried to smile. "It's not good," he whispered.

Luke leaned closer to hear his brother's weak voice. "I've seen worse." Of course, most of them hadn't made it. Gabe's attempt to smile did nothing to ease the fear burning in Luke's belly. He didn't acknowledge the feeling often, but when it was family…training went out the window.

His brother coughed weakly and his eyes flickered shut.

Luke pushed the panic back. "No way, Gabe. Don't you do it. Montgomerys don't give up. *You* don't give up."

Gabe's chest heaved and he squeezed Luke's hand. "Wasn't Jazz's fault. Make sure she knows it. Stand by her."

"How can you be sure?" Luke didn't know what to believe. He could see three options: she'd flat-out screwed up and missed; she'd tanked the shot; or she'd been sabotaged.

"Best shot there is." Gabe's lips tightened with pain. "She's all about protecting us, she'll blame herself. The team won't fight for her."

Gabe sucked in a weak breath, and the nurse working on his leg let her mask slip. Her grim expression chilled Luke to the bone.

"Keep talking to him," she whispered. "Don't let him go."

Luke urged his brother to hang on, but inside, recriminations tore him apart. The caller had warned him his family might be in danger. Was Gabe's attack a different kind of message? Had Luke's failure to discover the caller's identity brought more grief down on his family?

He knelt down next to Gabe's ear. "You're going to make it, little brother. Mom will kick my butt if anything happens to you, and Dad will kick yours if you meet him at the pearly gates before your time."

Gabe's eyes crinkled at the corners then he grimaced. His eyes closed and his hand went slack.

"No!" Luke's cry echoed over the roar of the helicopter blades.

The nurse took Gabe's pulse and gave Luke a cautious nod. "He's just unconscious."

"He'll make it?"

Pity crossed her face. "I don't know. He's lost a lot of blood. The surgeons are waiting for him. He's got a chance."

Luke gripped his brother's hand and squeezed, willing life into him. "You hear that? There's nothing to worry about."

At that moment, the lights of the hospital roof came into view. He sent a prayer heavenward. "*I'm* not giving up on him. Don't *You* give up on him either."

The cold mountain wind whipped against Jazz, but she felt nothing. She lay unmoving and focused, perched above and apart from her teammates.

She didn't know how long she'd been there. The air ambulance carrying Luke and Gabe had long since disappeared in the night sky.

As she waited, she replayed the events leading up to the stray shot again and again. Nothing stood out. Nothing had changed from the last hundred missions. Where had her bullet landed?

Finally Sarge's voice barked through her earpiece. "All clear. Blue One, report to Command Central double-time."

Jazz ripped off her camouflage cloak, grabbed her gear, and hurried down the hill toward the spotlights littering the front of the farmhouse. The team formed their usual line-up, silhouetted in front of the series of lights; a stark, empty space where Gabe should have been standing broke the human chain. She wanted to hide, but there was nowhere to run. She'd let her team down; she had to face them.

When she came to a stop in front of Sarge, he frowned at her, the disappointment and frustration in his gaze something she'd never seen before. "What happened?" he barked.

The words pierced her because she had no answer. "I don't know. He was in my sights. He should've gone down."

"Leave your rifle with me. There will be a full investigation."

His too-quiet voice sent a chill through Jazz. She stared down at the weapon in her hands, the custom-made stock, the perfectly balanced barrel, the one thing in her life that had never betrayed her, and her foundation crumbled. The Remington shook in her hands.

"Gabe?" she croaked out his name.

Sarge's expression grew cold. "Gangbanger caught him in the leg. Slashed Gabe's femoral artery. He bled a lot, and he's in critical condition. They're taking him into surgery. It's touch and go."

Sarge didn't state the obvious. If she'd done her job right, Gabe would be with them now. Swallowing around the lump in her throat at the knowledge she'd let everyone down, she opened her case and placed the Remington carefully inside, scope still attached. Afterwards, she chanced a glance at her teammates, certain she'd see accusation in their eyes. Some looked away, a few shook their heads in pity. Several glared. She saw the truth. They blamed her, just as she blamed herself.

She shut them out, as she had so many times before, and met Sarge's stare. "Which hospital?"

"University." He took the weapon case from her and tagged it with an evidence number. "Luke went with him. His family will be there soon. You may want to stay clear for a while."

She sent him a curt nod with no intention of listening to the advice. She had to be there for Gabe and Luke. And for herself.

But first, she needed to find out what happened. "May I go into the house and see where the bullet hit?"

Sarge studied her, and she knew he could see every doubt, every worry she tried to hide. Finally he nodded. "Redmond, Paretti, go with her. Wear booties and don't touch anything. IA will be all over this."

Her commander didn't trust her to go in alone. The realization cut into her. Why else would he send Redmond and Paretti with her? Was he afraid she'd tamper with evidence if it made her look bad?

"Parker," Sarge held Jazz back as her shadows gathered the protective equipment and moved to the house, "I'm doing this for your protection. IA can't come back and say we doctored the scene to cover for one of our own."

His face didn't crack an expression as he stared at his team. "Now figure out what happened."

Jazz followed her teammates into the house to the room where Suspect One had held the woman—to where the bullet should have met the target's head. There was no sign of the bullet or a hole. What was going on?

Careful not to contaminate evidence, she studied the broken window first, but couldn't see any obvious damage that would have caused the bullet to veer. She turned toward the paneled wall and let her eyes wander in concentric circles from the point where the shot should have landed. Three inches. Her heart skipped a beat. Six inches. Her throat tightened. Twelve inches. Sweat beaded on her forehead. She had to be a cop now. Her mind clicked through the events, as if she were checking and rechecking the sights on the shooting range. It didn't add up.

She turned to Steve and Carl. "I don't understand. No glass left in the window. Nothing should have deflected the bullet. It should have hit him."

Gone was the joking camaraderie from the van. Their faces held that speculative mask she hadn't seen since she'd first won her slot on the team.

Her insides turned cold. She'd known they would turn on her someday. She really could only count on herself. She returned her focus to the wall. This was crazy. Where was the bullet? If she didn't know better, she'd doubt she'd fired at all.

Her gaze continued its survey. Over a foot off the mark, she saw it. Her throat burned sour. "What the...?"

A hole. But how could it be her hole, her bullet? She hadn't fired that far off course—*ever.* Especially not at just a hundred yards.

She studied the impression, but knew she couldn't dig out the bullet. IA would have to do that.

"You found something?" Steve Paretti came to stand beside her. He placed an awkward hand on her shoulder, but she shrugged him off.

"Crap," he said. "Did the thing take a right turn at Albuquerque?"

His attempt at a joke fell flat. Nothing could excuse what she'd done. How badly she'd missed.

But she *never* missed.

The nausea in her belly churned as she walked to the window and looked up at the hill where she'd laid. "It can't be mine. It doesn't make any sense." Unless Luke had been right. Unless she'd been so rattled tonight that she'd lost focus.

The thought cramped her insides. She prided herself on maintaining control—and on going by the book. Sure, she'd been furious tonight, but she was not some shrinking violet. She didn't rattle easy. She was a professional. She could picture herself checking the elevation and windage, taking aim, breathing. Taking the shot.

Oh, God. With the mark that far off, anyone could've been hurt. If the hostage had been on the other side of the perp, the woman would be dead now. And Jazz would be responsible not only for Gabe going down, but also for murdering an innocent.

Sirens blared from outside. Redmond cleared his throat. "Come on, Parker. The finks are rolling up. Sarge shouldn't have let us stay this long."

Jazz took one last look at the damning wall and nodded. They left the farmhouse, but not before she scanned the scene one final time. She couldn't understand what had happened. How could she have been so far off?

The answer still eluded her when the team reached the sheriff's office. She hadn't looked any of them in the face on the strained ride. She'd ignored the few comments directed her way. As quickly as possible, she stowed her gear, got a loaner truck from the lot, and made the long drive to the hospital on her own.

After reaching the surgical floor, Jazz searched the hallway. The waiting room should be close. She hated the institutional green color of the walls. Granted, this wasn't an orphanage or a court house or even a way station for kids who weren't wanted. But the horrid green still gave her the creeps.

She finally found the right door, but didn't turn the doorknob. The Montgomerys were probably inside. She wanted to hide, but there was nowhere to run. She'd let Gabe down; she had to face his family.

With a deep sigh she pushed open the door. The room was empty. No mother, no brothers, no Luke. Her lungs emptied and she could breathe again.

Maybe they were somewhere else, a place where the *real* family waited.

Family.

The word made her shudder. Gabe had called her family, but she wasn't. Not really. And now, because she hadn't listened to him, he was fighting for his life.

The image of the knife played over and over in her mind until it was all she could do not to scream. How had she missed the shot?

She snagged the chair closest to the door and perched on the edge, ready to bolt. She tugged at the neck of her gray sweatshirt. She'd changed into civvies, not wanting to agitate an already tense situation when she saw the Montgomerys.

No, that wasn't the entire truth. She hadn't stripped off her SWAT team regalia so much for Gabe's family as for herself. How could she wear the uniform of her team when she felt as if she'd blown the unit apart?

Sarge had been right. Coming here was a stupid idea. She should have gone home and waited for news. She should leave. Right now.

The door slammed open beside her, hitting the side of the chair and blocking her from view. Luke strode in and she tensed. He hadn't seen her, but Jazz's heart twisted at the torment carved in his face. She'd never seen his hair so unkempt, like he'd tried to tear it from his head, and lines she hadn't noticed before grooved his mouth. But the pain in his eyes hurt the most. She'd seen them in passion, in aggravation, but never with the agony she witnessed now.

He rammed his fist into the wall. "Damn it!"

The anguish cloaked within the wrath made her ache for him.

Oh yes, she definitely should have left. But now, like so many other times in her life, she had no choice but to stay and deal with the consequences. "Luke," she whispered.

He whirled around, his body poised for attack, his aggression, frustration, and fury tearing across his face in waves. When her identity registered, he went still. "Jasmine? What are you doing here?" Disbelief edged his voice.

The urge to go to him, apologize, and hold him close appalled her. She had no right. This was her fault. "I'm so sorry, Luke. I shouldn't be here, but I just couldn't wait at home. I had to know how Gabe's doing."

Luke shoved his hand through his hair. "He's still in surgery. No news." He paced the room like a caged beast, body taut, ready to ambush anyone who dared bring him bad news.

Unable to watch him in so much pain, she followed her instincts, stood, and reached out a hand to clutch his arm. "Can I find your mother, your brothers? You need your family with you now."

He said nothing, just stared at her as if he couldn't believe she had the audacity to even breathe the same air he did. Expecting rejection, she turned to leave.

Luke grabbed her arm and spun her to him. "God help me, Jasmine. You're what I need."

He yanked her to him, the hard muscles of his body shaking with emotion she'd never seen in him before. He buried his face in her hair and she could do nothing but stand there, holding him, not knowing how to comfort this kind of grief.

"Just this," he whispered. "Give me a minute."

In all the time they'd spent together, she'd seen him frustrated, strong, intense, smoldering, but this was unfamiliar territory. She raised an unsteady hand and stroked his hair.

"It's bad," Luke's voice choked out the words. "He was so gray. I've seen that look too many times on men who didn't make it." He lifted his head and his bloodshot eyes bored into her. "The doctors aren't hopeful. I saw it on their faces."

Jazz didn't want to hear that. She refused to believe Gabe wouldn't survive. "He's strong."

"Strength doesn't always matter. My dad was invincible—at least I thought so. Then on his day off he walks into a convenience store and some punk kid with a stolen .45 blows a hole in his chest." Luke's jaw tightened. "My father died in this hospital. I'm not sure my mother can handle another doctor coming in with the same news."

Jazz didn't know how to respond, so she just wrapped her arms tighter and whispered words as much for herself as for him. "Gabe'll make it. He's got to."

Luke's cheek rested against her head and he pressed her even closer. They stood there, in silence, unmoving.

"Luke? Jasmine? Oh, dear God. What's happened?"

The woman's panicked voice wrenched Jazz from Luke's arms. She recognized the Irish lilt. Luke's mother stood in the doorway, her pale face tense with concern. Anna Montgomery hurried toward them, followed closely by Luke's U.S. marshal brother, Nick.

In an instant Jazz watched as Luke thrust aside his own emotions. His jaw strong and eyes calm he pulled his mother into his arms and hugged her close. "Gabe's still in surgery, but he's fighting. I've left messages for Seth. He's on a mission, and Zach's on location in South America. The studio will get in touch with him as soon as possible."

Anna nodded her head against Luke's chest as he comforted her, whispering words Jazz knew he didn't believe. Jazz backed away toward the exit. She *really* should have listened to Sarge. She didn't belong here.

"Jasmine." Anna's soft voice stopped Jazz, and slowly she turned to face Gabe's mother. "I'm glad you're here."

"I am *so* sorry."

Tears pooled in Anna's emerald eyes, and Jazz couldn't hold her gaze. Shame bowed her head. Anna cupped Jazz's face in her hands and the smile that trembled at the corner of her lips nearly buckled Jazz.

"I know you did everything you could, honey. Gabe knows too."

Jazz wanted to scream in denial. *No. It's not true. I missed the shot. I failed him.* But she couldn't form the words, and she couldn't pull away. Anna held her tight and Jazz's heart crumbled as, unimaginably, Anna comforted *her.*

Luke's hand stroked Jazz's back, and an undeserved warmth settled over her in this unexpected cocoon. She wanted to cry. She needed to leave before she broke under their kindness. Before she could escape, though, a large bear-like man strode in, his arms laden with a bundle of pink. Caleb Montgomery couldn't have looked more fierce, except that his eyes moved tenderly from the sleeping child to his mother. The blanket fell away from the angel's face and Jazz's throat tightened. Joy.

Luke strode to Caleb and lifted his little girl into his arms. "You shouldn't have brought her."

"We didn't have anywhere else to leave her," Caleb whispered. "The Baileys are on vacation, and I...I had to come. We'll worry about the hospital kicking us out later."

Luke swallowed and pushed aside the soft blond curls. He kissed her forehead and ran a tender finger down her cheek. "Jasmine, meet Joy."

The gentleness in Luke's expression and touch squeezed Jazz's heart. She'd never seen such love in anyone's eyes. She'd never felt that kind of love either.

Anna held out her arms, and Luke shifted the precious bundle to his mother. The little girl snuggled against her grandmother's chest, the stuffed clown fish tucked in her arms. Silent tears fell down the woman's cheeks as she stroked Joy's blond curls. Now three generations waited for word.

Caleb turned to Luke. "Gabe?"

"I'm ready to break down doors. No news since the last specialist went into surgery."

Caleb's face turned grim with purpose. "We'll see about that. I still have M.D. after my name even if I don't have hospital privileges here anymore."

Jazz hovered and turned to the exit, but Luke firmly drew her down beside him as if there were no question she belonged there. "Stay."

Guilt wracked her, but she couldn't leave. Not when she owed the Montgomery family for what she'd let happen to Gabe.

Within minutes, Caleb returned, his expression somber. "It's grim. They called in a vascular surgeon. He's lost a lot of blood. They're not sure how much muscle and nerve damage there might be. He may not regain full use of his leg...if they're able to save it."

Nausea burned Jazz's throat. She wanted to disappear, but then she witnessed something remarkable. With quiet grace, Anna pulled a string of rosary beads from her jacket pocket and bowed her head. In an oddly synchronous movement, all three strong men knelt beside her.

Soon low whispered prayers filtered through the waiting room. Jazz wished she knew how to pray for Gabe, but, growing up as she did, every ritual the Montgomery family performed in this sterile room was foreign to her.

So she simply bowed her head. *Please. Save him.*

A chilled breeze sliced along the hill next to the hospital, thrashing the piñon needles into a frenzy. Jazz Parker had looked devastated as she'd walked in.

Good. The bitch deserved that—and more.

The plan had been brilliant. Just a little turn of a knob, and Jazz Parker was a pariah.

One missed shot, and the SWAT team didn't trust her anymore. How wonderful it would've been to watch the cops scurrying around like rats wondering what'd happened to their precious plan. Fools. They should've known when they hired the daughter of a town whore that she'd fail. Jazz Parker—no, Jane Sanford—couldn't be trusted. She was a thief and a liar. Always had been. Always would be.

If only the cop would die. That would be perfect. If not, the hospital entrance was an open invitation. Death could be arranged. There were a lot of ways to die in a hospital.

Yes, Jane would feel pain like she'd never felt before. Pain she deserved. Someone Jane cared about *would* die.

Justice had a name, and it was vengeance.

Chapter Six

Luke didn't know how long his family and Jasmine had waited, but midnight had come and gone. He'd prided himself on patience in the field, but when it came to those he loved, he had none. The doctor's face had appeared more and more grim each time he'd updated them. All Luke could think about was his brother surviving. Then his mind would veer to tracking down the thug who'd done this to Gabe and snapping the guy into pieces.

"Daddy?"

At his daughter's sleepy voice, Luke shifted in his chair and shoved aside the stark thoughts of retribution. He couldn't let Joy sense the violent rage vibrating beneath the surface. Burying his emotions, he knelt beside the little girl, who'd fallen asleep using his mother's lap as a pillow. Tenderly he brushed the hair from his daughter's eyes. "Why are you awake, munchkin? The sun's still asleep."

The girl rubbed her eyes. "Where's my bed? I thought Uncle Caleb was taking me home."

"Daddy needed to be here, so Uncle Caleb brought you to me."

Joy's nose wrinkled up and Luke watched as her mysterious little brain processed the information. Sometimes he would just sit and watch as she discovered a new fact about the world and marvel at the capacity of a human being to grow and adapt. She gave him hope that good things existed in this world. Now he prayed she would be spared from learning the lesson of death much too soon. He still hadn't figured out a way to explain her mother's death to her. She knew she didn't have a mommy because her mommy was in Heaven, but she didn't remember Samantha, and that made it easier. For now.

"Is it church day? Is Uncle Gabe here too?"

"Uncle Gabe is sleeping right now, munchkin."

"But I'm awake, and I want to play with him." She threw her blankets aside and plopped down off her grandmother's lap. "Wake him up, Daddy. He won't mind." Joy hugged her stuffed clown fish to her. "Me and Hero want to fly to Uncle Gabe."

"He can't wake up right now, Joy." Luke's voice turned gruff. "You remember when we went to the park last Saturday?"

"You bought me a red balloon." Her expression brightened.

"And remember when you slid down the slide?"

Her lips turned down and trembled. She lifted her elbow and pointed to the faint cut that had almost healed. "I hurt myself."

Luke nodded. "Well, something like that happened to Uncle Gabe, so he's with the doctor who's fixing him."

Joy placed her small hands on either side of Luke's face and leaned forward to whisper in his ear. "Will he get a shot?"

"He might. He has a big hurt, Joy."

"You'll kiss it and make it better?"

Joy's words held such conviction that Luke wrapped his arms around her and buried his face in her hair, inhaling the fresh scent of baby shampoo. "I love you, baby."

Her lips pursed against his cheek, and she blew a butterfly kiss then squirmed in his arms. "Let me go, Daddy. You're squishing me."

"Sorry, munchkin." Reluctantly Luke released his daughter.

In little bunny slippers, she explored her new surroundings. She padded over to her uncles and one by one patted them on the cheek when they lifted her up. Luke's heart warmed. He didn't know what he'd done to deserve Joy in his life, but he thanked God every day for her.

Then Joy's attention shifted to Jasmine's hair. The little girl's eyes widened in obvious awe. She stretched out a tentative hand toward the long, blond braid brushing Jasmine's thigh.

"Are you Rap...Rap..." Joy glanced over her shoulder at her grandmother. "What's the name of the princess with the long hair?"

"Rapunzel?" Anna's voice was soft and laced with a smile.

Joy leaned closer to Jasmine. "Did you have to cut your hair when you escaped?" she whispered, her voice conspiratorial.

Jasmine's panicked gaze flew to Luke's, but his daughter refused to be ignored. She stroked the shimmers of blond bound by the braid. "Were you scared when you ran away from the wicked witch?"

Confusion painted Jasmine's face. "What witch?"

"The one who stole you from your mommy and daddy," Joy said as if the answer was obvious.

A shaft of pain flashed in Jasmine's eyes, and Luke winced. He knew very little about her childhood, but it couldn't have been easy since she'd wiped away not only her name, but her entire identity. For all he knew she *had* escaped from a wicked witch. "Joy, don't bother Jasmine. She's sad right now."

Joy's eyes widened with alarm. "Are you going to cry? Do you need your mommy and daddy?"

Luke could see Jasmine struggling to maintain composure, her hands clenched in her lap. "I don't have a mommy and daddy, Joy."

"Who tucks you in at night?"

Luke stepped forward to pull Joy away, but his daughter's wrinkled forehead made him pause. He could tell she was working some problem out in her unique three-year-old mind.

She looked down at Hero and then up at Jasmine. "Is it scary at bedtime?"

Jasmine blanched. The sniper was gone. A vulnerable woman had replaced her. She tried to smile at Joy. "Sometimes."

"I get scared too," his daughter said, leaning in to Jasmine. "I don't like the dark," Joy whispered.

"Me either." Jasmine's hand shook; her eyes turned haunted. "I...uh...have to go now."

"Wait." Joy lifted her chin and stuck out both hands, cradling the well-worn orange and white fish. "You can have Hero. He'll keep you safe."

Then Luke saw something he'd never seen before. Jasmine's eyes glistened and she bit her lip.

"I can't take Hero. He belongs to you."

That stubborn Montgomery glint shone in his daughter's eyes. "It's okay. I have Daddy *and* Gamma *and* Uncle Gabe *and* Uncle Caleb *and* Uncle Seth *and* Uncle Nick. And I even have Uncle Zach. He's the Dark Avenger," she whispered. "He flies and catches bad guys."

Helplessly, Jazz glanced at Luke. "What should I—?"

"Take good care of him. He needs lotsa hugs every day." Joy shoved Hero into Jasmine's arms. With a small hiccup Joy ran past Luke and into her grandmother's arms.

Jazz stared at the stuffed toy. "I...uh...don't know what to say." Her voice had gone hoarse. "Th-thank you, Joy."

A thunder of footsteps echoing down the hall nearly drowned Jazz's words. Gabe's teammates filled the opening of the waiting room.

Sarge stood framed in the doorway and studied the situation before stepping inside. He strode across the room and nodded his head in greeting. "Mrs. Montgomery."

She stroked the blond hair of the child resting in her lap. "Sergeant Carder. Thank you for coming."

"How's Gabe doing?"

The rest of the team moved forward and shed curious glances at Jasmine.

"He's still in surgery. It'll be a while," said Luke.

As the team shifted to offer their best wishes to his family, Luke watched Jasmine draw away from them. No one came toward her. Couldn't they see what they were doing to her? Each second they were in this room ignoring her devastated her even more. As it was, she retreated inwardly, inch by inch, before his eyes.

She dug into her pocket, obviously going for a Life Saver. He hated seeing her like this. If it weren't for his mother and daughter, he'd knock a few of these idiots into doing the right thing. As it was, he'd have to be covert.

He pulled Paretti aside. "What the hell does your team think it's doing, treating Jasmine like the enemy?"

Paretti grimaced. "We tried. She distanced herself. As usual."

"Well, try harder. You all should be supporting her. Gabe told me you wouldn't fight for her. I didn't believe him until now. Guess I'll be the one standing by her since her teammates are too cowardly."

"Step back, Luke. You don't get it. There are a few jerks on the team, but most of them wanted to give her a chance. Have given her more than one. She pushed us away. Makes it hard to watch her back."

"Still—"

"Her shot was over a foot wide with no possibility of deflection," Paretti snapped. "The whole operation cratered. Gabe assumed the target was down. Instead he caught the bastard's knife."

Luke stared at Jasmine, who'd turned her back to the team and still sat alone, almost shrinking into the chair. Snipers *could* miss a target. It was unusual, but not unprecedented. A foot wide, though? He'd never heard of a shot that far off in all his years overseas.

And Jasmine being off that much. He didn't buy it. The only other option made his stomach knot. Sabotage. He'd been inside the SWAT den. The weapons were locked up, access limited to members of the sheriff's office. Proof of corruption, perhaps? Jasmine and Gabe might both be victims of the cancer spreading through the ranks.

"She doesn't miss. Ever." Luke spoke the words loudly enough that a couple of SWAT team members turned their heads.

"She missed tonight," Paretti said under his breath.

Luke caught Jasmine's expression and knew she'd heard at least part of the exchange. She carefully cradled Hero in her arms, stood, and, with her shoulders hunched, walked out of the room without saying a word to anyone.

"Shoot," Paretti muttered, "Maybe I—"

Luke stopped him with a glance. "Don't bother. If you want to do any good, talk some sense into your so-called team. I'll go."

He sent a quick glance from Joy to his mother. She nodded her understanding. Joy would be okay. His mother would see to that.

Luke stalked out of the waiting room and didn't pause for the elevator. He plowed down the stairs two-by-two until he reached the lower floor just in time to see her exit the glass revolving doors at the hospital entrance. Luke broke into a run, ignoring the censure of the white-haired gargoyle guarding the information booth.

When he finally shoved outside, the woman he'd raced after had already crossed the parking lot.

"Jasmine!" he yelled.

She didn't slow down, and he sprinted after her. When he caught up to her, he spun her into his arms and pulled her close. She shoved against his chest, but he wouldn't let her go. He pinned her to him, unwilling to release her.

"Let me go, Luke. Your family needs you."

"You didn't have to leave."

"How could I stay?" She sagged in his embrace and ducked her face against his chest. "Don't you get it? It was my fault. I lay on that hill tonight, far above the action, with just one job. One friggin' job. Take out the bad guy. Well, I screwed up, and Gabe paid the price. I know it. The team knows it."

"That's bull. In one night your car got vandalized, a sniper took a shot at you, and you missed a shot. There are no coincidences. If you blame anyone, it should be me. Everything started with my investigation and the article I wrote about you."

She shrugged him off, shaking her head. "Protecting them was *my* responsibility. You asked me if I was ready. I honestly thought I could handle it." She lifted her chin and met his gaze. "I made a mistake. I was wrong. Now Gabe might die."

"He won't die. You said it yourself, he's strong. He's a fighter. So come inside with the family."

"I can't." She clutched at his shirt. "I want you to know I'd trade everything to have Gabe safe and well. For you and your family. I'm so sorry."

She was so set on being alone, so determined to take all the blame. He framed her face with his hands and stared into her tired eyes. "You belong in there. With the people who care about Gabe."

"A sniper who misses can't be part of the team. They can't be counted on."

"I don't think you made a mistake. I think someone sabotaged your weapon."

"It doesn't matter. The weak link gets you killed. It's my job to be perfect."

"No one is perfect. And a team is supposed to watch each other's back." He kneaded her shoulders and rubbed the knotted muscles. "No one can do it alone. No one expects perfection. Gabe didn't expect it. He *told* me not to let you blame yourself."

"Well, I do. My team does. I've failed them."

"Are you telling me none of them ever came up short?"

"It's not the same. I have one responsibility. How can they ever trust me again?" She bowed her head. "It's over, Luke. My career, my place on the team. My whole identity."

He lifted one hand and tucked a strand of hair behind her ear. "I can't tell you there won't be fallout with your team, but don't give in. Where's that fighter I know is in you?"

"You don't know me." She shoved against him to escape his embrace.

"You're wrong about that."

His lips swooped down and fastened to hers, hard and demanding. Butter rum burst between them. The taste flooded him with memories of Saturday mornings nestled in warm covers, losing himself in Jasmine's passionate touch, making the world fade to nothingness.

God, he wanted that for her right now.

She softened against him, and the chaos of emotions engulfed his senses. He pressed his body closer, where, for just a moment, he lost himself. Present, past, future, they all faded away in the sweetness of her lips. Nothing existed but her mouth. Her hands roamed his back, eliciting a rumble of pleasure in his chest.

Struggling to control the primal need burning inside him, he raised his mouth and stared at the woman who'd just melted in his arms. He wanted to unbraid her hair and tangle his fingertips through those silken strands. He longed to feel her legs wrapped around him and her breasts pressed against his chest with nothing between them but heat and desire. She could make him forget like no one ever had.

Now was not the time or the place, but he would have her again. And soon. He didn't want to give up touching her, so he let his hands roam down her arms, down past her waist to the soft curve of her hips. Her eyes blinked open, soft with desire, and he pushed back a wisp of hair.

She swayed against him, shaking her head. "Oh, God. I can't do this," she choked. "I won't be like her. I swore I would *never* be like her."

Her words didn't make sense, but the panic in her voice, the torment in her eyes tore through him. "Who?"

"My mother," Jasmine said. "I used to hide in the dark, forgotten, while she entertained them. A man, any man, meant more to her than I did. She only remembered me once they left."

She pushed away from him, her cheeks drawn, her body stiff, and he let her go. The fight within her died right in front of him. He wanted to shake the passion back into her, but her small revelation stopped him. He could only imagine the horrors she'd faced, and he could do nothing to protect her from the past.

"Look at me, Luke. My teammate is helpless, maybe dying. It's my fault, and all I can think about is escaping into your arms. I'm no better than she was." Jasmine shook her head slowly. "I may not know who I am anymore, but if I become like her, I really *am* nothing."

From the hidden lookout above the hospital, a hand reached out and ripped a branch from the tree. Hatred seethed through every pore. Luke Montgomery had kissed the bitch.

A red haze clouded blurry vision. No. No. No. This wasn't right. He was ruining everything. Jane Sanford was supposed to be humiliated, abandoned, and alone. Her team didn't want her around anymore. The cop had said so.

Whitened fingers balled against camouflage pants. The slut was just like her mother.

Montgomery was like all men. He couldn't wait to get into her pants. He'd been warned, but he'd fallen into the Jezebel's arms. Well, he'd regret that mistake. The ones he cared for most—his family—would forfeit the ultimate price. They would be destroyed.

A satisfied smile twisted determined lips. Soon, Jane and Montgomery would both pay. In blood.

The August moon hung above the sheriff's office, suspended like a fading spotlight in the early morning sky. Night and day, past and present, trading shifts.

As Luke steered his SUV down the block, he banged his hand on the steering wheel. Gabe was in a medically induced coma and holding his own, but Jasmine had vanished. Run off like before, like Samantha had.

Samantha. He hadn't thought about Joy's mother in quite a while. Not until recently. The affair had started out so much like his and Jasmine's. They'd connected. Too fast.

They'd liked each other, had fun together, and then she'd turned serious. She'd wanted him to give up his foreign travel. Stay home. Find a life in Denver, near his family. She hadn't understood why a war across the world was so important to him, and he couldn't explain. He hadn't wanted to explain those darkest parts of his soul. He'd left her, promised to return, and been captured by a group of insurgents. For several months even his family hadn't known if he was alive or dead. When he came home, Samantha was already gone. He hadn't looked for her, though; he'd been relieved. He hadn't wanted to hurt her, but he hadn't known that by not following her, he'd lost a child he didn't know existed.

Well, no more letting go. Not anymore. He shouldn't have let Jasmine leave the parking lot. Not in her state. He'd hoped a few hours of rest would snap her back to herself. Had she gone to her apartment? Of course not. Stubborn woman. He'd been searching for hours. She hadn't been at any of her usual hangouts either: the gym, running in Apex Park, or even the corner convenience store that stocked butter rum Life Savers for her. The cop shop was the only place left to look. She had to be here.

He'd been mulling over the situation all night. He'd contacted his researcher to take the search on Jasmine one step further. He'd even authorized travel to New Mexico to hand search the archives.

She'd lied about her past, that much was clear, but he also knew a fundamental truth about Jasmine. She wouldn't have sacrificed her team—or Gabe—for anyone or anything. The miss last night had devastated her. She hadn't tanked the shot.

Hell, he was violating his own rules by not having proof, but at heart she was a protector like him. He and Jasmine were alike in so many ways. They fought with all the strength they had for right and the innocent.

He also understood something today that he hadn't considered two years ago. He'd terrified her with his blind resolve to ferret out the truth about Derek. She'd recognized he wouldn't quit searching if he'd gleaned she was hiding her own dark secrets. Well, the thing she'd hated most about him was about to come in handy.

He pulled into the parking lot. Nothing mattered except finding out who was doing this to her. And why. Had Jasmine been the target? Had Gabe? Was this about the corruption investigation...or something else? Too many loose ends.

Luke didn't like it when pieces didn't fit. Hadn't liked it when he commanded his Ranger unit. He didn't like it as a journalist either. Trouble tended to follow.

Out of the corner of his eye, he caught the flick of a cigarette lighter. A cop out for a smoke? Close to the parking lot's exit, the tall, broad-shouldered figure, face obscured by a ball cap and an overcoat, stood hunched near an old red Pinto.

Something about the man's stance and the Pinto bothered Luke, but he couldn't quite place the car. Had he
seen it before? He maneuvered the SUV into a parking
space, but his Ranger instincts revved into overdrive.
What was he missing?

At that moment Jasmine emerged from the station.
She carried a rifle case in one hand. Simultaneously the
man standing next to the Pinto dropped the half-smoked
cigarette, snuffed it out with his heel, then picked up the
butt and pocketed it, his movements quick and furtive.

Unless this guy was anal about littering, normal people
didn't usually tuck away their cigarette butts. Surveillance
might. Or a predator who didn't want to leave behind
traceable DNA.

Jasmine crossed the parking lot, jumped into a beat-up
pickup truck she must have scrounged from a junkyard by
the looks of it, and, before Luke could react, tore onto the
street. A second later, the man Luke had been watching
ducked behind the tinted glass of the Pinto, and the old
car lurched once then pulled out after her.

The guy was following her.

Luke floored the gas and raced after the red vehicle.
He grabbed his cell phone and punched a number on
his speed dial he'd never bothered to delete. It rang then
went to voice mail.

"Damn you, Jasmine. Pick up."

As the red Pinto weaved through traffic, always maintaining at least one car between him and Jasmine, Luke
pressed on the accelerator to keep up. He squinted to
read the small car's license, but it was covered in mud.
The guy knew what he was doing.

Luke redialed several times, but Jasmine still didn't answer. Obviously unaware of the tail, she turned toward the outskirts of Golden then pulled on the road to the rifle range.

Her destination clear, the red Pinto slowed but didn't stay with her. Luke gritted his teeth and debated whom to follow, but he had no real choice. He couldn't let the unknown subject get away.

With a quick turn, he tailed the Pinto onto a side street, barren of traffic except for the two of them. Within minutes, the car whipped through another quick turn, then took a second left. Luke cursed. He'd been made. And the guy knew how to evade.

Luke swerved to make another sharp turn, but when the SUV straightened, the obviously suped-up Pinto had vanished. His muscles taut with urgency, Luke retraced the last several hundred yards, looking down side streets and alleys for any sign of the red vehicle.

Nothing.

He'd lost him! If the guy doubled back to Jasmine… she was alone.

Luke yanked his SUV around and flew toward the firing range. He would get to her in time. He had to.

Wind gusted between Jazz and the target, buffeting her clothes with sand. Her elbows pushed into the cold dirt as she lay belly down on the ground. She'd been up for over twenty-four hours, but it didn't matter. Nothing mattered but the truth. Fighting bone-numbing fatigue, she shifted her hips and tried to replicate her position from the night before.

Tower had cornered her at the crack of dawn for an official sit-down. His interview had been brutal. He'd relished every moment of having her in the chair across from him, knowing she couldn't leave. He'd grilled her with question after question. About the weapon's scope settings, its windage, its elevation, her own emotional state. The worst part was she'd asked herself those same questions over and over again since last night. Did he think she hadn't wondered if she'd made a mistake? If she'd lost it?

She hated the doubts that crept into her mind, but she couldn't stop them. She'd fought so long and so hard to find a place where she would be respected. She didn't expect love or friendship or family. Those were out of reach, but she could hit a target. Better than anyone.

At least she had until last night.

Using the back-up weapon Sarge had given her, she'd know in the next few minutes if she'd lost everything. Could she take it if she missed again?

The tripod cradling the gun didn't take the pressure off her triceps as she maintained position, attempting to mimic everything—the cramped muscles, the stiffness, the pressure—before taking the first shot.

Without looking at her watch, she knew it was time. She'd waited long enough. She clasped the stock, blinked the grit from her eyes, and focused. She didn't need the cool air whipping through her shirt to tell her which way the breeze blew. Through the scope, at a forty-five-degree angle to the right, she could see the wind mirage, rolling like waves across her view.

Jazz held the gun into the optical illusion to compensate for the gusts of air. On a clear, still day the bullet would move to the right a bit. Centrifugal force would do that. In this weather, she had to make additional adjustments, but each move was like second nature.

The target should be easy. She'd made tougher shots more times than she could remember. Never had any shot felt as important.

Gazing at the concentric circles of the target, she focused on the ten ring, the bull's-eye. Deep breath. Another, and another. Jazz exhaled slowly and, between heartbeats, squeezed the trigger.

For a brief second after the shot rang out she closed her eyes, unwilling to see another hit off target. Heart pounding, hands damp with sweat, she opened her eyes and stared through the scope. Dead center of the ten ring.

Thank God.

Something large and dark lifted from Jazz's heart, and her arm sagged, letting the barrel drop a few inches. Unexpected tears burned in her eyes. Despite what she'd told Tower, until this very moment she hadn't been certain. Not really.

Jazz cleared her mind and focused. She raised the barrel, sighted the target, and fired. Again and again and again.

After the last round hit, Jazz walked out the hundred yards and removed the target from its backstop. She held it up to the sun, but even with the paper flapping in the twenty-mile-an-hour wind, the tight pattern of holes streamed sunlight on her face. Twenty out of twenty, less than a centimeter off the ten ring's center.

"Tower, you son-of-a-bitch. I haven't lost it."

She tacked up another target at 250 yards and strode back to her weapon, her steps quicker, her concentration more focused than it had been since the moment Gabe fell. She'd do it again, this time faster.

She pushed aside the sleep deprivation and lay prone in the dirt. The world around her disappeared; the wind faded to nothing. The past, the future were driven away by a single piece of steel flying through the air at 2,800 feet per second.

Twenty more shots; twenty perfect hits.

Jazz lowered her weapon, centered in her skill. The fault wasn't her aim. Something else had happened. Sabotage, as Luke suspected? Soon she'd be able to tell him…wait a minute. Why did proving herself to Luke matter? Had Luke ensnared her emotions again? She couldn't let that happen. She needed to show Sarge. She had to stay focused on discovering what happened to Gabe.

She stood and made her way down the range to the second target, then hunkered in front of it. The center ring holes had melded into one, just a few millimeters from the first target's cluster. She whizzed through the calculations in her mind. Perhaps adjusting the grain of the full metal jacket would give her a bit more precision.

She pulled off her ear protectors just as a man's shadow raced across the paper. Jazz whirled to her feet, her body poised for combat.

Luke yanked her into his arms and hugged her tightly against him, his lips brushing her hair.

"Don't you ever turn on your cell phone?"

She must've imagined the slight tremor in his voice and shaking in his body.

He grabbed her weapons and clasped her hand, dragging her into a run toward their vehicles. "We've got to get out of here. Fast."

"Is it Gabe?" she breathed, terrified of the answer, struggling to balance the targets and keep up with his long stride.

"They think he's gonna make it. But someone tailed you from the station. Red Pinto. Muddied license plate."

Jazz stumbled slightly then righted herself. "Red Pinto?" she gasped. "I noticed a red Pinto on the street near my apartment before the truck was vandalized."

"Then your buddy's back. And he could be watching us." Luke scanned their surroundings. "Pray to God he's not the sniper. Move it."

Chapter Seven

Luke couldn't believe he'd been so careless. He could have lost Jasmine. If the guy in the red Pinto was the sniper, he could've taken them both out. They'd been exposed, sitting ducks. He should never have let her out of his sight.

His fingers drummed on the steering wheel. He could see Jasmine's loaner truck not too far ahead of him, but he wanted her with him. Now. His hands itched to hold her. His lips missed the taste of her.

He'd known this would happen. He didn't want to fall for her. He had too many questions; there were too many secrets between them. But his body didn't care. One inhale of her clean fragrance, one touch of her smooth skin, one smile or sparkle in her hazel eyes, and he was a goner.

Until he found out who'd targeted her, though, he had to stay on mission. He couldn't let his desire distract him.

Following her as they headed to the sheriff's office, he searched for tails, particularly the red Pinto, but he saw nothing. He needed another lead. Unfortunately he only had one option. He snagged his phone and dialed a number he'd memorized but hoped he'd never have to use. "Come on, Grace. Pick up."

"H…hello?"

The tentative greeting infuriated him all over again. When Grace had called him about the corruption within the sheriff's office, she'd risked her life by ratting out her purported family. The crime syndicate they ran was into drugs, prostitution, gambling, gun running. If it was profitable, they had a piece. Grace wouldn't chance leaving her husband, no matter how much Luke had argued. Not unless her husband and the head of the family could be stopped.

"It's Luke Montgomery."

A soft sigh filtered through the phone and she cleared her throat. "Okay, I'll answer your survey if it won't take too long."

He heard a loud curse in the background and then the sound of a closing door. Damn, he wished Grace would let him help, but short of kidnapping her and her son he couldn't do anything. If he discovered enough information, though, he *could* involve the FBI.

"I'm outside just in case the place is bugged. I've got a few minutes before Charles gets frustrated."

"Grace, I can help you. I'll put you in touch with a U.S. marshal and witness protection."

A derisive laugh escaped from her. "The family can get to anyone. The last person who tried to help me is dead. That's why Steve Paretti turned his back on his father and the organization in the first place. I'm still shocked he hasn't been eliminated. No, it's better if I'm here until the end. It's safer for me and Bobby."

"I hate seeing you trapped."

"I won't always be," she said softly. "I'm glad you called, though. You're being followed, Luke. I saw the photos.

They want to know who tipped you off...and what you've found out."

"How'd they find out about the investigation?"

"You questioned the wrong person. They have ears everywhere."

"I've received threats. Is there a hit out on me?"

"Not yet. They want to scare you, but if you get too close..." The silence grew thick. "Maybe we should forget the whole thing. If you let it be known you've stopped—"

"No way. We'll make you safe." Luke rounded a corner, only a few miles from the sheriff's office. "Have they mentioned Jazz Parker?"

"She's the sniper on the news, right? She's never been here, and I've never heard them talk about her."

Thank God. Luke hadn't realized how desperately he'd wanted to believe in her. At least now he had one less reason to doubt.

"How about Brian Tower?"

"Him, I know. He attended a *very* private party last week. Tons of security. He was an arrogant jerk. I had to smile and be nice. Like always. How'd you know he was here?"

"Was he with his father?"

"I haven't seen the sheriff in a while. The son came on his own, and the family fawned all over him. I don't know why, but it must've been important."

"Interesting. Brian Tower and no sheriff. Could he be the one following me?"

"Maybe, but I can't be sure," she said. "I need to go, Luke. Don't call here again. Please. I'm going to have to explain as it is."

"If you hear anything about Sheriff Tower or Brian or Jazz, let me know. Anytime. Day or night. Lives are at stake."

"For both of us," she said softly. "I'll try to find out more. If I can."

The line went dead.

Luke flipped on his turn signal. Brian Tower. A key to his investigation into the sheriff's office and maybe more of a player than he'd imagined. No longer just a deputy with a grudge, Tower now seemed to be linked to Luke's investigation into Grace's family. Was Tower's IA interest in Jasmine connected at all?

Or was it a coincidence?

The entire situation sat wrong, but there was no proof of anything except that Tower possessed enough information to hurt Jasmine. Luke never wanted to see her shrink the way she had in that hospital. That wasn't his Jasmine.

His Jasmine. Oh, man. *She's not yours. She never was. Get it through your thick skull and deal with it.* He should focus on who was out to get Jasmine, and then he needed to stay away from her. If he could.

Her truck turned toward the sheriff's office and he followed, slowing down, validating they hadn't been tailed. He pulled into the parking lot, and with a quick scope of the area to verify their safety, he jumped out of his vehicle to help her gather her weapon and the targets.

She wrenched open the rusty door of the truck. "I didn't see the Pinto. You?"

"We weren't followed, but it doesn't matter. He knows you work here."

"This is crazy." She dug into her pocket and pulled out an empty Life Savers wrapper. "The day just keeps getting better and better."

"Someone is out to get you. We need to find out who and how before the situation gets worse. If they are willing to sabotage your rifle, they'll do anything."

"You believe that? You don't think I lost my cool? That I made a mistake?"

"Whatever has happened between us, Jasmine, I do know some things about you, and I believe you would do *anything* to protect the team. Just like I would. You're a hell of a good sniper. Maybe the best I've ever seen. A foot off isn't a normal miss. Whoever did this knows what they're doing, and they don't care who gets hurt. Gabe's the proof."

Impulsively she leaned over and kissed his cheek. "Thank you."

The touch of her lips re-ignited the unwanted heat so close to the surface. "You are always...unexpected."

The air between them sizzled. His heart thudded as he stared into her green eyes, then he lowered his gaze to her lips. She swallowed and licked their fullness.

To hell with good intentions. Without waiting for permission, his lips claimed hers, and she surrendered, shoving her hands in his hair, returning the kiss with an intensity that made him shudder. He wanted to give in to the longing that threatened to overpower him and throw her into the back of the SUV and make her his. He longed to sink into her and lose himself in the heat.

It wouldn't take much to drag her into the back of his SUV and let himself peel away her clothes piece by piece until she lay beneath him, skin glowing, eyes soft, lips swollen from his kisses. His body throbbed with desire, and he arched against her hips, letting her feel the strength of his need.

Panting, she wrenched her mouth from his. "I thought we agreed this was a bad idea."

"We did. And it is." He thrust his hand through his hair. He wouldn't acknowledge the turmoil between his heart and mind. No matter how much he wanted her, he couldn't risk his heart—or Joy's—with someone who'd walked out of his life once already. If he'd had a choice, he'd have walked away. But he had no other option. And neither did she. "I'm going to take care of whoever's doing this to you, Jasmine. I'll *make* it work out."

"Save the fairy tales for Joy. My life isn't made up of happy endings."

Jasmine stepped away, and a veil came down between them, that barrier of protection he recognized so well. All for the best. She turned on him and grabbed her targets and gun from the truck.

"And yet," he said, "you still believe in justice. Even though it's clear the person who sabotaged your rifle has access to the SWAT den and was probably a sniper. To get anything past you would take some serious skills. My bet's on Brian Tower at the moment. I doubt he's working alone, but he's involved."

"He's a sniper. He hates me, but he's a cop. He took an oath. We all did."

"Now who's living in a fairy tale? Cops turn bad. Tower's got means and opportunity," Luke said. "I think he might be playing both sides. Half cop, half organized crime stooge. I don't have proof, but I've got indirect evidence. If we could tie him to the Pinto, we could prove his involvement, but we can't assume anything. Anyone on the SWAT team—past and present—is a suspect. Sergeant Carder and Sheriff Tower were both snipers."

She shook her head. "I won't believe that. My team might not have faith in me anymore, but they wouldn't sacrifice Gabe. And Sarge would never give up any of us."

"I hope you're right. For the record, I've known Carder for years. Our parents were friends. I doubt he's the one."

"Is that facts or your gut, Luke?"

"The last few days have reminded me that confirmation isn't always there when you want it. Sometimes all that keeps you alive is instinct."

He walked with her into the sheriff's office and watched her nod to a stiff desk sergeant. The jerk didn't return her greeting. They'd judged her already, and it annoyed the hell out of him. They deserved a lecture on teamwork, that's for damn sure. But Jasmine. She just walked on by. He admired the pride in her step, the lift of her chin. She didn't let them see how much they'd hurt her.

Just as they were about to push through the double doors leading to the SWAT den a voice from behind jerked them back.

Brian Tower sauntered toward them as if he owned the place. "Parker. I figured you'd run for the hills."

The bastard had some nerve. If Luke found corroboration Tower had *anything* to do with his brother or Jasmine, he'd bury the guy. For now, Luke fought to play it cool.

"I assume those are yours?" Tower nodded to the targets rolled up in Jasmine's hand.

She stiffened next to Luke. "And if they are?"

"I'd like to see them." Tower held out his hand.

Jazz wanted nothing more than to wipe Tower's Cheshire cat grin off his face. It had become far too familiar yesterday during her debrief. Now, as he plucked the targets from her hand and unrolled them, his smile deepened. Cold fingers ran up her spine. Why should an almost perfect target make him so happy?

"You're coming with me. Down to ballistics. There's a little test Internal Affairs would like you to perform."

Tower's sneer of victory sent chills through her. What was going on? She searched Luke's gaze for reassurance.

"Not without representation, she's not," Luke said, clasping her hand, compelling her to meet his gaze. "He can't force you."

"Maybe not. Of course, most of the men here would want to prove themselves," Tower goaded. "Still, I'm a bit surprised you're unwilling to eliminate yourself as culpable so my team can identify how Gabe ended up in the hospital fighting for his life. But it's your choice."

"Jasmine—"

Luke's tone cautioned her of the risk. She knew, but it didn't matter.

"I don't have anything to hide. It'll be fine."

Silent fury flashed in Luke's eyes, and she could tell if they'd been alone, he'd have dragged her out of here. He didn't understand that she needed to do this. Tower had called her out; she refused to back down or let Luke fight the battle for her.

"Let's go," she said.

Luke moved to follow, and Tower sent him a small smirk. "Sheriff's deputies only. Wait here."

. With one last, backward glance at Luke seething, she exited the office. Side by side, she and Tower walked to the elevators. He didn't speak, but Jazz couldn't ignore his sneer. "What do you think you're going to prove?"

Tower punched the down arrow and waited for the metal doors to slide open. When they'd both entered and he'd pressed the button to take them to the basement, he faced her. "That the daughter of a whore doesn't belong on our team. Did you follow Mama's example and sleep your way into the paper just like you slept your way into SWAT?"

No. This couldn't be happening. How could he possibly know about her mother? No one knew. No one.

Jazz's fingers closed into fists.

Tower snorted with laughter. "Come on, Jazz. Hit me. You know you want to."

Every instinct screamed at her to take him out, to use all the training at her disposal to squash this little worm, but as she studied where to best punch him she sighted the badge tucked into his waistband. She couldn't give him what he deserved. That was what he wanted. "I won't play your game."

"You have self-control, I see." He smiled at her. "Better than I thought, considering your white trash background."

She froze in place. She could almost hear Luke's voice. *Don't let him get to you, Jasmine. He wants you to crack, to do something stupid.*

"You didn't think I'd find out? Oh, babe, I know a lot more than appears in those flimsy files in IA. How do you think your SWAT mates will feel when I tell them what a fraud you really are? That you've been arrested for ripping off your Johns? Think they'll respect you then?"

No. Impossible. No one should've been able to dig up her juvenile arrest files. Sheriff Clarkson had destroyed them along with the newspaper articles. Someone else had to be feeding Tower information. But who?

The elevator doors slid open. She couldn't move. She just stood there, stunned.

He cracked a smile. "After you. I'd say 'ladies first,' but we both know you're not one."

She stiffened and leveled a laser gaze at Tower. "Back off, or I won't be held responsible for my actions."

"Threatening an investigating officer? That won't look good on your record."

He walked ahead of her and opened the ballistics lab door. "Johnson, she's here."

The ballistics technician acknowledged her presence with an embarrassed nod.

The whole thing felt like a set-up, and she'd gone and let Tower tick her off. Between her shock and anger, she was shaking. She had to rein in her emotions. She needed to be the Ice Queen.

She closed her eyes and pictured that lake, those hot springs washing everything away but the moment. One, two, three deep breaths and she opened her eyes.

"What do you want me to do?"

Tower nodded at her beloved Remington, resting behind the glass window separating the lab from the testing room. Her old friend. "Give us ten shots at the target."

"That's it?"

Tower smiled. "That's it."

Confused, she opened the door and looked back at Tower and the tech. Tower appeared every bit the commandant watching his worst prisoner take the final steps toward a firing squad. The tech just looked uncomfortable.

Jazz's stomach roiled, but she wouldn't let Tower intimidate her. A quick gauge of the distance, and she did her calculations. "Forty-five yards?"

The tech's eyes widened and he nodded.

Jazz picked up her Remington and fought the urge to wipe the stock with a rag. No telling who'd handled her baby. She checked the chamber and put on the shooting muffs. Her fingers adjusted the windage and elevation for distance before she tucked the perfectly balanced weapon to her shoulder.

She glanced through the glass at a condescending Tower and mouthed, "Ready?"

He nodded.

Jazz breathed in deeply, sighted the target, and squeezed the trigger.

The muffled sound of a bullet hitting the backstop brought a gasp from her. She stared through the scope. Where was the hole?

She lowered the weapon slightly.

"No," Tower shouted. "Nine more shots, Parker."

They'd tampered with her scope. They must have.

Jazz's hand trembled and she positioned herself behind the scope. Now she knew what Tower had wanted from her. Nine shots erupted out of the Remington's barrel. Ten missed targets and she could do nothing about it.

Finally, after the last boom sounded in the room, she lowered the weapon and stared at the target. Hands trembling, she struggled to raise each foot as she walked the length of the concrete room, a strange echo stalking her.

The pristine ten ring screamed at her, and disbelief whirled through Jazz. Her gaze lit on the nestle of holes about seven inches directly left of the target. The same relative distance as on the wall at the farmhouse.

Jazz stared back and forth from the target to her weapon. It couldn't be. There was no way she could have made that kind of mistake.

She rushed back to the Remington where Tower now stood, his gleeful expression almost high.

"So I see you missed yet again. Why am I not surprised?"

She couldn't think; she didn't care what Tower thought. All she cared about was proving her theory. "Let me have it."

Tower shrugged, and the technician watched as she focused in on the windage. "What was the measurement at the farmhouse? Exactly how far was the bullet off-target?"

"What do you think it was, Parker?"

"Just spill it, Tower."

"Fifteen inches."

A flash of understanding lit through her. "Fifteen at one hundred yards," she whispered. She rounded on Tower and the technician. "Did you adjust the scope's windage knob?" Messing with the left-right adjustment was the only way the bullet's impact would be consistently off-target.

"Until you, no one has touched the scope since it was brought in." The tech's face cleared in comprehension. "You think the windage was fifteen clicks off. A full revolution?"

"It has to be." She stared at her scope, her Remington, the friend who had never let her down. Or could she have—no, she refused to consider the thought.

"Hmm." The technician stared at the weapon and pulled out a magnifying glass. "You can't tell if it's three hundred sixty degrees off unless you test it. Sure, if it's a click or two, but a full revolution is impossible to see without firing."

Jazz moved to adjust the windage, but Tower stopped her. "I don't think so, Parker. Now we know what happened out there. You choked under the pressure and screwed up your settings. This gun is evidence you may be able to hit a bull's-eye, but you can't be trusted." He took her weapon and walked back into the lab before placing the gun in the gun case and resealing it. "You'll have to explain your negligence to a board of inquiry."

"You know I couldn't have done this." But her voice held less certainty than she'd hoped. Deep inside, some part of her had to consider—had *she* made the mistake?

"Do I? Who else would've had access to your weapon?"

Who else indeed? She studied Tower through her lashes, speculation running rampant. Was he really cold enough to have sabotaged her scope? Did he hate her so much he would've jeopardized innocent lives?

Tower made a few brief notes. "As the IA investigator assigned to your case, I'm authorized to order you to see the department psychologist for an evaluation of your fitness for duty."

"You're kidding."

He tucked his pen into his pocket and smiled. "No, not at all. I'm sure no one wants you behind any sort of weapon until we're all convinced you can handle the pressure. Understandable considering your—shall we say—colorful childhood." His eyes went icy. "You blew it and a man almost died. You're through."

He strode toward the door and looked back at her. "Come on, Parker. Sergeant Carder needs to acknowledge what a screw-up he chose."

They didn't speak in the elevator, but Tower shot her a satisfied smile as they exited the confining space. "You and your career are finished. I will personally see to it that you're thrown out on your ass. You can't expunge *these* records. You're not a minor anymore."

The blood drained from her face as they pushed through the doors to the SWAT den. Luke and Sarge met them just as they entered. Jazz had never seen either man so angry, but Luke vibrated with barely harnessed violence.

He grabbed Tower's collar. "What did you say to her?"

"Take your hands off me, or I'll have you arrested for assault. Don't think I won't do it. I'd enjoy putting you in a cage."

The muscle in Luke's cheek spasmed. Jazz fully expected him to ignore the warning, but he let Tower go with a scathing glare. "You're not worth the aggravation... or the lawyer's fees."

The man should've been quaking in his boots. Tower had to know Luke's background. As an Army Ranger, he'd forgotten more ways to kill than a cop would ever know.

Tower just shrugged, the fool.

"As I was about to tell Sergeant Carder, I've proved a point I've been trying to make for a very long time. That department judgment," he glared at Sarge, "is severely lacking. Parker buckled under pressure on the last job."

"Into my office, Deputy Tower," Sarge said, his voice clipped. "Now."

Tower followed, ambling through the double doors leading to the SWAT den.

All gazes in the lobby swept to Jazz. She could feel them boring into her. Her skin prickled, and unwanted memories flooded her mind. Stares at a little girl with bruises on her arms, wearing dirty clothes because she'd used the Laundromat money to buy milk and bread instead. Why couldn't she just disappear again? What did it matter if she fought or ran? Tower would tell everyone soon enough. Luke would learn the truth. She'd lost everything already. "I've got to get out of here," she whispered.

Luke tugged her against him, his stance protective, as if he might do battle. For her. What was she doing? She was a cop, not that scared girl anymore. Even Luke believed in her skills, her identity as a sniper. She couldn't let Tower win.

When Luke pivoted her toward the front door, she shook her head. "Wait. I've got to talk to Sarge first."

"Do it later. You don't have to stay."

"I. Can't. Run."

Luke lifted her chin and stared into her eyes. He smiled slightly. "I get that, but be smart. You shouldn't have gone with him without a rep. Tower's not stupid, and he's out to bring you down. Don't play into his game."

"It won't happen again. From now on, I control the moves."

Luke clasped her hand in his, and together they entered the SWAT den. Sarge's door was closed, his blinds drawn. She sank onto a bench and Luke settled down next to her, his thigh touching hers. He kneaded the back of her neck, his fingers lingering on that small spot at her nape that made her legs tingle. The comfort of his touch made her want to lean against him, soak in some of his strength. But she couldn't show weakness. Not here.

"Okay," he said. "No audience for the moment. What happened?"

"He had me shoot the Remington. The scope's windage was off by one complete revolution."

Luke let out a low whistle. "It'd be a quick and easy adjustment, but you'd need expert knowledge to know what to do."

"The scope appeared to be aligned perfectly. Nobody would've been able to tell until the weapon was fired that it'd been sabotaged."

"Tower has the skills," Luke said.

"I can't prove he did anything, but if he did, he's not in it alone. Someone's feeding him information about my past, Luke. He knows things he shouldn't know. Things no one should know."

Sarge's office door flung open. Jazz snapped straight, and Luke's hand dropped. Her skin cooled at the loss of his caress as Tower strode through the room, triumph exuding from every pore. "I'll set up the hearing date, Sergeant. Incompetents don't belong on your team."

Sarge didn't call her to his office. He came to her, which didn't bode well. "You thinking sabotage?"

"For a few minutes during that ballistics test, Tower made me wonder. But I couldn't have made that mistake, Sarge. A full revolution. It's impossible."

"Tower's probably involved," Luke said. "Everything that's happening to Jazz is no coincidence. The vandalism, the shot fired at us, and two hours ago someone tailed her to the gun range."

"Why would Tower go to the trouble?" Sarge shook his head. "I don't buy it, unless there's something you're not telling me, Luke."

Luke said nothing, but a knowing stare passed between the two men.

"Fine," Sarge said. "I'll be the first one to blink. The IA investigation came up too quickly. Usually I get wind of that sort of thing, but this flew in out of nowhere. It's suspicious, but Tower's father is a powerful man. You go down this road without more evidence, Jazz's career won't survive." He speared Luke with a glare. "Your career will be over too."

"You think I care about that when this bastard might have contributed to landing my brother in the hospital?"

"Your theory could hold water if you tie Tower to the tail *and* the sabotage."

Jazz struggled to focus. She hadn't slept in over twenty-four hours, but there had to be something she'd missed. "Tower comes down here all the time, especially lately," she mused. "For someone with experience, turning the windage knob wouldn't have taken a few seconds. One turn and the shot's off fifteen inches."

"He'd have had to get your rifle out of the vault," Sarge said.

Jazz bit her lip in thought. "Not if it was already out…" Her voice trailed off then she raised her chin in triumph. "I know when Tower could've done it. The day you called me into your office about the IA investigation, I left the Remington on my desk to clean it. When I came out, Tower and his redheaded girlfriend were at my desk."

Jazz let her mind drift back to the razzing the guys had given Gabe. "The woman. She flirted with Gabe… She could be working with Tower as his distraction. That would make sense. The next time I used the Remington was at the hostage site."

Sarge frowned. "I'll look into what started the IA investigation—carefully, slowly. For now, I'm ordering you out of here, Jazz. Nothing is going to change before tomorrow. You're a mess. You have to face the department shrink in the afternoon. Go home and recharge. Tired people make mistakes, and that's something you can't afford to do."

"But Sarge—"

"Get out. I need time to go over some options that won't see us both fired."

"You need to get rid of a dirty cop," Luke snapped.

Sarge rose. "And that would make your exposé, wouldn't it?"

Luke's face turned to stone, a sure sign Sarge had surprised him.

"You think I haven't heard about your little investigation?" Sarge said. "There are no secrets around here. If that shot at Jazz's apartment *was* aimed at you, there are a lot more suspects than you imagined. Take my advice. Don't go off half-cocked and get yourselves into a situation that we can't control. I don't plan on losing my best sniper because of Tower's personal vendetta. Let me do my job so Jazz can keep hers."

She hadn't heard the words aloud before. Hadn't even let herself think she might really lose her place on the team. The pain was so swift and intense Jazz swayed on her feet.

Her commander frowned. "See that she gets some food and sleep, Montgomery. She looks like hell."

"I'll take care of her," Luke promised, "and we'll find out who's behind this. I won't stop until we do."

Jazz looked up into his determined face. The once-broken nose, the strong jaw, they all told her more than his words. He wouldn't give up. Ever. Mostly for Gabe, she knew. He would fight for her too, but for how long? He seemed to believe in her *now*, but he didn't know the whole truth. What would happen when he learned who Jazz Parker *really* was?

Chapter Eight

The noonday sun streamed through the windows of Luke's SUV, and the sheriff's office disappeared in the rearview mirror as he ended his cell call and plugged the dying phone into the charger. "Good news. Gabe's doing better. He's still unconscious, but he's no longer in a coma. The doctors are more hopeful about his leg too."

"Thank God," she said as she leaned back against the seat and closed her eyes, her bag in her lap.

Luke watched as she unconsciously stroked the stuffed clown fish peeking out of the zippered top, her fingers fondling the soft toy as if searching for comfort. "You seem as attached to Hero as Joy."

Jasmine's hand stilled, and she turned weary eyes toward him. "He grows on you. Something about him makes me feel...I don't know—"

"Cared about?"

She put the toy aside, as if to prove to Luke and to herself that she didn't need the crutch. He doubted he would've recognized the tell when they'd been together before. He'd seen her strength and her skill as a warrior and he'd experienced her passion, but he hadn't looked for her vulnerabilities then. Being a father had changed him. Joy had given him a window to the world he'd never known existed, where relationships mattered more than ever.

During missions, he'd counted on his unit. He'd trusted them with his life, but not his soul. Even though Joy's mother had betrayed him, Joy held his heart in her small hands. Could he ever trust Jasmine that way? How could he now, when she guarded her secrets so fiercely?

"Tower spooked you back there. What did he say?"

Her leg bounced, and he recognized her control slipping. Lack of sleep tugged at her camouflage. Drawn-out battles did that to a person. Eventually the masks fell away, revealing the truth.

"He knows details about my past that I'm not proud of," she said. "Only one man on earth ever knew the complete story, but Sheriff Clarkson would never give me up."

The message behind her words shouldn't have felt like a .38 caliber ripping through his heart, but it did. "Unlike me."

"How can I trust you after the way you went after Derek?"

"You're not the only one taking a risk. Derek, one of my oldest friends, lied to me. Joy's mother, Samantha, lied to me. She never told me she was pregnant. She never gave me a chance to be a father. If she hadn't died, I wouldn't even know about Joy. You lied to me too. Exactly how am I supposed to trust *you*?"

"Then why torture each other? We're better off apart."

"I thought so too. Once." Luke let his hand rest on Jasmine's thigh and he squeezed slightly. A delicate shiver fluttered beneath his fingertips. "There's something between us, Jasmine. There always has been. Always will be. Besides, right now, we're stronger together. Like it or not, your past and my investigation are connected. If we don't find out how, whoever's responsible could win. Do you want them to come out on top?"

"Of course not."

"So help me inside the sheriff's office. We'll nail them as a team."

Her fingers curled into a fist and she bit her lip. She didn't like considering that her precious cops' world might've been infiltrated. He got that. Nobody liked to be betrayed.

Finally she let out a slow breath. "If I'm sure someone's dirty, I'll tell you."

"That's more than I thought you'd agree to. Truce?"

She turned away from him and stared out the window.

A few blocks later, Luke recognized a restaurant he hadn't visited since they'd parted. A whiff of tomato sauce and the scent of a grill wafted to him. Jasmine needed food. It was perfect. Good food, a buffet, and fast. The only rub…it was *their* place.

Her stomach rumbled and she clasped at her belly with a grimace. "Sorry."

That decided him. He pulled over in front of the red-and-white-checked décor of the restaurant. "You need to eat."

She stared out of the car window and bit her lip. "You can drop me off at my apartment. I'll be fine."

"And risk you ingesting the science experiment budding in your refrigerator?"

A smile tilted her lips, and he returned the grin. *Truce.* Their relationship hadn't been all bad. It had taken a lot of cajoling on his part. He'd enjoyed finding ways to surprise her. The circus. A hot air balloon ride. An amusement park. Eventually they'd laughed. They'd teased. They'd loved. It had been too good for a while. Perhaps that's why her leaving had hurt more than he'd ever let on.

He scanned the street for anything suspicious, but nothing caught his attention. He opened the restaurant door for Jasmine, and soft strains of Italian opera danced on air scented with spices and tomato sauce. As she walked through the opening, he placed his hand on the small of her back to escort her to a table, and just that small touch brought memories flooding back. As if by rote, they veered toward a very familiar corner of the restaurant.

"Not there," she said, her voice low and private. "Anywhere else."

The location shouldn't have mattered. It was only a table in a restaurant. But it did. "How about that one?" He pointed to a spot at the opposite end of the building.

She nodded and they seated themselves near the buffet. Within minutes, they'd filled their plates and settled in. Luke shifted his chair so his blind side stayed to a wall and he could keep an eye on the entrance.

"Even now, you never go off alert," she said, pointing to his posture.

"Habit. Five years infiltrating enemy territory taught me to never turn my back. In more ways than just the physical."

Luke swirled up some pasta, and the rich tomato sauce with just a hint of pepper exploded in his mouth. "I'd forgotten how good this place is," he said, savoring the bold flavors.

Jasmine, on the other hand, after a few bites, rested her fork on the plate. "You didn't have to go back to Afghanistan with the damage the bullet in your shoulder caused. Why put yourself in danger?"

"I could ask you a similar question."

"I'm not at risk. Not really. I sit above the action, just trying to protect my team."

"You're wrong. Everyone on a mission is part of the whole to find justice, to protect the innocent." Luke stabbed the greens of his salad then looked up at her. He'd never told anyone the whole story, but she needed to understand why he needed her trust. "You want to know why I *really* went back?" He sat down his fork and leaned forward. "My last year in Afghanistan, I was twenty-three with an attitude. Thought I knew it all. So this forty-something reporter with a wife and two kids gets assigned to our unit. To tell the *truth* about the war. We were all ready to hate the guy, but his first week embedded we got pinned down. Frank pulled one of the guys into cover. He became part of the team."

"You were impressed."

"Hell, yeah. The guy grew up with a silver spoon but ate MREs like they were gourmet meals. He was one of us. All Frank wanted to do was tell the world about what we were doing. No filters. Just the truth. My dad would've liked him."

"Frank was with you when you were ambushed?" Jasmine asked, her voice a mere whisper.

"He'd made friends with our translator. He trusted the guy. I trusted him too." Luke's gut burned. "You know what happened next."

"The translator outed your location to a group of insurgents," she finished. "They attacked, ambushed your team."

"Ten minutes later, I was shot to hell. What I never told anyone before is Frank died sprawled on top of me, while I was left for dead. I should've been killed, but for some reason I survived. I swore to come back and find the son-of-a-bitch who'd betrayed us. It took months to recover. Even though my days as a Ranger were over, to honor Frank, I vowed to come back as a war correspondent. Took me years to get a degree and get assigned." Luke raised his gaze and met Jasmine's. "I found the translator. This time his lies didn't work."

"What did you do?"

"Let's just say his next 'ambush' had a different outcome. His *comrades* weren't pleased. He got what he deserved. I thought retribution would bring peace. It didn't. Frank's kids still didn't have a father. Nothing had changed. So I decided to come home for a while. Visit family. Exorcise a few more demons."

"Why journalism? Why not a cop?"

"I thought about it, but Frank's last stories were printed after he was killed, and they were amazing. Gritty. Horrific. Inspiring. He revealed the truth. All of it. I'd seen too many cover-ups and too much deceit to follow the rules and laws cops did. They wouldn't let me touch some of the stories I needed to focus on. Sounds cliché, but I wanted to clean up the world of lies. I blew it with Derek, though. I was still too brash, too sure of being right. I wish I'd handled it differently, made it possible for him to get out instead of believing he was alone." Luke took a swig of iced tea. "I can see now that I pushed too hard with you too. I regret that."

He reached for a roll just as Jasmine did. Their fingertips met and the heat between them sparked once more. He slid his hand over hers and captured her gaze. "I know you're tired and feel like you've been beaten up, Jasmine. I could help, if you'd only talk to me. Trust me. I won't quit. I'll do whatever it takes to find out why and how this is happening. Whether it takes a few days or a decade."

She shook her head and pulled her hands from him. "You have a daughter to protect, Luke. I'll handle it. My way."

She pushed away a half-eaten plate of food. "I'm finished. I need to go home. Alone."

Luke paid the bill, his mind made up. No way was he letting her stay by herself. Not until he convinced himself she was safe. He'd do whatever it took to protect her. He refused to let Jasmine fight this battle alone.

Breaking into Jazz Parker's apartment had been too easy. She was a failure as a cop, just like the rest of her life. Just like her whore of a mother.

Not that a lock or two would've stopped the plan. Now all she had to do was bait the trap. She flipped open her phone and dialed her cop's number.

"Hello?" His too-eager voice rumbled with anticipation.

"Hi, lover boy. You ready to be bad with me?"

"You know it, honey." His voice lowered. "I'm ready for you. Big and hard and ready. Just the way you like it."

Her stomach rolled when she thought of his horrible hands all over her, but for now she needed him.

"Lover, I could really use a favor. It's naughty, but I know you can do it."

A soft laugh sounded through the phone. "The naughtier, the better."

"Oh, you." She forced herself to gift him with the incipient giggle that turned him on so much. "I probably shouldn't be telling a cop this, but I accidentally knocked my car door into this Pinto and I didn't have anything to leave a note with. I want to try to contact him. I memorized his license plate. Can you get me his name and address so I can give him my insurance information?"

There was a long pause on the other end.

"Please. I'll do anything you want. Even what you asked for last night."

The sharp intake of breath brought on a smile. He was hers. She controlled him.

"Give me the number."

"Oh, lover, you're just so smart and so wonderful. See you tonight. I'll give you a whole lot more than I promised." Her voice grew low and sexy. "I'll ride you like you've never been ridden, so be ready."

He groaned. "I'm ready now."

With a last giggle, she pursed her lips and made a disgusting kissing sound then hung up the phone.

And so the next step began.

She scanned her enemy's possessions. The place was too neat. She could see the cop now, arranging all the books and bottles just so. She pulled down the wall unit.

Books and manuals flew across the room, crashing into the wall. The few mementos of Jazz Parker's life, shattered.

Methodically she trashed room after room, finally pushing open the bedroom door. Everything necessary to frame Jazz would be in here, and her enemy would soon pay for what she'd done. She rummaged through the closet, slashing her clothes, destroying her life.

Then she saw them. A pair of Arvada Police Academy sweatpants lay in the middle of the floor. Perfect. The irony would be poetic.

The phone ringing interrupted the celebration. "This is Jazz, you know the drill. Leave a message."

Her voice sounded through the machine: clear, calm, content. Well, that would soon change.

"Jazz, it's Anna Montgomery. I wanted to let you know that Gabe's much better. Also, I'm looking for Luke and haven't been able to reach him. He's searching for you, so if you see him, tell him I'm taking Joy to Lake Arbor Park this afternoon. We'll be home before dark."

Everything was falling into place. The lying bastard's daughter and mother would be at a park. Alone. This entire day was a sign. A wonderful, glorious sign.

A quick search of the bathroom and closet for a weapon and the job would be complete. And there it was—like Excalibur waiting for the chosen one who would wield it for justice.

An iron crowbar lay tossed in the corner. Vicious, deadly, wonderful.

A quick pivot out of the closet brought her face to face with her reflection above the vanity. Her recently dyed auburn hair was scraped away from her face to prevent even one hair from escaping.

Her mother's eyes stared back at her.

No. No. No. Mama, the weak, trusting fool, was dead. She wasn't here.

Panicked, she swung the crowbar with all her might at the mirror. Shards splintered, but the accusing eyes didn't disappear. A thousand images reflected back at her. Eyes watching her. Everywhere.

"I promised you I'd kill the killer! I will. I'll keep my promise, Mama."

Breathing labored, she sucked back a sob as the crowbar dropped to the floor with a thud. "Jane Sanford will die."

Dinner hadn't ended quite as Luke expected. He'd hoped Jasmine would agree to his plan. They were still negotiating, though Luke had no intention of losing. He pulled into the parking lot of her apartment building. Last time they were here they'd been a target. This time, his body tingled with something other than danger. He let his fingertips graze her arm as she exited the SUV. She shivered as the heat sweltered between them. Would she acknowledge the attraction? Would she fight it?

As they climbed up the stairs toward her apartment, a place they'd made love countless times, the electric awareness crackled even above the irritation.

"For the last time, I don't need a babysitter."

So, all business. Part of him sighed in relief, part in disappointment. He could keep their relationship professional. He hoped.

"I'm not leaving," he said. "Whether I plant myself in your apartment or in the hallway, I'm here for the long haul."

They exited the stairwell to Jasmine's wide-open front door. "You've got to be kidding," she said.

Luke palmed his HK and shoved her behind him. "What the devil is going on now? We need backup."

She peered past him as he eased toward the door, step by step, listening for signs of an intruder. He wanted this son-of-a-bitch so bad he could taste the kill.

"I can't believe I'm calling 911. Again." She reported the break-in then pulled the Glock from her bag. "Who's doing this?"

"I don't know, but I've had it," Luke said. He hoped the bastard was inside. He'd end this sick game once and for all.

They edged around the open door. Jasmine's breath caught. Nothing remained untouched. Her sofa had been shredded. Shelves were upended. The few knickknacks she possessed had been scattered and broken.

"Forensics is going to be furious, but I'm not taking a chance he'll get away," Luke said, hoping he'd have the pleasure to settle the lopsided score.

"I'm going with you."

"Stay close. No heroics."

"Ditto."

The apartment was oddly silent. Luke's shoulders tensed as they picked their way through the devastation.

The mess didn't stop her from being a cop. She'd become a master at compartmentalizing. He recognized the skill. He'd developed it as a soldier; she'd honed her abilities surviving her childhood. She was so strong; she impressed the hell out of him.

Methodically they searched the kitchen, the coat closet, anyplace an intruder could hide.

Finally they reached the bedroom door.

"Last room," she said softly. "Last chance."

His moves quiet and subtle, he rounded the corner and quickly swept the room with his HK. Empty. When he saw her bed, he recoiled. Her mattress and pillows had been hacked just like the sofa and truck. The viciousness of the attack sickened him. Every destructive inch screamed personal vendetta, not professional hit.

A small hitched breath sounded behind him as she took in the full scope of the hatred. The violation had wounded her. Luke's jaw ached as he fought to restrain his fury. He stepped toward the bathroom. *Let him be there. Five minutes is all I need.*

He entered the room. Empty. Again. But the message was clear. He stared at the wall, a flood of curses erupting and echoing through the tiled room. The mirror had been violently shattered, a threat scrawled in red on the wall for impact.

Killer Cops Die Too.

Jasmine stilled next to Luke. Careful not to startle her, he placed a hand on her shoulder, kneading slightly. She wasn't alone. She had to know that.

"It's not lipstick," he said.

"No," she said. "It's blood."

Jazz waited in the hall until Detective Neil Wexler left her apartment. "You've got yourself an enemy, Parker, and not a sane one. First the truck, the gunshot, and now this. Add to that your...work troubles...and your life seems to be unraveling mighty fast. Any chance they're connected?"

"I don't know." She shoved her hand in her pocket. Empty. Man, she could use a Life Saver.

Wexler flipped open his notebook. "I'm primary on the vandalism and this break-in. Do you know of anyone who has a personal grudge against you? Anyone who got caught because of one of the SWAT operations? Any recent parolees who'd want revenge?"

Did she dare mention Tower in an official investigation? It could cost her. Sarge had made that clear, and Jazz reluctantly agreed. "No one's brought anything to my attention in months. You could check on the new complaints, I guess."

"There was a red Pinto following her earlier today," Luke interrupted. "Some guy was waiting for her when she left the station this morning."

"You saw him?" Wexler's eyebrows rose.

"Yeah. He looked like a cop or maybe ex-military." Luke sent Jazz a pointed stare.

She glared back and then looked away.

Wexler slapped his notebook against his thigh. "Okay, what are you two not telling me?"

"We may have a suspect, but it's just speculation." Jazz cleared her throat. "It's difficult."

"Go on."

"He's a cop. IA."

A low whistle sounded through Wexler's lips. "Brian Tower." Neil didn't put pen to paper; his expression turned serious. "Listen, Jazz, I want to get the jerk doing this to you, but are you sure you want to open that can of worms? Messing with Tower won't be pretty. He's got connections."

Luke gestured toward the apartment. "You think what this guy did was pretty? Only a psycho would slash up a bed like that. If Tower's the one, he should be strung up without a trial."

"Luke—" Jazz said.

Wexler planted his feet in challenge. "We're getting into some deep and smelly waters here, and you're hiding information. Why do you suspect him?"

Jazz held her breath. What could she say?

Finally Luke lowered his voice. "I'm assuming you've heard, but I'm investigating corruption in the sheriff's office," he said. "I have it on good authority Tower's involved. I'm still unsure about how deep."

Jazz stared at Luke, stunned. How long had he been certain Tower was mixed up with the bad guys and hadn't told her? Her stomach flipped at the betrayal. Even with their deal, she couldn't trust Luke to be straight with her. When would she learn she couldn't count on him to be there for her one hundred percent?

Wexler's expression turned cold. "Really? Exactly who is this 'informant'?"

"I don't have to disclose anything. I *can* tell you this person is vulnerable to organized crime by even talking to me, and I'll do whatever it takes to protect my source. I provide the identity, and someone will die."

"You're giving me nothing. What am I supposed to do? Wait for you to ruin a cop's life on rumors? Do you have any evidence? At all?"

Luke listed their suspicions, but even as he did, Jazz recognized how flimsy the case was against Tower. Jazz could tell Wexler didn't want to listen. She couldn't blame him. Luke was withholding. She wasn't giving the detective the whole picture either. She'd taken the easy way out—the safe way out—and not mentioned that Tower knew details about her past. Wexler may not know what they were holding back, but his instincts must be screaming at him.

"It's thin," he said. "What about the Pinto. You see it, Jazz?"

"Not today, but I glimpsed one the night my truck was vandalized."

Wexler made a few more notes. "It's not much to go on. We may get lucky and find some fingerprints. At the very least we should get some DNA from the blood on the wall." He rubbed his chin and cleared his throat. "Look, Jazz, I'll keep an eye on your suspect. But I'm going slow and easy. For your sake as much as my own. If you come up with anything else, let me know." He shot Luke a chilling gaze. "And if you have any *concrete* information, maybe you'll share it with me. Before more than an apartment or vehicle is sliced up."

"We gave you a suspect, Wexler. Don't worry, I'll provide you anything I can that will help you do *your* job." Luke faced him toe to toe. "But if you don't follow through, I'm giving you a heads up. I'll do whatever is necessary to protect Jasmine."

"Keep it within the law." Wexler ducked under the crime scene tape then turned back to Jazz with a concerned look. "Have you got a place to stay until we're finished here?"

A wave of exhausted realization hit her. Her apartment was a crime scene. That meant she had no clothes, no home. She shivered and lifted her chin. "I'll be fine. Thanks." She'd figure out something. She always did. "Let me know what you find out."

"Will do." He glanced at his clipboard. "Take care, and watch your back until we catch this psycho."

Wexler disappeared into Jazz's apartment and she confronted Luke. "Your informant named Tower? You lied to me!"

Luke pulled her away from the door. "Lower your voice. I never lied."

"So what's your latest definition of a lie, Luke?" She crossed her arms and glared at him. "As I recall, when you went after Derek, the definition included pretty much anything that wasn't the whole truth and nothing but the truth."

"I can't tell you everything. I'm shielding someone who can't protect herself," he whispered. "Or her son. If her husband learns she called me, she's dead. I can't let that happen. She's a mother protecting her child."

"Damn you." A wave of hopelessness swept through Jazz. She understood. She'd done far worse in the name of protecting someone who couldn't protect herself.

Luke turned her to him, shifting her body against his and rubbing her arms. "I'll find a way to help you, Jasmine. I promise, but we have to broaden our thinking.

As much as I initially believed these attacks were about my investigation, I was wrong. When the perp slashed your truck and destroyed your apartment, those acts are much more vicious and personal than a deliberately missed shot. Put that together with Tower knowing details about your past that no one else knows, and this situation is more complicated than I realized."

"But why come after me now?"

"Maybe the news coverage reached someone from your past who recognized you, or Tower put out inquiries. I don't know. But I won't stop until we find out who's responsible and you're safe."

She shivered at his dogged confidence. How could she appreciate his determination on one hand while that very trait chilled her soul? How could she trust him with her past? She'd never been one to give up control of her life. She hadn't even let Sheriff Clarkson destroy those files and the newspaper articles about Jane without witnessing their shredding. She didn't have faith that Luke wouldn't turn his back on her when he learned the truth. Everyone else had judged her—from the time she was born to the day she'd taken her new name.

Nothing had changed. From the moment Luke and the SWAT team had learned just one snippet of her story, she could tell they looked at her differently. And if they knew everything? Luke wouldn't stand by her. He'd judged Derek as guilty for far less than Jazz had done.

She lifted her hands to Luke's shoulders and pushed away. "This isn't just about your investigation anymore. This is about me. So unless you have another suspect in the wings—"

. "Nothing solid." He studied her face, his churning speculation evident in his eyes. "What are you planning?"

"The only lead left besides Tower and his accomplice is the car. Maybe it'll give us a break. I need to run the Pinto myself. I'm going back to the office."

"Carder will kick you out if you try anything before you get a good eight hours' sleep. You need a safe place to rest," Luke said, his voice firm. "My mother's been bugging me to let Joy sleep over. Stay with me tonight. I've got the equipment to run searches on the Pinto."

"I don't know." Talk about walking into trouble. She bit her lip. "I'd better go to a hotel."

"If you get a room, I'm stuck there with you. Less time and privacy to investigate. If you research at the sheriff's office, everyone will know, and it could get back to him." Luke let his hands run down her sides and slipped his fingers into her empty pocket. "Besides, I've got a stash of butter rum," he said. "And you seem to be all out."

"The butter rum clinches it." She hesitated. "No sex."

"I wouldn't dream of it."

He put his hand on her back. "Much," he muttered beneath his breath.

Chapter Nine

Luke unlocked the door to his house with relief. At least she'd be safe for a while. Actually, on the ride over, Jasmine admitted it was Luke's computer setup that had finally convinced her to come home with him. He didn't care why she'd agreed. She was here now.

A soft click of the front door and a twist of the dead-bolt shut them in. He slipped the key into his pocket and watched as she strode past a jam-packed wall of family photographs and into the living room. He couldn't remember a time they hadn't headed straight for the bedroom when they had come to his house. The fire between them had burned hot, but not deep. He'd never known her. Not really. He knew how to touch her and caress her to drive her wild with passion, but he hadn't seen her heart. He'd understood her dedication to the job, had admired that she'd fought for a place on SWAT, but he hadn't look past the external cues. He'd been a fool.

Her gait stiffened over the hardwood floors as she navigated around a pink princess puzzle, several stuffed animals, and Joy's latest sparkly, twirly dress. "This wasn't a good idea, Luke. What if I bring the trouble here?"

"My investigation's already done that. Now we've got to fix it. Have a seat," he said, nodding toward the sofa.

He sat down next to her and sighed as he took in her features. The lack of sleep showed. Dark circles rimmed her eyes; lines of fatigue etched her face. Delayed shock had done the rest. Her body was shutting down. He stroked his thumb across her cheekbones, just under the shadows beneath her eyes. "How long since you slept?"

"I have no idea."

"While you rest, I'll use a few computer tricks to look for the red Pinto. It'll take some time. Do you realize how many there are in the greater Denver metropolitan area? It's easier since the company discontinued them, but I need to narrow the search. I'll start with Tower and hope something pops. Then we work with what we know: a person in your past who knows everything about you."

She squirmed in her seat and shook her head, avoiding his eyes. "I'll look at the list when I wake up to see if I recognize anyone."

"We don't have time for secrets. Not anymore. Whoever ransacked your apartment has gone over the edge. He wants you dead. If it's Tower, he's a cop. He's a sniper. He could kill you at any time. And we need to identify his accomplice." Luke lifted her chin and forced her to meet his gaze. "Time's up, Jasmine. You have to trust me. I'll help you if you just tell me the truth."

She shoved him aside and stood, her body trembling as if the worries of days, even years, vibrated just beneath the surface. "You're lying. You didn't help Derek. You judged him."

"That was different. He broke the law when he withheld information. He became a criminal. I promise you, I'll be there for you."

"No one's ever stood by me," she scoffed. "No one but Sheriff Clarkson. Why should I believe you? What if *I'm* a criminal, Luke? What would you do then?"

"It wouldn't happen."

"Really. How about we test your theory? What if I told you that when I was fourteen I was scared and desperate and did things I'm not proud of just to survive? What if I told you I was arrested?" She turned her back to him, her spine stiff and defensive.

"Why are you doing this?" he asked. He'd never seen her this raw, this close to a meltdown.

"Doing what?" She spun and faced him. "I thought you *wanted* the truth. 'The truth will set you free.' Isn't that your credo?"

"Jasmine—"

"Did you know it's hard for a fourteen-year-old with a past to find work or a place to live? I had nowhere to go." Her voice shook with pent-up emotion as the flood of what she'd hidden all those years exploded. She shifted her gaze from his face, staring instead into space, as if the memories were playing in front of her. "Sometimes the hunger got so bad my stomach would cramp until I couldn't stand up from the pain. But other times...I thought I would just rather go to sleep and die."

"Oh, Jasmine."

She stepped back and stared at her feet. "No. Don't... say...anything."

What had gone so wrong that she'd been left unprotected? Fourteen. A child. How had she survived? Luke couldn't bear to think of his Joy fighting for her life that way. But Joy had his family. Why would Jasmine believe she could depend on him now? She'd been all alone, with no one to count on.

His battle experience did him no good. Somehow he had to convince her to trust him when she wouldn't even look at his face. Her entire body stood erect, the tension palpable, warning him not to come near, even though his every instinct screamed at him to hold her.

"When it got that bad, I had no choice," she said. "I walked the streets. I didn't sell my body," she rushed out. "I couldn't bear to become like my mother, but I did set up the Johns. I was tall for my age. I played the part, lured them in, then kneed them in the family jewels and took what cash I could for a few meals. Clarkson caught me."

He'd known she possessed a fighter's heart, but he hadn't realized the true level of her courage. Luke could barely stand still. One wrong word or move from him, and she'd spring for the door. She waited for him to judge her. Well, he'd prove to her that some people in this world were steadfast.

"Sheriff Clarkson didn't look at me like I was dirt, the way everyone else had. He gave me a second chance. He believed the system had failed to protect me, and he wanted to set things right. No one else had ever cared. He looked out for me...and he never asked for anything in return—never touched me, never insisted that I..."

Luke didn't want to think about what she must've faced, but the images flew through his mind like a horror movie. He longed to touch her, to pull her into his arms, but he feared she would bolt. He was beginning to understand, to see the story of her life before Colorado. He hated that he hadn't been there to protect her.

"I always thought eventually Clarkson would demand *benefits*. In my world, no man gave anything without wanting something in return." She shuddered. "I was so scared. Like a wounded animal unable to trust anyone. After he took me in, some nights, I'd hear a noise and would be sure it was him. That tonight would be the night he'd show he was just like all the men my mother *entertained*. But he never did."

A few minutes alone with the bastards who thought they could victimize a child like her—that's all Luke wanted. Clarkson had saved more than her life. He'd saved her soul.

She lifted her gaze. "Do you really think Sheriff Clarkson would ever speak to anyone?"

"No," he said. "That kind of man wouldn't betray you. Is he why you became a cop?"

"I wanted to save people." She rubbed her eyes. "And I wanted to start fresh. Sheriff Clarkson helped me gain emancipation, expunge my juvenile record and change my name. We erased my past. Or so I thought. After two years fighting the system, he brought me here when I was sixteen to start over. He found me an apartment in a building his old war buddy, Mr. Peterson, owned. The sheriff even set it up for me to get my G.E.D. and apply to Metro State."

"He was a good man."

"The best. He believed in the gray. In me. It's legal to answer 'no' to any questions regarding juvenile arrests if your record's been expunged. So did I lie to the cops? Did I lie to you? I didn't tell the entire truth." She shrugged. "Sometimes it's the only way to survive."

"Jasmine—"

"Now you know the truth," she said. "I've stolen. I've been arrested for prostitution. My mother was a whore. I changed my name to escape my past. Are you *still* going to stand by me?"

He couldn't begin to tell her how wrong she was about him. He simply stared at her, stunned.

"That's what I thought," she muttered.

Jasmine raced for the door. She swiped at her eyes with her sleeve and fumbled at the deadbolt, giving Luke just enough time to reach her and whirl her in his arms, pinning her against the door. Her face, streaked with tears, tore at his soul. He had to make her believe him.

"What will you do if I don't let you leave? If I *do* stand by your side? What then?"

She paused, open-mouthed. "I don't understand."

"It's your turn to listen to me. You know what I've learned about you? I don't see a thief or a liar. You've overcome more obstacles than most people will ever face in a lifetime. The girl you were shaped the woman you are, and she's amazing and beautiful and...you're a hero."

Her face crumpled and she sagged against him, shuddering with an emotional avalanche.

"Jasmine, if you wanted to frighten me off, you failed." He wiped a tear from her cheek. "Because you're not even close to scaring me away. You've made me want you more."

He shifted, sliding his jeaned leg between hers so she could feel the power she had over him. She shivered against him, pressing into his length. His entire body hardened in a desire he could barely control. He'd been waiting for this since the moment he'd seen her again.

Hell, he'd been waiting since she'd walked out the door two years ago. Her alone with him, just a few steps from his bedroom.

"I want you, Jasmine. Badly." He lowered his head, nipped lightly at her ear and nuzzled her neck, smiling as her pulse jumped beneath his lips.

She sighed and went limp. He kissed her forehead, her eyes, her cheek. His hands stroked her arms and he linked his fingers with hers. When he glanced down, he couldn't tell where her hand stopped and his began. He squeezed tight so she'd know he was there. Unmoving, not leaving.

"Even after what I told you?" she whispered.

Luke pulled back and studied the top of her bowed head. With a gentle hand, he tilted her chin up and stared into the caution on her face. He lifted her hand to his lips and turned her palm over to kiss the inside of her wrist, relishing the racing pulse, knowing he was the cause. "I want you now more than I've ever wanted anyone."

Jasmine gulped in a tear-choked breath. "I didn't think…"

"What? That I wouldn't want to taste you?" He nuzzled at her wrist, worked his way up her arm to her elbow, and breathed in deeply. "Inhale your scent?"

His entire body throbbed with longing. He met her gaze, trembling with desire. "Need you?"

She wrapped her arms around his neck, her hold almost desperate. She grabbed his shoulders, running her hands down his arms, his chest, circling his waist, and finally to his hips. "I want you too," she said.

"Your wish—"

She fastened her lips to his, her mouth begging for entrance. He let her have her way with him. He gloried in the taste of her. With a low groan, Luke scooped her into his arms, cradling her against his chest, reveling as she turned into him, her lips exploring his chin, his cheek, his temple. Shoving aside any doubts, he held her fast and kicked open the bedroom door.

It was a perfect afternoon. The child and her grandmother playing, without a care or worry.

The peace wouldn't last long. The terror would begin soon.

A stand of trees shielded all the intentions. Plastic gloves protected an identity Jane would know soon enough. There would be no fingerprints.

It had been a good day, and it was about to get better.

A duffle bag dropped to the ground, in it the pair of Arvada Police Academy sweats and a crowbar, as well as the GPS tracking device to be used later. Last, and most important right now, a bright red ball peeked into view.

A perfect lure for an innocent young girl.

With a few swift strokes of a magic marker, a quick message—one Luke and Jane would very much understand—decorated the ball.

The lovers needed a wake-up call. Once Luke Montgomery understood the price of associating with the enemy, Jane would learn what it was like to be all alone, to lose everyone.

The blond-haired imp laughed as a bright swing flew higher and higher. The grandmother smiled indulgently with each push of the toy. They were naïve. They were happy.

As she had once been. Too long ago to remember. Before Jane Sanford had ruined everything.

The girl jumped from the swing and whispered to her grandmother, who nodded and turned toward a tree, hiding her eyes for an obvious game of hide and seek.

The child ran toward the grove.

Intent hands rolled the red ball onto the grass a few feet from the trees. *Come to me. Come closer.*

The little girl veered off toward the ball and picked it up.

"You found my ball. Thank you. I thought I'd lost it."

"It's pretty. I like red," the child said.

Sweet voice, innocent voice.

"Do you? You can have the ball if you'd like. I have more at home."

The girl's face lit up. Joy. That was her name. It fit. For now.

"Thank you!" Joy said, coming closer, until the trees blocked the grandmother's view. "It's red like your hair."

"And your dress."

Joy smiled brightly. "Can I show it to Gamma?"

"Of course, dear. You should definitely show it to your grandmother. Your daddy too."

"Joy Marie Montgomery!" The grandmother's worried voice split the air. "Where are you?"

"Here, Gamma!" Joy called. Then she turned back. "Do you want to play with us?"

"Not today. But I'll see you again. Very soon."

Perfect.

This had to be a dream. Luke still wanted her. Jasmine hadn't told him everything, of course, but she'd been so certain he would turn from her in disgust. He hadn't. He was here. With her.

He *wanted* her.

A weight lifted, freeing a desire she'd clamped down for too long. She craved his touch, his caress. Her body screamed for the sensation of his lips and hands exploring her, making her body sing songs only Luke could evoke. With a sigh of anticipation, Jazz kissed his neck as he carried her to the bed.

A low growl rumbled in his chest. He gently laid her down, and she sank into the soft mattress. Unwilling to relinquish his touch, she drew Luke down with her.

He let her.

His finger trailed down the side of her face, and she shivered at the intensity in his eyes. He wouldn't look away. He held her gaze as if staring into her soul.

She couldn't look away. Everything she'd ever wanted was buried in his gaze. No doubt, no judgment, just desire.

Her body trembled in eagerness, her nerves vibrating with expectation. He didn't move. He simply watched.

"Aren't you going to kiss me again?" Jazz didn't recognize her voice, husky, longing, needing.

"I'm memorizing you," he said. "The green flecks in your eyes, burning for me. The flush of your cheeks. Your lips."

Ever so slowly, he lowered his mouth to hers. "Are you sure?" he whispered, his mouth hovering above her lips.

Her body on fire, Jazz shook. "I want you. Now." Her hand traveled down his shirtfront, slipping the buttons free, past his waist and lightly over the bulge in his jeans.

His chest rumbled and he cupped her face in his hands. "I'm happy to oblige."

Her lashes fluttered closed as Luke lowered his mouth with a kiss full of promises. His lips demanded entrance, parting hers with a sweep of his tongue, reminding her why she'd finally succumbed to his seduction. Two years ago, and now.

He demanded without hurting, celebrated her without doubts. He wrapped her in his arms, cradling her body, but plundering her mouth. She could barely think; she only knew she wanted more. Now.

Jazz's hands circled his torso and she slid his shirt down his shoulders until it fell to the floor, leaving his bare chest for her to savor. She ran her fingertips down the spiderweb of scars at his shoulder. Her mouth skirted the ridges of his old injury, and Luke let out a slow, fervent moan.

Yes. She could make him groan, make him tremble. She let her hands roam down his chest, fingertips brushing his nipples. He shuddered at the touch. She knew where to touch him.

He nipped at her collarbone. A quivering breath escaped her.

He tugged off her top. "Beautiful," he whispered, his voice reverent.

He cupped her softness in his hand as he tasted her skin. Jazz reveled in his exploring kisses. She wanted him to taste her, to touch her, to give her what she'd missed. She was so tired of being alone.

Luke teased her breast and his mouth toyed with the peak. He latched onto her softness and her body purred in response. "I've missed this, Jasmine," he said. "I've missed you."

He pushed at her clothes and yanked at his own until finally they lay skin to skin. She stared at his strong body, his hard desire.

"I'd forgotten how beautiful you are," she murmured as she caressed him intimately, relishing the way he surged into her palm.

"Don't go too fast." Luke let out a groan. "I'll never last."

"I don't know if I want you to." Jazz smiled and squeezed him gently.

"Believe me, sweetheart, you don't want this to be over too soon." He held her wrists captive and moved over her, parting her legs and settling between her thighs. His body probed until he slid against her wet softness. She clasped him to her and drew him in.

In one stroke he settled deep inside her body. He filled her as if they were made to be together. He sighed as if he'd just come home. Jazz wrapped her legs and arms around him to hold him there. They fit. Perfectly.

"I don't want you to move, ever. I want you to stay just as you are," she whispered.

"Sorry, honey." Luke shuddered beneath her hands. "I've got to have you. I've waited too long."

With a groan, he withdrew and pressed back into her again and again, until they were wild with the passionate friction he created. She gripped him to her, desperate to hold onto him.

He folded his fingers through hers and raised them above her head. She couldn't think; she could only feel. He drove her higher and higher, his every thrust lifting her to a place she'd never been. With one last thrust, the world turned bright, and she shattered with the force. They were one.

When the blinding intensity slid away, all she could sense was the quivering rhythm within her and an aura of utter contentment. Luke turned his head and kissed the hollow where her pulse still pounded. "Mmm. You okay? I didn't hurt you?"

She shook her head. "That was better than I remembered."

"We're not finished yet," Luke smiled. He opened the nightstand drawer and she peered over his shoulder. Stashed next to the box of condoms was a roll of butter rum Life Savers. He palmed it and handed it to her. "Just like I promised."

The side of her mouth twitched upward. "I didn't really believe you." She opened up the end and popped one in her mouth. Her eyes closed. "I needed that."

He stole another quick kiss, and butter rum sweetness mixed with the taste of Luke exploded on her tongue. He pulled her hips to spoon her to the curve of his body. So right. They fit together.

The shrill ring of a cell phone shattered the moment.

"I have to answer in case it's the family." Luke kissed her cheek as he leaned over the side of the bed and dug in his pants for the small phone. "Montgomery."

Jazz watched as Luke's face went pale. He jerked back and scanned the room as he pressed the speakerphone button so they could both hear every word.

"I hope I didn't catch you with your pants down, Mr. Montgomery."

"Who is this?"

"Oh, don't worry. I can't see you and your whore. You have plenty of privacy."

The mechanized voice curdled Jazz's blood. She wrapped the sheet around her and swallowed. Luke reached for his pants, and she could see him fighting for control.

"You've made your point," he said. "Now what do you want?"

"Me? I don't want anything. I just thought I'd tell you how adorable your daughter looks today. The red polka dots really make her blond hair shine in the sunlight. You should tell her grandmother not to let her swing so high, though. Little girls are so easily hurt, especially ones who accept gifts from strangers."

Luke's face lost all color. "If anything has happened—"

"You'll what?" The laugh turned maniacal. "You don't know who I am, but I know everything there is to know about you, your slut, your daughter, your entire family— including your poor, unconscious brother. His heartbeat was a bit erratic today. You should watch him more closely, I think."

"Anything happens to my family, I'll hunt you down. Nothing will save you."

"I doubt it. You want a scoop, Mr. Montgomery? You decided to align yourself with Jane. Now someone you love will pay the price, and I guarantee it'll make the front page."

The phone went dead.

Luke stared at the receiver in his hand, and Jazz sat frozen in shock. She couldn't think, couldn't speak. Joy and Gabe were in danger. Because of *her.*

Jazz glanced at Luke, and he didn't waste a second. His jaw clenched, and he pressed two on his speed dial. "Come on, Mom. Answer."

"This can't be happening," she said, unable to think or to feel, only knowing that somehow she'd put Luke's daughter in danger.

The speakerphone's ring echoed through his bedroom. Each time the sound repeated, his breath hitched. He sagged on the bed as if bracing himself for the worst.

"Hello?" Anna Montgomery's voice echoed in the room, unhurried and unconcerned.

"Mom. Listen to me. There's someone at the park, watching you and Joy. You've got to get out of there."

"Oh, my God!" Anna yelled out, the panic in her voice hard to listen to. "Joy...Joy! Run to the car, we've got to go."

Jazz grabbed Luke's arm. "No," she whispered. "Not the car. There could be a bomb. They need to take cover and wait for the police," she said, and then snagged Luke's landline to make the call to send a squad car to the park and the hospital.

"Mom. Don't touch the car. It might be tampered with. Find some cover near the parking lot and stay there. Jasmine's calling the cops."

Jazz didn't know how he kept his voice composed, but he was a rock of calm.

"Luke?" Anna said, her voice close to cracking. "What do I do?"

As Jasmine hung up, Luke grasped her hand and squeezed so hard it hurt, but she didn't complain. She wasn't the one in trouble. Why did they have to be so far away?

"Mom, help is on the way, and I'll be there soon. Just keep talking to me."

As Luke worked to calm his mother, Jazz threw on her clothes. Who'd been on the phone? Who would go so far to hurt a child? Her mind went blank. Why couldn't she think?

The sound of sirens filtering through the telephone came as sweet relief.

"The police are here, Luke. Hold on," Anna choked out.

He breathed a sigh. "Thank God."

Random voices mumbled from the speakerphone, and a few seconds later his mother came back on the line. "We're in the police car, safe now. They're taking us to the Lake Arbor precinct while they search the area."

"Jasmine and I are on the way." Luke's voice had gone hoarse with emotion. "Put Joy on."

"Daddy?" The little girl's voice wavered a bit.

Jazz could barely restrain herself. She wanted to leap through the phone and hug Joy. She couldn't imagine what Luke must be feeling.

She placed her hand on Luke's shoulder as the innocent voice came through the line. "Gamma and me are going in a police car. Are they gonna put us in jail?"

Luke's hand turned white as he gripped the phone. "No, munchkin. They're taking you for a ride, and I'm coming to get you at the station. Do what the policemen say, okay?" His voice broke. "I…I love you, baby."

"Me more, Daddy."

Luke flipped the phone closed. His narrowed focus and rage were palpable—that of a man who would fight and die for those he loved.

He yanked on a knit shirt and old leather shoes while Jazz tugged on her sneakers, keeping up with his frenetic pace.

"Let's go. I'll call my brothers on the way. Gabe can't be left alone."

Jazz snatched Hero from the floor. Joy would need him.

One thing she knew for certain as they raced out the door. Whoever had done this was dead. If Luke didn't kill them, law or no law, she would.

Chapter Ten

The drive to the Lake Arbor Police Station took forever. Luke wouldn't truly believe Joy was safe until he saw her for himself. "What was I thinking, ignoring the dangers, putting Joy's life at risk for an article in a newspaper?"

"You were trying to fight for justice, for a woman who couldn't help herself," Jasmine said quietly.

"Well, I could've helped her in some other way. I was selfish. Wanting to prove myself as some kind of warrior with a pen for a weapon."

Well, no more. After he made sure Joy and Jasmine were safe, he'd make some changes. They both deserved more. They deserved to be safe.

"This was why Samantha—Joy's mother—didn't trust me to be a good father," Luke said, ramming his hand against the steering wheel. "She said I was addicted to the adrenaline rush. She was right."

"If that were really true, you'd still be overseas and your mother would be taking care of Joy. You love her. You'd do anything for her. Right?"

"Hell, yes. From the moment I got that call in the middle of the night from Arizona Child Protective Services about Samantha's accident I vowed I'd keep Joy safe. Great job I'm doing."

"This isn't your fault."

"My investigation started it off. That's the sort of thing that worried Samantha. When I returned to Afghanistan hell-bent on making things right for Frank and my unit, she begged me to stay, to give up the dangerous jobs, and let go of what I couldn't change. Ironic, huh? We're not so different after all—fighting the past."

"Could you have stayed in Denver?"

"If I'd asked, probably. But I wanted revenge for the ambush. I couldn't let my unit down. I made it out alive, and they didn't. I had to prove my survival had a purpose. Samantha wanted me to love her. She wanted a future, to be a family."

"She was already pregnant," Jazz surmised.

"I didn't know, and by the time I got back, she'd left. I lost Joy's first year of life. I won't chance losing her again."

"I'll do whatever I can to help."

He clasped Jasmine's hand in his, but he'd never ask her to put herself out there. His investigation had dragged her life into chaos, and somehow he had to fix it, for Jasmine, and for Joy.

Luke's SUV careened into the parking lot. Jasmine at his side, he ran through the automated doors leading into the precinct. He skidded to a halt at the sight of his pixie daughter holding court with a bunch of guys in uniforms. He grasped a chair to steady himself. That little girl could scare him like no insurgent ever could.

Joy sat on a large desk behind the main police counter, her freckled face wreathed in smiles as she took in every detail. Four police officers catered to her every need, all the while their steady hands nearby in case she teetered off her perch.

"Joy." Her name croaked out of him.

Her grin, if possible, widened, and her eyes twinkled. "Daddy. Come meet my new friends. They put the siren on for me."

For the first time since the mechanized voice had created a nightmare vision in his mind, Luke could breathe again. In two strides he reached her, scooped her into his arms, and held her tight.

He cleared his throat and ran his hands over each limb, assuring himself that she really was all right.

His mother touched his shoulder, and he reached out and pulled her to him too. Her body trembled. He knew her fear, understood the terror. He dropped a kiss on her forehead then whispered, "Thank you for protecting her."

Anna's eyes shone bright, but she wiped any sign away and turned to Jazz to squeeze her arm, pulling her into the embrace.

For a moment, Luke simply let himself take in the fact that Joy and his mother were safe, that Jasmine was here. Soon, though, Joy kicked her legs against his body and squirmed in his arms.

She'd obviously had enough of being squeezed as if he were holding on for dear life, but by God, he was. Stemming a flood of emotion he couldn't afford, he gave his mother a reassuring smile then knelt down with Joy until her feet touched the floor.

She grinned up at him. "The policemen let me and Gamma ride in their car. It was fast and loud."

He cupped her face, needing to touch her again. "I'm glad you had fun, munchkin."

Joy's attention shifted to his side and her expression brightened, her face beaming. "You brought Rap...Rap... punzel with you. Hi."

Jasmine knelt beside Luke, and her tremulous hand fingered a curl of Joy's hair. "Hello, Joy. I brought someone who missed you."

From behind her back, Jasmine drew out the stuffed clown fish.

"Hero!" Joy squealed and grabbed the soft fish to her, twisting her small body to and fro in hugs. Then she stopped, her little face turning serious. "Are you sure you're not gonna need him anymore?"

"Positive." Jasmine smiled at Joy. "He took good care of me, but I'll be fine now. I think he wants to come home."

Joy launched herself at Jasmine and hugged her tight.

Did Jasmine understand how much it meant to Luke that his daughter clung to her? The most terrifying thing in the world was being a single dad, but for this moment he didn't feel quite so alone.

Joy pulled back from the hug and tugged at Jasmine's hair. "I'm glad you came." Her voice lowered to a childish whisper that Luke could easily hear. "I think I saw the wicked witch. She gave me a ball. She was nice at first, but then her eyes got scary."

The wicked witch?

A woman? Tower's accomplice? If so, it was a smart move. With all the mothers in the park, a woman would barely be noticed.

"I know I shouldn't have taken the ball, Daddy."

"You're right. We don't take presents from strangers. Next time, stay close to Gamma." Luke picked Joy up, sitting her on the officer's desk.

She held on to Hero for dear life and buried her face into the soft toy. "We were playing 'Seek and Go Hide.' I was hiding when I saw the witch's ball."

Luke lifted her chin up and looked into his daughter's eyes, his heart thudding at how close he'd come to something happening to her. He reached for Jasmine's hand. "Joy, what did the wicked witch say?"

"She told me I could keep the ball. At first I liked her, but then her face got mean. She turned into the wicked witch and I ran away. But I kept the ball, even though she wrote on it."

"Where's the ball now?"

Joy looked around. "I gave it to him." She grinned at the gray-haired officer behind the desk. "I like him. He gave me a donut."

Luke caught Jasmine's gaze, and she nodded and went behind Joy to the cop's desk. When the cop pulled out an evidence bag containing the ball, Jasmine's face turned ashen. She tilted the ball toward Luke so he could read the message written there.

Is Jane worth her life?

Cold, dark anger froze Luke from the inside. The bitch had threatened his daughter. He struggled to clear away the fury for Joy's sake and took her small hands in his. "Munchkin, can you tell us what the wicked witch looked like?"

The large cap on her head fell down past Joy's nose. She shoved at it until she'd pushed it back up. She shrugged. "Her hair was red. Like my dress."

Slowly, patiently, Luke pieced together a description of the woman from Joy. His daughter's mind could be such a puzzle, but little by little he created a picture of who they were after.

"The description matches the woman who came to the precinct with Tower the other day," Jasmine said. "She's obviously involved in much more than warming his bed or being a simple distraction."

Luke's gaze kept wandering back to Joy and his mother. If anything happened to either one of them... Then he took in Jasmine's tense features. If anything happened to her and he could've done something to stop it, he would never forgive himself. "Tower won't get away with this. He brought a crazy woman in contact with my daughter. He'll wish he'd never started down this path."

"You should get Joy away from here, someplace safe. Post a guard to look after Gabe in the hospital." Jasmine's eyes went flat. "Tower's the key. I'll force him to identify the redhead."

"No. It's too dangerous. You're in their sights already. No telling how far they'd go if they're cornered."

"I'll have backup. Sarge and Wexler will have to listen to me now. The entire SWAT team saw the woman with Tower. She's threatened a three-year-old girl. They'll have to bring Tower in for questioning. Once we get him, we'll have a good lead on the woman."

An awkward cough dragged them apart. "Sorry to interrupt, but Joy is asking for you, Mr. Montgomery," the cop said. "Also, the captain wants to know if you'd be willing to let Joy work with a sketch artist."

Luke shot a quick glance at the daughter he'd sworn to protect. "I'm taking her out of town before anything else happens. If you can get someone over here now, and if I can be there with her, then you can try. But she's only three."

"One of our sketch artists specializes in working with children. Don't worry. She'll make it seem like a game. I'll call her in."

The officer left to make the arrangements, and Luke took Jasmine's hands in his. "Come with us. I can protect you."

"We both have a job, Luke. You're a father. I'm the law. You do your job. Let me do mine."

He knew that look on her face well. She'd already decided to go headfirst after Tower. Probably alone. Oh, she'd get help. After she'd found him. Well, Luke wouldn't let her put herself at risk. She might think she'd won this battle, but as soon as Joy was safe, Luke would be there for Jasmine. Before she got herself killed.

A park could hide an abundance of sins. The woman merged into the nighttime shadows along the Apex Park jogging path. Over the nests of piñon trees, an apartment building was visible. Tower was due in half an hour. Tonight he'd experience a show he'd never forget.

Smiling, she pulled her newly dyed blond hair back then adjusted the Arvada Police Academy sweats. She wandered into the open and, keeping her face averted, did a series of calf stretches, attracting the attention of some late-night joggers. A few even waved, as if they recognized her.

Perfect. The pursuit of revenge was oh so sweet.

She took off in a measured jog and passed one or two courageous souls who were willing to brave the park at night. Before long, she'd rounded the path and said a few words to a slow-paced elderly couple. They would remember the woman who'd taken the clip from her long blond hair and let it swing down her back. The woman who'd bent over and displayed the outline of her curves even beneath those sweats. The old man had practically been drooling.

She glanced at her watch. Tower would be here soon. She slipped back into the grove and waited. She watched him walk toward the meeting place and exhilaration filled her.

"You here, Red?" Anger tinged Tower's voice. "What the hell is going on? I had a chance to bring that bitch down legally, and now I'm being pulled in for questioning. You better have a damn good explanation and even better evidence to bring Jazz Parker down."

Silently she eased up behind him. "You're going to have to think of a new nickname for me. 'Red' isn't going to cut it anymore."

Tower whirled around and glared at her, then took in her blond hair and sweats. "Holy...you look like Jazz."

She took his hand and slid it up under her sweatshirt until he cupped her breast. "I know. I thought I'd give you your darkest fantasy. You're screwing her at work, but tonight you can pretend you're screwing her right here."

He pulled his hand free. "You're sick. You know that?"

She slid her hand down the front of his pants and smiled as he sucked in a breath. "No, lover. I'm just horny and in the mood for some games."

She backed into the shadows and beckoned him to follow. She forced her voice to remain low and husky. "Wouldn't you like to give her everything she deserves? Take her hard and fast...and rough as you like?"

After stepping back farther, she slid the sweatpants down and kicked them away. The sweatshirt skimmed the top of her thighs. She leaned back against a large boulder and smiled. "I'm waiting."

Tower cursed and stayed on the now-deserted path. Was he really going to pass this up? He looked around and finally came to her in the small thicket. He pressed his lower body against hers then slid his hands up under the sweatshirt to grab her breasts. His touch was much rougher now, and she fought not to wince. His eyes were dark and intense, full of lust. Oh, yeah, sex was definitely on his brain.

"You like me like this?" she asked, cupping him, molding him, rendering him her slave. "Looking like her?" She squeezed and released. "Do you want to teach her a lesson? Do you want to—" She whispered crude words in his ear, and he jolted.

"You are so hot," he choked, groping her, running his hands all over her.

She shuddered. She hated being touched, much less doing the touching, but justice required sacrifice.

Tower put his hand behind her neck and yanked her toward him, chest to breast, hip to hip. He clamped his wet mouth on hers, thrusting his tongue against her teeth.

She kissed him back, making him believe she loved his disgusting tongue down her throat.

"Man, I knew the assignment to set up Jazz for the corruption charge would be fun, but not this much. It was easy. I'm IA. I can access most anything in the office, and once I discovered her background investigation file on her name change, I knew she was the perfect stooge. Set up doubt. Plant evidence. Kill her. Blame her. Then you came along. You gave me more. You made it easy. Until now."

She squeezed him and he winced, eyes glazed with lust.

"You really like it rough, don't you?" He pinched her nipple, and she forced a moan of pleasure when all she wanted to do was retrieve the crowbar hidden in her bag and end this.

"Let's find a room. Now." He thrust his erection toward her and she rubbed him again. He swelled against her hand.

"I can't wait," she whispered. "Let's do it here."

She turned away from him and leaned over the boulder, offering him a tantalizing view of her ass. "Come on. Pretend I'm her. Give her everything she deserves."

"You're insane, but I don't even care," he moaned.

"Then do it. Right here. Right now."

He swore, his breath coming in uneven gasps. "Hard and fast, huh, babe? You got it."

He moved behind her and shoved the sweatshirt up over her hips, then fumbled with his zipper and slid his pants down around his knees. "It's gonna be good for you. I'm big, and I'm ready."

He clasped her bare hips and kneaded the flesh she'd offered to him. She winced at his rough touch but gulped down the nausea. Lord spare her from men who thought they could make her want them. At least soon she would feel his touch no more.

"It's going to be *very* good." She slipped her hand into her hidden bag and grasped the crowbar. She shifted and swung the weapon at his head. Metal connected with bone, the sound sweet and wonderful.

Blood spattered across the sweatshirt and the grass beyond. He crashed to the ground, stunned and barely conscious. Smiling, she stared at the body lying face down among the pine needles.

"Was it good for you too, lover? *I* certainly enjoyed it."

She slipped Jane's sweatpants back on then turned to Tower. He'd started to stir, moaning. "Sorry, Deputy, but I have justice to serve, and for that I need a corpse."

She smashed the crowbar hard on his skull to finish the job. Again and again and again.

Her breathing came fast and quick as sobs mixed with curses. He. Would. Never. Touch. Her. Again.

She pummeled his body with the metal until her arms lost their strength. She looked down at him. Good. He could still be identified. Just barely, but that's all that mattered. Her own body throbbed with satisfaction.

"Soon," she whispered. "Soon, Mama, justice will be ours."

The night lights of Denver glared off Jazz's eyes as she bounced in the loaner truck. Luke's SUV had been more comfortable, but it hadn't seemed right to keep his vehicle. The clunker was more her style anyway. And its battered body matched her mood.

Wexler had invited Tower in for a nice interview all right. Tomorrow morning. She knew the detective didn't completely believe her theory. Twelve hours gave Tower—and his accomplice—way too much time to come up with an alibi. Jazz intended to corner Tower tonight and get his girlfriend's name, no matter what. For Joy's sake.

She gripped the steering wheel, her focus keen. First she had to find him.

She'd scoured the station house, the gym, his apartment, a few bars he'd been known to drop some bucks in. The last time anyone had spoken with him, he'd mentioned a hot date. With the redhead no doubt. The last sighting had been hours ago. Since then, nothing.

Jazz glanced at her watch. Ten p.m. Shift change at the precinct. Maybe one of the grave-shifters knew where he'd gone. If she had to, she'd bunk in front of Tower's apartment until he showed.

Sirens blared behind her and she pulled over to allow two fire trucks to pass. Jazz hung a left and followed the engines to see if she could help. Several sets of emergency lights flashed a few blocks down. Her gut clenched. They were very close to her place. This couldn't be happening. Not again.

Smoke billowed into the sky. She drove closer. The orange flames engulfed the upper floor of her building. "No!"

Jazz whipped the truck to the curb, pulled the keys from the ignition, and jumped out. Had everyone escaped the blaze? She raced down the street and held up her badge to the uniforms cordoning off the scene surrounding the conflagration. Firefighters scrambled to secure hoses, and ladders lifted high into the sky, but red licks of flame raged from the third-floor windows. The old building had gone up like dry tinder.

She shoved through the chaos until she reached the fire command post and flashed the badge clipped to her shirt. "I live here. What happened?"

A cop frowned. "According to the witnesses, it looks like it started in the corner apartment on the third floor. A witness thought he smelled gasoline."

Her place. Her knees quivered, and she locked them in place. Someone had torched *her* place. Her neighbors had lost everything. Because of her. Unable to avert her gaze from the crackling inferno, she simply stared, bewildered. Everything she touched she destroyed sooner or later.

"Jasmine!" Luke's voice roared over the crowd. He rushed to her and dragged her into his arms. He ran his hands up and down her back, as if convincing himself she was in one piece. Shoving his fingers through her hair, he fastened his lips to hers in a kiss of desperation. She clung to him, ashamed of her relief at his presence.

He hugged her close and kissed her forehead. "I've been looking everywhere for you."

"Why? I thought you were leaving with Joy." Jazz pulled back. "What are you doing here?"

"Nick took Mom and Joy to our cabin in the mountains. They're safe. I'm here to watch your back."

"Luke, your place is with your family. I can handle finding out who came after Joy."

"No way. Look behind you. This just escalated to a new level. I'd wager a year's salary it's arson. There is *no* way I'm leaving you alone."

She should push him away. She couldn't let him see how much it meant to her that he was here. "Someone said they smelled an accelerant."

"Not a surprise."

A crash reverberated behind them and they turned toward the fire. A side wall had collapsed. Jasmine's heart broke a little as the life she'd known since she was sixteen collapsed. Mr. Peterson's apartment was the first place she'd ever felt truly safe and secure. Not a home exactly, but certainly a haven. Now it was gone.

Wexler emerged from the crowd of gawkers, his face grim. "I should've known you two would be here. How long have you been on site?"

"Five minutes maybe," Jazz said.

Wexler pulled out his notebook. "Were either of you in Apex Park or Heritage Square in the last few hours?"

"What's going on?" The tension in Wexler's back and shoulders, the aggressiveness of his posture set Jazz off. She didn't like anything about the detective's demeanor.

"Answer my question," he rasped.

Dark apprehension flooded Jazz. "I was out looking for Tower to ask him some questions. I stopped in a few places, but never found him. Why the interrogation?"

Wexler turned to Luke. "What about you?"

"After the threat against my daughter, I packed her up and got her out of town. Then I heard about the fire and high-tailed it over here."

The detective swore, sending Jazz a pointed glance. "So you have no alibi." He turned to Luke. "And you threatened Tower directly in front of me a few hours ago. Are you two *trying* to get arrested?"

"What's going on?" Jazz said.

Wexler shifted into an official stance. "Brian Tower is dead. He was murdered on one of the jogging trails nearby. This apartment building is visible from the crime scene."

Jazz whirled to look at Apex Park. Sure enough, search lights glowed among the piñons and willows.

Wexler stepped forward. "With the bad blood between the two of you and Tower...I'm taking you both in for questioning. Let's go."

Chapter Eleven

The gray walls of the interrogation room closed in on Jazz, and she struggled to maintain control. The god-awful paint color and the confining walls reminded her too much of the closet her mother used to lock her in when customers came calling.

Jane had been trapped then.

Jazz felt trapped now.

Tower was dead. Their only solid lead.

Jazz's head thudded with pain. She prayed Tower's murder was just a coincidence, some cosmic bad luck, but she knew better. His body found near her apartment, her apartment burning to the ground, their confrontations. If she'd been assigned Tower's murder, she'd arrest herself.

She hadn't done it, but all the events of the last few days aligned to one possibility…a setup, but who was framing her? The woman? The mob that appeared to have infiltrated the sheriff's office? Had she seen something she shouldn't have and not realized it or terminated someone and triggered a vendetta? Was she paranoid?

She rose from the chair, catching sight of her haggard reflection in the two-way mirror. Well, she was only delusional if they weren't out to get her, and someone sure as hell seemed to be.

Circles shadowed her eyes, her fatigue evident. They were watching her, hoping she'd break. She closed her eyes and focused, pushing back the tide of despair that surged through her. She wouldn't crack in front of them. She'd survived Truth or Consequences, she'd survived the streets. She refused to cave now.

Jazz turned away from the mirror. She was more concerned about Joy and Luke. He was in one of these rooms being interrogated. He should be with his daughter, protecting her. Jazz should be finding the woman who'd threatened Joy.

Jane's name had been on that ball. Why? Were her past and Luke's investigation connected? Too many questions. She needed answers, and instead she was in nearly the same situation she'd been in twelve years earlier. Sitting in jail.

Except this was worse. She had more to lose. This time she wasn't a juvie, and she wasn't here for solicitation or petty larceny for the scam she'd run. This time the rap would be for murder of a cop, and there'd be no friendly sheriff stepping in to save her.

Unlike the last time around, however, she was innocent.

Wexler strode in and sat across from her. "I'd get an appointment with your rep, Parker. And soon."

She flipped her chair around and straddled the seat. "I didn't *do* anything. Can't you see what's going on? I'm being framed."

"A few hours ago you believed Tower was the one setting you up." Skepticism dripped from his voice. "He's dead now. What's your new theory?"

"Tower's death doesn't mean he wasn't responsible. Talk to Luke. Tower was involved in something dirty. Maybe he pissed off an accomplice. Maybe he just got mugged."

"Montgomery is answering some tough questions of his own. Worry about yourself." Wexler pulled out a photo and laid it in front of Jazz.

She gasped at what was left of Brian Tower's body. He'd been brutalized.

"This was not a mugging gone bad, Parker. He was beaten to a pulp. His wallet was still in his pocket, his service revolver still on him. This was a crime of passion. By someone who hated him. Someone like you."

"I didn't do this. I couldn't," she whispered.

"You're a sniper. You kill people for a living."

She winced. She only did what was necessary to protect the innocent. She didn't pull the trigger for revenge. She'd never do that. "Why would I murder Tower? Or vandalize my apartment and torch the building? None of it makes sense. You think I used my own blood to write myself a message?"

"We know it wasn't yours." He slammed another file on the table. "This is a preliminary report. The blood on the wall was feline."

"A cat?"

"Reported missing by a couple who lived on the second floor of your apartment building."

Jazz could barely think through the disbelief. The cops she'd trained with and battled beside had abandoned her without any resistance as far as she could tell. "Do you honestly believe I'd do this? Wreck my apartment, butcher a helpless animal, kill a cop?"

"We're receiving reports from all over town that a woman matching your description was looking for Tower tonight, and she seemed mighty determined to find him. Several witnesses placed you in the park near the time of death."

"I wasn't at Apex Park. I'll admit I was searching for him, but I never found him."

"You had the means, motive, and a questionable alibi. How about this theory? Tower discovered corruption in the department and pegged you. You lied about your past, so maybe you were blackmailed, but he had the goods on you. You killed him. Then you and Luke cooked up this little scenario to get you off. Hell, maybe *you* hired the redheaded woman in the first place."

"I'd never put a child at risk, Wexler. Never." Jazz slammed her hands on the table. "I didn't kill Tower. I didn't do *any* of this."

"Listen carefully, Jazz," Wexler said. He leaned forward, focused and intense. "As far as Sheriff Tower is concerned, he's figured the whole thing out. You're guilty. You understand what I'm saying? According to Brian Tower's IA investigation notes, you have a juvie record. We're checking into it to see if there's anything relevant. Any more scandalous facts and the sheriff *will* use it to bring you down."

His words and tone sank in as she stared at his unwavering expression. He didn't like what he had to do, but he didn't have a choice. She'd been a fool to believe she could escape where she'd come from. Her whole life was unraveling, and she couldn't stop it.

"Those records were expunged," she said, her voice weak.

"Murder changes things. Call. Your. Rep."

"Someone's framing me to take a fall, and there's only one person who might be able to tell us what's going on. The redheaded woman. She's the only connection to Tower. Have you investigated her?"

"I know how to do my job, Parker. We have the sketch from the girl's description. Your *ex*-teammates have confirmed the woman who threatened Montgomery's daughter was Tower's lover, though they know her only as 'Red.' Thanks to their input, we've refined the drawing and sent it over the wires. She's a smart cookie, though. She obscured her face from all the cameras in the sheriff's office, which makes me wonder exactly what she's up to. We'll find her."

"Maybe she's working for the crime syndicate. Maybe *she* killed him."

"We'll bring her in for the Montgomery case and check her alibi for tonight. That's all I'll promise. In the meantime, worry about yourself. You're at the top of the suspect list. And I don't think that'll change unless some damned impressive information falls in our lap."

Stunned, Jazz sank back into her chair. He couldn't do a thing for her. She was on her own unless she could prove she was being framed, and how would she do that from a cell? She'd be locked up within hours if the pattern of the last few days continued.

Tower had wanted to bring her down. She'd bet he hadn't planned to do it from the grave, but he could get his wish. Whoever killed him was smart and vicious.

She might not be able to save herself or her career. Too much had happened, but Jazz didn't care about herself. She didn't matter. Joy was in danger, and Jazz had to protect Joy and Luke. She refused to let that little girl lose her father. She'd promised them, promised herself. She wouldn't fail.

The noose was tightening. One more deadly blow to destroy Jazz Parker, and Jane Sanford would finally pay.

Fools. They had no clue who they were dealing with. They would.

She scanned the rundown neighborhood, waiting. The street had probably been quaint, once. Fifty years ago. Now she'd bet every other house had either a fresh supply of crack or meth. The hovel she stood in front of had fared little better. She watched from below a broken street lamp as a rusty red Pinto pulled into a dirt driveway.

The house's gray paint was peeling. Missing boards left gaps in the sagging porch, and the screen hinges were askew. She knew he didn't live here. This was his cousin's safe house. She'd made it her business to know everything about this man with a few too many secrets.

She took a step forward as his muscular body unfolded from the car. *Not bad.* At least he had the physique to be of some use. "Deputy?"

The man jerked and went for his weapon.

"Calm down, sugar. I just want to talk."

He clutched the Bowie he'd pulled from its sheath. "I saw you. You vandalized Jazz's truck."

"And I saw you. You took a shot at them. You've been a very bad boy. Oh, by the way, did I mention I like to take pictures, *Deputy?* Pictures that I put in safe places and get paid money so bosses and newspapers don't see them?"

He clenched the knife tighter. "I could turn you in."

"And wouldn't your colleagues love to know about your double life? It didn't take me long to learn who your father is. It wouldn't take them long to realize you never left the family business."

"What do you want?"

"A little cooperation. I need a partner. To bring Jazz Parker down. You seem to want the same. If she's dead, your little side business at the sheriff's office gets blamed on her. You get off free and clear, right? That was the plan, wasn't it?"

He couldn't hide the surprise, and she just laughed. "You guys aren't as smart as you think you are. Tower talks a bit too much in the sack, but I would've figured it out anyway. Why didn't you just kill her? You had the shot that day at her apartment."

"I wasn't after her."

Lisa chuckled. "Men. You can't think on your feet. You were there to warn off Montgomery, and you didn't see the opportunity to just take out the perfect patsy for the investigation. Fool."

"You seem pretty sure of yourself. So why do you need me?"

"Even I can't be in two places at once. So, *Deputy*, you help me finish *your* job *my* way, and I'll give you the location of those pictures I took at her apartment. No one ever needs to know your dirty little secret. You kill me or you don't help me, they end up at the FBI and the newspaper."

He re-sheathed the knife and sent her a calculating look. "My assignment hasn't gone as planned," he said. "I'm interested."

She pulled out a small GPS tracking device from her bag. "Do I need to tell you how to use this? I need some people followed…for starters."

Alone in the stark interrogation room, Jazz rubbed her eyes with her hands. She was free to go? She'd been here for hours. Wexler had pushed at her until it became obvious there would be no resolution—yet. He hadn't served an arrest warrant, but it was only a matter of time. He'd warned her not to leave town and then walked out of the room.

Only Luke's statements had saved her from jail. Wexler and his cohorts couldn't explain the attacks against her and the threat on Joy. He was her alibi to all three events, though they were skeptical of his story. The missed shot was her fault—a mistake by a woman on the edge. They still wouldn't accept sabotage.

She laid her head against the table, trying to figure out where her world had gone wrong. Only days ago she'd been up for a promotion and now she was fighting a murder rap.

A brisk knock sounded at the door and Sarge strode in, his face stern, his eyes pained. She'd never seen him so uncomfortable, so ill at ease in his skin.

"I'm sorry, Jazz. I need your gun and your badge. You're suspended pending a full investigation and disposition of this...ah...situation."

"I didn't kill him, Sarge."

"Until that's proven, I don't have a choice...and neither do you."

The words slammed her harder than the recoil of a .458 Winchester. She gritted her teeth until her jaw hurt, rose, and retrieved her coat from the back of an empty chair. Forcing her hands steady, she unzipped her pocket, reached in, and pulled out the badge. She'd worked her tail off for that star. It defined her identity as Jazz Parker. Without it, she'd become invisible again. Just a kid from the wrong side of the tracks. The daughter of a murdered whore.

The bronze star glinted in her hand. "Receiving this was the proudest day of my life until I got my SWAT pin." She handed her badge to Sarge. "I swear I haven't dishonored it."

"Your gun too."

This time Jazz couldn't stop the slight trembling.

"Wexler took it."

"I'll get it from him." Regret clouded Sarge's face. "I guess that's it then."

A numb fog floated around her. The room, Sarge, it all seemed like a very bad dream, one from which she couldn't wake.

Sarge started toward the door then turned. "Maybe things will work out."

Jazz nodded, ignoring the pain as he left. His voice told her he didn't hold much hope. Right about now, neither did she. Stiff, aching, and heartsick, Jazz struggled to maintain her composure when a rookie, who had obviously drawn the short straw, escorted her through the bullpen like a newly released felon. Probing glances tracked her progress and angry whispers followed her out of the door of the station, into the darkness beyond.

Cop Killer.

Dear God, some of them obviously believed that of her. A lump formed in her throat. No one offered her support. She was on her own. As always. Determination tightened her jaw. She *would* track down the real murderer.

Jazz paused on the sidewalk in front of the stone building and peered into the moonlit night. It would be dawn soon. A new day for the real killer, and Jazz didn't know where to start looking.

"Jasmine?"

At the sound of Luke's voice her heart skipped a beat. He opened the door of his SUV, its interior light shining like a beacon, but she couldn't move toward him.

"Go away, Luke. Keep your family safe. You heard the threat when that maniac called about Joy. I'm poison to you."

The slam of the SUV's heavy door echoed like a gunshot. Within a few strides he was there, looming over her. "Get in the car, Jasmine. We don't need to put on a show for the boys in blue who are doing their utmost to string you up for a murder you didn't commit. If I hadn't been able to prove I was packing up Joy at the time of the murder, we'd be in the same position. Wexler still wonders if we're co-conspirators. Like it or not, we're in this together."

Shaking with anger, hurt, and despair, she held her ground for a minute, then cursed and strode to the vehicle. A moment later, they were both enclosed in the SUV, the air crackling like heat lightning between them.

"Did you just plan on walking out on me?" Luke said. "Again?"

"I'm tracking down a killer. Alone."

"Not while I'm still breathing."

She turned in the seat to meet his fury, wanting so badly to fall into his arms and let him hold her. She couldn't let herself. With all the strength she could muster she steadied her voice. "The sheriff is using Wexler and the IA investigation to pin his son's murder on me. I don't know how the redhead is involved, but I do know I have to find her. First to protect Joy and second because that woman's my only hope to clear my name. This may have started out as your investigation, Luke, but it's mine now."

She laid her hand against his cheek. "I need to stay away from the people I care about before I get them killed. Go to your daughter. *I'll* find out who's doing this and bring them down."

"And how are you going to do that? You have nothing to work with. You're wearing the same clothes you've been wearing for twenty-four hours. You have nowhere to go. No home. No money. No resources. Nothing."

"I didn't have much more than this when I landed in Denver with Clarkson, and I made it."

"With help from friends. Just like I'm offering now. You can't run me off, Jasmine. You need me and my contacts now more than ever, and you're going to have to accept it."

Cracks splintered through the ice she'd molded around her heart. "Luke, you have to stay safe. I can't take it if anything else happens to you because of me."

"And I'm supposed to just stand by and not care what happens to you?

"Yes," she snapped. "Just let me do my—"

"Job? Is that what you were going to say? Wexler told me you've been suspended. You had to turn in your gun and badge."

She pulled away. "He had no right to tell you."

"What? You wouldn't have said anything? Or would you have lied? Let me think you were still on the force? That you had backup and a gun to protect yourself?" At her silence he slammed his fist against the steering wheel. "Christ, Jasmine. Are you *ever* going to trust me to help you?"

She turned to the door and yanked it open. "I don't need you, Luke."

"No, you don't need me. You've made that clear. You're friggin' Wonder Woman. But the world doesn't revolve around you. *I* need to get this woman. For Joy. So face it, 'Jazz', I'm investigating, whether you're with me or not. I'd just feel a lot better if we were watching each other's back. Joy doesn't need to be a three-year-old orphan."

Jazz gasped, her insides clenching at the thought of Luke being killed, of Joy without her father. "Anyone ever tell you that you fight dirty, Montgomery?"

"Only when I need to. So are you in?"

She stared at him, but fear took root. Could she really protect Luke and his family from a killer with no conscience? Or would everyone she loved be taken from her...again? "You die on me, Luke, and I'm going to be extremely irritated."

"Back at ya, babe." He started the SUV then shifted into gear. "We'd better not go to my house. Nick suspected someone was watching it earlier. We'll get a room and hook up my computer. I've got some serious hacking to do."

Jazz barely held herself together for the remainder of the ride to a Victorian bed and breakfast Luke knew. They didn't speak; he didn't turn on the radio. Odd how she could be so comfortable in silence. Either Luke understood she needed the quiet or he was doing the same thing she was. Trying to make sense of everything that had happened.

She'd gone over and over the details with one inescapable conclusion. The person who'd called Luke and written on the ball in the park had called her Jane. Not Jazz. Jane. Tower knew her first as Jazz. She didn't believe he'd made that call. She could only deduce he'd hooked up with someone from her past who hated her enough to involve a three-year-old girl. She didn't know who, but she could think of only one reason why.

When they reached the bed and breakfast, she burned with humiliation as the proprietor checked them in, frowning at their filthy clothes and more so when they told her they had no bags. She remembered too well those disgusted, judgmental looks from her childhood.

God, she couldn't break the sensation that she was hurtling back into that oppressive place again. Every option closing off—one by one—until she was reduced to the streets. Starving. Desperate. Relying on primal instincts, like an animal, to survive.

Heartsick, she followed Luke and surveyed the pristine bedroom. The white comforter gleamed bright on a four-poster cherry bed. A small sitting area with large, overstuffed chairs invited a body to sink into oblivion. She didn't belong here. She was unclean, unworthy, inside and out. She glanced at Luke, saw his closed-off expression. He'd recognized the truth too. That she didn't belong here or with him.

"I need a shower," she choked.

The look in his eyes held too much sympathy as he nodded. "Take as long as you want. I'll set up the computer and see what I can find."

He'd backed off from challenging her. He was walking on eggshells, and she didn't blame him. She was so ready to crack. She staggered to the bathroom and closed the door. The antique lock didn't work. Great.

She stripped off the smoky, filthy clothes and dropped them on the white tile floor. The whole place was white, making her feel even dirtier. She turned the water on in the tiny shower enclosure and shuddered at the thought of going in there and closing the curtain, blocking off most of the light. It was barely the size of a closet, and she was struggling enough to fight off nightmares of the past.

Bracing herself, she stepped inside. Water beat down on her in the tiny space, and she fought to contain a growing panic. She grabbed the soap, desperate to finish and get out, only to drop the bar. Crouching down, she watched the dirty water swirl around the floor drain and suddenly the tears and horrible memories started to flow.

The years disappeared. She huddled in the dark. Locked in a closet. Waiting for the bad man to come. That last time, he didn't come for her mother.

He came for her.

Luke's laptop lay open on the rolltop desk, the screen black. The quiet room should've been the perfect place to concentrate on the investigation, but he'd gotten nowhere. He kept glancing at the closed mahogany door. Jazz had disappeared behind it too long ago. She'd held it together, barely, but he'd recognized the symptoms of someone on the edge.

Only putting the pieces together—and quickly—would save her. But the puzzle didn't fit. He needed more information. His investigator hadn't had any luck at the *Sentinel's* archives. Jane was a ghost, but obviously not to everyone. There had to be something more. Something Jazz hadn't told him. An expunged arrest record didn't engender this kind of stalking. And how was Tower connected?

Desperate for a break in the case, Luke snagged his cell and placed a restricted call to Grace.

"You've reached a number that has been disconnected or is no longer in service—" He slammed the phone next to his computer. He just prayed it was Grace who'd cut the phone off and not her husband.

Which meant he'd have to push Jazz. He needed to know everything, and they had no more time. His nerves raw, he paced the floor and finally paused near the bathroom door again. An unfamiliar sound mixed with the drum of the pounding spray.

Crying?

Every instinct screamed at him to break down the door. He laid his hand flat against the dark wood, as if he could touch her through the barrier, and closed his eyes. Should he pretend he didn't hear, back away and give her space?

Another muffled sob decided him. He rapped once before turning the knob. He eased open the door and his heart twisted in agony. Through a break between the curtains, he saw her crouched in the corner of the shower, huddled against the white tile, her head buried in her arms. Her body shuddered as she gulped in air.

He didn't hesitate or take time to strip. She needed him. He wrenched open the curtain and stepped under the streaming water into the cramped space. His clothes soaking, he hunkered down beside her and placed a gentle hand on her shoulder.

"Jasmine."

Her body jerked away from him. "Don't hurt me! Don't—" Her eyes flew open, her expression wild. Then, to his relief, the panic cleared, and she recognized him. "Oh, God. I thought you were…"

Nausea burned the back of his throat. He'd seen that look before. In Afghanistan. On women and children who'd been assaulted and raped by the insurgents ravaging their towns. He'd never thought to see it on the face of someone he cared about.

He reached out to her, but then clenched his fist and dropped his hand. "Who did this to you?"

She shook her head and turned away from him, curling into a tight ball of misery, hiding as much of her body as she could from him.

Luke shut off the shower and slowly, calmly, backed away from her, giving her some room. He could hardly bear to watch her sink into herself, and he didn't know how to comfort her. This wasn't a skinned knee. This was a deep secret that had devastated her soul and that she'd kept hidden for a lifetime. Blindly he reached for a towel then gently covered her.

"Please go," she whispered, letting her hair fall across her face, shielding her expression from him. "I don't want you to see me like this."

He dropped his hands, knowing he couldn't alleviate this kind of pain. "I...I'll wait for you outside," he said and backed out of the room, closing the door behind him.

Chapter Twelve

She couldn't face him.

Jazz's hands trembled as she dried her body. Her entire soul was brittle, shaken. Empty.

She dropped her dirty clothes into the sink and filled it with soapy water. She couldn't put them back on until they were clean. Terrycloth hospitality robes hung on the back of the door, and she pulled one on, grateful for the warmth and the fact that it covered her nearly head to toe.

Emotion welled again and she fought back tears. She had to stop this. She owed Luke an explanation, but she dreaded it. She'd never meant for him to know everything. Never wanted anyone to know.

She stared at the closed door, wishing she could scrub away the past and never face the world. But even in this room, there were too many memories. With a resigned sigh, she grabbed the brass handle.

Wearing an identical robe, his hair still wet from his unplanned shower, Luke sat in one of the overstuffed chairs across the room. Waiting. He said nothing, just stared with tormented eyes.

She took the chair facing him, arranging the terrycloth precisely so no bare skin showed. "I haven't had a flashback in years."

"Jasmine, I'm sorry."

She raised a hand to stop him, to ward off the crushing panic that threatened to steal her breath again. "It wasn't your fault. Too many things have happened. And I haven't slept."

Shame burned hot within her and she looked away. "I never wanted you to know."

"Did you believe I'd think less of you? Blame you for something that wasn't your fault?"

"I'm not...I pretended I wasn't that person anymore. That...victim. That helpless creature that others could control."

"And you're not."

"But I feel like her again, and I hate it." She heard her voice helplessly crack. "I hate being out of control."

He started to get up.

"Don't." If he touched her, she'd break. "I...can't do this if you're close to me."

He stopped, eyeing her warily, then settled down. "What can't you do?"

"Tell you the rest of the truth," she whispered. "About the man I killed."

Luke sank deeper into his chair. "Talk to me."

Jazz's nails bit into her palms. She had to get through this, but she wanted to stop. To hide from the way he would look at her soon. Like she was white trash. No, far worse than that. "Growing up, we never stayed in one place long. Usually we were run out of town or escaped in the night because we couldn't make the rent." Struggling against the flashback, Jazz forced herself to continue. "When I was ten, my mother and I lived in Truth or Consequences,

New Mexico, on the wrong side of the tracks. Literally. Men who came to our house wanted to get laid or have a punching bag who wouldn't report them to the police if they got a little rough. Mama always promised that someday we'd make it big. We'd leave town, change our names, and start over. I wanted to believe it. I wanted to believe every word."

"Jasmine…"

Jazz tried to keep the tears from falling, but they simply flowed. She could do nothing. If she released her hold on her robe to wipe them away, she'd shatter into a thousand pieces. "One night, a man named Gary Matthews showed up. Drunk, horny. Itching for some action."

In her mind the bed and breakfast morphed into the grimy shack she and her mother lived in, the moldy scraps in the refrigerator, the mixture of fear and anticipation when a client would visit them. Would they bring food? Or maybe a treat to keep her quiet? Would they come after her when Mama was too drunk to notice? Or care.

"Mama locked me in the closet, like she usually did when her men came over. This time, she hadn't been drinking, but Matthews had. This time, he wanted me. She said, 'No.'"

Luke's face went white, and the muscle in his jaw throbbed, but he said nothing. Thank God.

"Matthews was drunk and angry. They were shouting, and I was so scared." Even now, her body shook. The images in her head were sickeningly real. "I was huddled in the closet with a baseball bat gripped in my fists. He unlocked the door and yanked it open. I just froze. My mother screamed and threw herself at him. He punched her. I saw her go down. He hit her, again and again and again, but I did nothing."

Luke knelt by her chair and tried to pull her against him. "You were a child."

She shoved him back. "It was my job to stop him. That's why my mother gave me the bat. If anyone started hurting Mama, I was supposed to scare them away. Protect her. I pushed my way out of the closet, but there was so much blood. I couldn't move. Couldn't even think."

"Jasmine, you were ten. He was a grown man. What could you have done?"

"I should've helped her," she said in a broken whisper. "I should've hit him *then*. Instead he grabbed the bat from me and whipped it across the room. I'll never forget the sound Mama made when it hit her. She cried out, clutching the side of her head as she fell. Then he dragged me to the kitchen and...he...He'd hit me before, but this time...there was no one to stop him."

Silence filled the room for a long time.

"He came back at dawn," she finally whispered. "I was bleeding and broken. Mama had died in my arms. I didn't know what to do."

"What happened when he returned?"

"He waved the six-pack around, then kicked Mama and yelled at her because she wouldn't get up and share it with him. He was so drunk he didn't know she was dead. I'd been hiding, but when he kicked her, I lost it. I started screaming that he'd killed her. I pummeled him with my fists. He backhanded me, called me a liar, and then forced me down to the blood-spattered floor. He'd nearly choked me to death when my right hand hit something hard and round. I latched onto it. That time, I swung the bat.

"I wanted him dead." She sagged into the chair, drained. "I killed him."

She couldn't look at Luke. Couldn't risk it. Then he was there. He pulled her to him and wrapped his arms around her, stroking her back, murmuring into her ear.

She couldn't process his words, all she could do was let his warmth seep into her frozen soul. She sighed against him, and he lifted her into his arms and took her to the bed. Carefully, as if she were fragile as glass, he laid her down and settled in beside her, nestled in the safety of his embrace. His heat and comfort lulled her into oblivion, sleep overtaking her, pushing aside reality.

She knew she must be dreaming when she heard him whisper, "Ah, love, I'll protect you. I'll never let you go."

People in her life didn't protect her. And they never, ever stayed.

The computer screen taunted Luke. He'd left Jasmine to much-needed sleep, determined to fight this attack on her past. After hours at the keyboard, his back muscles had cramped up, and he'd gotten nowhere. The phone on the desk vibrated, and he looked at the screen. Blocked. Not again.

He stepped into the bathroom, trying not to think about the pain he'd witnessed from Jasmine. He'd never forget. The image of her fear had engraved itself on his mind.

"Montgomery," he said. If he heard that mechanical voice...

"It's Grace."

"Are you okay? Your phone—"

"I had to ditch it. I don't have much time. It's chaos here. Someone screwed up."

"Brian Tower?"

"He wasn't supposed to die. The female sniper is. They have to pin the corruption on her. Dead, she can't defend herself. They don't know who killed Tower. I've never seen them so furious."

"Grace, get out of there."

"I found another way. I won't contact you again, Luke, but I had to warn you before I leave. Your friend is in real danger. The family's got a back-up plan. The last of their plants in the sheriff's office is taking the lead. I don't know who, but he thinks he can salvage the operation. If they kill your sniper, they'll wrap the entire mess up in a nice neat bow. Blame her for Tower's death, and the sheriff's office will reveal she was taking bribes. Problem solved. No more leak."

"Is Sheriff Tower involved?"

"According to my source, his son played him. They'd planned to make him the fall guy before the sniper fell into their laps. No other name, no story—except a sniper gone bad."

Luke shoved his hand through his hair. She was right. Without any other evidence, Jasmine was in the crosshairs, and he'd hit a dead end, unless... "Did you hear any mention of Tower's accomplice? A woman? She threatened my daughter. She might have information."

"No. I'm sorry. I have to go, Luke. Be safe."

"Grace, give me your numb—"

The phone went silent.

Luke's frustration settled into an ache just above his right eyebrow. He was no closer to identifying the woman, and Jasmine was still being set up to take the fall. He wouldn't rest until he found the traitor in the sheriff's office. To hell with the story. For Jasmine. He needed to come up with a new strategy.

He cracked the bathroom door, and his attention fell on her. During a fitful sleep, the covers had twisted around her. She'd cried out more often than Luke could stand.

Suddenly she sat bolt upright in bed, her eyes wide with panic. Her gaze swept the room and settled on Luke. The fear drained out of her. He hated to be the one to tell her things had just gotten a whole lot worse. He laid his phone on the nightstand and crouched next to the bed.

"You okay?"

She nodded, but they both knew she lied.

She pushed her hair out of her face. "Did you find anything?"

He caught her up to speed.

"So I'm an easy target and we have an unknown stalker out there we can't identify."

"I checked out Gary Matthews. His wife, Kathy, and their daughter moved away after he died. I haven't found them yet. They aren't in New Mexico, but I've got a search running. Hopefully something will pop."

Jasmine sagged against the headboard. "We're nowhere."

"I checked out the Pinto, but there's nothing so far on that either," he went on, "other than to determine that the section that wasn't covered with mud seems to match Colorado's plates best."

He went to the computer and moved the mouse so it reactivated. The logo for the Colorado Department of Motor Vehicles flashed on the screen. "According to the DMV, there are thousands of red Pintos in this state. I ran Tower, but nothing hit. I'll need to look at the owners name by name and see if I recognize anyone."

"You hacked into the DMV?" she said, looking over his shoulder.

"Searched for police records involving Tower and a red Pinto too." He brought up another screen.

"So do I arrest you now or..." She blanched. "Guess I can't do that, huh? I'm not really a deputy anymore." She laughed, a bitter, anguished sound. "Lucky for you, Montgomery. You get away scot-free."

"There are too many lives at stake to follow the rules."

The tension between them grew, and Luke held his breath. Would she want him to keep searching or follow the letter of the law?

"Since you're already in," she whispered, "what did you find?"

Turning back to the computer, Luke clicked a few buttons, and a composite drawing materialized on the screen. It was the redheaded woman. The SWAT team had filled in more details, and the sketch artist had captured a chilling likeness that stirred Jazz's recollections.

"I can't place her." Jazz's voice trailed off. A shiver rippled through her. "But there's something about her eyes..."

Silence filtered through the room, broken only by the soft whirr of the computer. Seconds, then minutes ticked by.

"Why can't I remember?"

The words held such despair that he turned in his seat and stood up. "You will."

He longed to touch her, to hold her, to comfort her. Would she let him? Tentatively he reached out and laced her fingertips through his. With a feather-light hold, he eased his hands up her arms to her shoulders and pulled her into his embrace.

Her head fell against his chest, and a shudder ran through her as she nestled against him. Luke let his temple rest against her hair. "We'll figure it out, Jasmine. I promise you that."

Each movement slow with caution, Luke lowered his lips to her cheek and kissed her. When she tilted her head to meet his mouth, Luke's entire body sang with relief, and he let himself sink into the kiss. Her tongue danced with his, and after a moment his body responded to the sensual call of hers. He groaned and lifted his head, holding back his desire.

She couldn't want him now. Not after what she'd been through today.

He stepped back, his breathing ragged. "No more, honey. You're too..."

Pain flashed across her face. "It's because of what I told you, isn't it?"

For a moment he couldn't understand what she was saying, but then he grabbed her to him. "God, no. Never think that anything that happened to you changes the way I feel. But your flashback, everything that's happened. I can understand if you just want to rest. We don't have to make love. I'll hold you, nothing more."

She shook her head, holding his face in her hands. "Don't treat me like I'm damaged goods. Nothing's changed except that now you know everything. I want you. With no more secrets."

She kissed him. Her lips explored his jaw and worked their way down his throat, giving to him in such a way he was in awe of her. After everything, she wanted him to love her.

"I want you," she whispered. "Now. Don't make me wait."

He couldn't deny her. "Then take me, Jasmine. But this time, you have power." He wanted to give her the control, to make sure their lovemaking was nothing like the past.

"Your touch doesn't call the demons back, Luke. Your touch drives them away. Make love to me." She placed her hands on the sides of his face. A laugh of exultation escaped him, and his dark gaze lit with a joy she'd never seen.

Luke fell onto the rumpled bed, drawing Jasmine into his arms. She tumbled on top of him, her touch and mouth reminding him of just why he would never get her out of his system. He lay there and let her revel in his body. She explored every inch, letting her lips explore his neck, the pulse at his throat. The softness of her mouth made him tremble. Her hair tickled his bare skin as she moved across his chest.

She didn't shy away from the scar on his shoulder, instead bathing him with her mouth and tongue until he was shuddering. She drove him crazy with each caress.

He reached for her and she smiled, a mischievous grin that made his heart thud in anticipation.

"Let me," she said.

He forced himself to lie still beneath her. As if she were indulging in the most decadent delicacy, she worked her way down his body, to his abdomen, to his hips, and finally her mouth nestled against his rock-hard desire. He arched toward her touch. "You're a witch," he gasped as her lips teased him unmercifully.

Then she moved away, her hair fluttering across his hypersensitive skin. He let out a sharp moan, but she gave him a flirty grin and worked her way to his thighs, massaging the muscles.

He'd never have believed his knees were erogenous zones, but every caresses, every soft breath made his body surge, seeking her touch.

"I can't wait," he panted.

Finally she rose above him, her hair falling in a curtain around her face and settled just above his aching body, tempting, promising, seducing.

He wanted her. She had to take him.

"Jasmine, please."

Her eyes closed in satisfaction when she lowered herself on him, her body surrounding him, clutching him.

They were one.

He groaned and pulled her down, burying his face in her shoulder. He let the passion overtake him and lost himself. His body surged into hers, taking him to heights he'd never been.

He couldn't stop the rush of emotions gathering as each thrust drew a heated groan from her, all giving, all accepting. Nothing between them any longer. She belonged to him.

"Jasmine. Mine." With a last, intense thrust, he buried himself deep inside of her.

"Yours," she gasped. "Yours always." She shuddered against him and collapsed on top of him draped in exhaustion.

The small final pulses of her body squeezed his heart. She didn't move away, just stilled, with him inside her, her head on his chest and her hair streaming down his body and tickling his hips, content. Slowly she shifted, resting her leg between his thighs, and kissed the sensitive skin near his nipple.

He groaned. "You're going to kill me if you keep doing that."

"Well, if you want me to stop—" She eased away from him, and he dragged her back into his arms.

"Don't you dare."

Luke swooped in for a kiss just as his cell rang. He cursed, grabbing the phone off the nightstand and flipping it open. "Montgomery."

Steve Paretti's voice came over the line. "Gabe's awake. I think you'd better get here fast."

~

The hospital smelled of the same antiseptic. The barren walls were just as devoid of joy since the last time Jazz had visited Gabe, but at least now he was out of intensive care. That fact didn't make her stomach less queasy, though.

As she and Luke strode on the linoleum tile toward his room, looking worse for wear in their rumpled clothes, dread bubbled up within her. Would he be okay? Had his leg shown more improvement? Did he blame her?

Luke put his hand on her back in a show of support. "Gabe's going to be fine, but we're not saying anything to my brother about the trouble. Agreed?"

She nodded, but one look at Gabe's face told them that he already knew a lot. Flanked by Seth and Caleb, Gabe appeared weak. Except for his eyes—they burned in anger. Guilt flared in Jazz's gut.

"It's amazing what one hears when people assume they're unconscious." The corners of Gabe's mouth creased with irritation. "It's also amazing what those same people won't confirm, and it really ticks me off. If one of you guys doesn't start talking soon, I'm getting out of this bed and will find the answers myself."

Despite his threats, they all knew he wasn't going anywhere. His leg had been rigged with some contraption, immobilized and elevated. Then again, with Gabe you never knew. He was stubborn enough to find a way.

Gabe's pointed stare nailed Steve. "You've known our family long enough to recognize my brothers are a bunch of wimps. Spill it, Paretti. Now."

Paretti shot an apologetic glance at Jazz. "Okay. In a nutshell, you got knifed. Everyone at the sheriff's office knows about Luke's investigation and they are pissed. Joy got threatened. Brian Tower was murdered. Luke and Jazz got hauled off as suspects after Jazz's apartment building burned down. And a few minutes ago, Wexler got a call that the arson investigator found bloody Arvada Police Academy sweats in Jazz's size and a mostly wiped-clean crowbar near the smoldering rubble."

"Why am I not surprised?" Luke muttered.

All eyes shifted to Jazz.

Another nail in her coffin. "I didn't kill him."

"No one here thinks you did," Steve said. "Though few would've blamed you for offing Tower. If you'd done it, you're too smart a cop not to cover your tracks better than that. Unfortunately the media and the top brass, including Tower's father, are out for the easy arrest. There's no warrant yet, but it won't be long."

"This is ridiculous," Luke snapped. "She's innocent."

"Are you going to arrest me, Steve?"

"No, I'm getting as much information as I can about this case and will see what I can do to help you. You're being railroaded, and I don't like it."

Everyone around the room nodded in agreement. Stunned, she realized that none of them looked at her with accusation. Their faith humbled her. "Thank you. All of you. But once the warrant's issued, I'll have to turn myself in."

"Then there's no time to waste. Start talking," Gabe bit out.

Luke filled them in on what they knew. "We know they want Jasmine to take the fall for the corruption investigation. But this crazy focus on her past doesn't fit. The vandalism, the phone calls threatening me, using

Jasmine's birth name. Those actions are personal. The shot that deliberately missed us. That was unemotional and professional."

"Two motives," Seth said, nodding. "Two perpetrators."

"There's no other way to explain the inconsistencies. Someone with a grudge against Jazz somehow hooked up with Tower. Of course, he didn't count on ending up dead. Which sucks for us, because he was the linchpin."

"Then who killed him?" Gabe asked.

"My informant claims the mob didn't waste him. Wexler showed me photos of the body. He was beaten to a pulp with the same viciousness as the truck and apartment," Luke said.

"Personal," Jazz muttered.

"Which brings us back to our mystery woman and the guy in the Pinto," Luke said. "We couldn't tie the car to Tower, and there's not much time for me to break into the DMV again..."

Steve raised a brow, and Luke's voice trailed off. He cleared his throat. "But maybe there's some sort of connection to one of Jazz's old cases or to the IA investigation."

"I suppose..." Steve shoved his hand through his hair. "I could run the Pinto against the IA files, see if something hits."

Jazz saw doubt in Steve's gaze. This had to be hard. He couldn't go to his family to verify their information either. If he did, he was dead. But they *were* asking him to risk everything he'd given up his family for.

"It's not fair for you to take this kind of chance with your career," Jazz said. "If they find out, you could end up getting tarnished with the same brush as me."

"Hell, what's life without living on the dangerous side. Besides, it's worth a shot. If it pans out, I get a promotion. But unless I hit triple sevens, it won't stop the brass from coming after you, Jazz. Unless they can't find you," he said innocently.

Silence battered the room.

"You think she should run?" Luke asked.

"I'm just saying I wouldn't be opposed to having a little more time to do the search."

Luke walked over to Jazz and grabbed her hand. "It's a good idea. You're in danger. If there's a plant in the sheriff's office, we should avoid them. It's not like you have an address anymore. They can't expect to locate you immediately."

Jazz recoiled from the idea. "I'll look even more guilty. Wexler told me not to leave town."

"Luke and Steve are right," Seth said. "The cops can't arrest you if they can't find you. We need the time, and you'll stay safe."

"I don't know."

Caleb, who'd been silently watching, spoke, his voice raspy as he tugged at his scraggly beard. "What if the Pinto belongs to the woman who went after Joy?"

"Then we're in trouble. We don't know who she is," Jazz said. "Luke pulled up her composite sketch, but I didn't recognize her. It's possible I knew her when I was a kid, but I lived in a lot of places, and people change as they age."

Luke paced the room in frustration. "If only we knew the woman's name." He turned to Gabe. "Could she have touched something while she was in the SWAT den, something that would have her fingerprints? I heard she climbed all over you."

"She touched me in a few anatomical places I won't mention in mixed company, but nothing that would help."

Jazz rubbed her face with her hands. "It's a dead end. We have a face with no identity."

"We're going to get you out of here while Steve heads to the station to run those names." Luke gripped her shoulders. "I'm still looking into what happened to a family from Jazz's past. If we all hit another blind alley, we'll regroup and try something else. We won't stop until we find out who's doing this." He looked around the room. "Right?"

"Oh, yeah," Gabe said. "Don't you worry, Jazz. Once the Montgomerys sink their teeth into a problem we never give up."

"Ever," added Seth and Caleb simultaneously.

Steve turned to Luke. "Where can you go? They'll be looking for you soon. You can't head to your place. They'll probably try there first. You need somewhere out of the way."

"Easy." Luke said. "The cabin. Nick took Joy and Mom there. It's isolated, and nobody but friends and family know about it."

Steve nodded. "Good idea. Then I'm out of here while you guys plan your attack." He paused in front of Jazz and cuffed her arm. "You hang in there. We'll take care of whoever is doing this to you."

"I hope so." Jazz shoved her hand in her pocket. Empty.

Luke gave her a small smile and pulled out a roll of butter rum Life Savers. He knew. He understood. She took the candy from his hand. Oh, how she wished she could let herself love him like he deserved. Who else on earth had ever been there for her like Luke Montgomery?

No one. She had to make sure his family was safe. This might be her last chance.

The woman toyed with the front of her stooge's camouflage jacket as they crouched in a thicket outside the Montgomery cabin. She loved the way her red-tipped fingernails looked like claws waiting to strike. "You did as I instructed? Luke and Jane are coming here now?"

His eyes narrowed. "I'm not an amateur. Luke's family is drugged and bound. They have been for a while. Now give me those pictures."

Her teeth grated. This was *her* plan. *She* was in control. Not him. "All but the girl will die? Right? I need her alive."

"I know the dosage. They won't survive much longer. The girl will live."

"Good." Luke Montgomery had to pay. With his brother and mother dead, he'd finally understand how much ignoring the rules cost. "How long before Luke and Jane get here?"

Irritated, he glanced at the GPS monitor. "About thirty minutes."

Relief washed through her. The pilot was on stand-by. Well paid to ask no questions. She still had time to finish the setup. "The flat tire was a good move. Gives us plenty of leeway. What about the explosives?"

Paretti pulled out a bag, no larger than a baked potato.

"That's it?"

"PETN packs a punch. With this amount, you could blow up an entire house."

She smiled. "Excellent. Now let's check out our bait."

With quick and sure steps through the pine needles and past a cluster of aspens she headed toward the cabin, pulling on a pair of surgical gloves as she went. No sense leaving fingerprints. After opening the unlocked door, she scanned the room.

The man and the grandmother lay on the floor, still. The little girl rested, cuddled on the sofa, hugging some stupid stuffed fish. A pink blanket covered most of her.

Placing two gloved fingers against the kid's throat, the woman smiled at the thready pulse. The Liquid K had done its job well. The kid would be out for at least another few hours. "Perfect. We're ready." She turned to him. "Throw the kid in the backseat of my car."

He frowned at her. "What are you talking about? Jazz and Luke haven't arrived. You said we'd take care of them here."

She slid a .44 Magnum from her bag and pointed it at him. "I lied."

Chapter Thirteen

Luke couldn't reach the cabin fast enough. He needed to get Jasmine to safety, and at least there they'd be defensible. He skidded around another bend. In a half hour they'd be safe.

She stirred in the passenger seat and opened her eyes, unfocused with sleep. "How long have I been out?"

"Not long. Check the cell phone for service. We're close to where we should be getting something. Remind me to buy a satellite phone after this."

She tilted the phone so she could see it. "Looks like a signal, but it's weak." A tone sounded. "You've got voice and text messages waiting."

"Hopefully it's good news."

They rounded another bend, and Luke pulled over to maintain the signal. He took the phone and scanned the incoming calls list. "Five from my editor—probably wanting that article. Three from Seth. He must've found something."

"Or there's a warrant for my arrest."

The thought had crossed Luke's mind, but he hadn't wanted to say it aloud. He hit the speed dial for Seth, and when his brother answered, Luke pressed the speakerphone. Static crackled across the lines. "It's Luke and Jasmine."

"About time." Crackling cut off his next words.

"Seth, this is a really bad connection. I can barely hear you."

"I said things are happening fast here. I called in a favor, hoping to get facial recognition info on the woman, and I put the Pinto in the request at the same time. I think I found the owner. It's not good."

"What's wrong?"

"A familiar name owns a registered '74 Pinto with Colorado plates. Jeff Gasmerati."

A cold shiver tingled at the base of Luke's neck. "Jeff Gasmerati? Steve Paretti's cousin? The one Steve disowned because Gasmerati stayed in the family business?"

"The one he *said* he'd disowned," Seth said. "That's not all. Steve lied to us. There was a warrant issued for Jazz's arrest just before he came to the hospital. Sergeant Carder told me Paretti knew. My guess is the family got to Steve—if he ever bailed on them at all. Just like they got to Derek's father."

"It can't be," Jasmine said, her voice a bare whisper tinged with hurt. "He was helping us. I trusted him."

"Son of a bitch," Luke muttered. "He knows we're headed to the cabin. He knows everything we're doing. You got a location?"

"No clue," Seth said.

Static cut through as the call dropped.

Luke banged his fist against the steering wheel. "I hate the mountains sometimes." He turned toward Jazz.

"I grew up with Steve. I can't believe he'd do this. He knows Joy's at that cabin."

"He wouldn't hurt her," Jazz said. "She'll be okay."

He tossed Jasmine the phone. "Call Nick and warn him and my mother."

A chime from Luke's cell signaled a text message. "Maybe Seth has more information."

Jasmine hit a few buttons. "It's a text message from Nick."

She went silent.

His stomach lurched.

She shifted the phone so he could see the screen. One word, *HURRY*, screamed at him from the tiny window.

"Damn it." Luke thrust the car into gear. Too much time later, he whipped the SUV around the curves leading to the cabin. Tall ponderosa pines served as the only rail, and more than a few times he nearly overshot the turn.

"Come on, baby, come on." Jazz hunched over the cell phone. "We have a signal back!"

"Get Nick. He's speed dial four."

She pushed the button, then send, and swore. "It's ringing, but he's not picking up."

"Call him again! No, call the police."

"The signal's gone again." Panic tinged her voice.

"Damn!"

Hurry. Hurry. Hurry. The word pounded through Luke's head, even as terror raked his soul. Joy. His baby.

The car skidded, tires shrieking as the vehicle slid sideways. At the last second, the wheels caught, and the SUV catapulted forward again. Luke took the turnoff to the cabin on two wheels then yanked hard to the right to pull into the drive. Gravel flew from beneath the tires like shrapnel, and he jammed on the brakes when he reached the cabin. No one exited the door to greet them, and his throat turned dry.

Jasmine flicked the safety off the gun Seth had given her as they left the hospital.

Luke opened his door and crouched behind it, his HK in his hand. "We don't know what we're facing yet. If there are no shots fired, we'll move in. Paretti's a professional. He knows what he's doing."

She nodded then mimicked his actions.

"Let's go," Luke hissed.

They belly-crawled toward the cabin. Moments later, Jazz made her way to the window and peered in.

"Steve!" Her anguished cry echoed through the clearing.

Luke took off at a run and slammed through the front door, then skidded to a halt as he saw the pool of blood. His lifelong friend lay on the floor in front of him, still as death.

"Oh, Steve," Jazz said. "If you'd only trusted us. We could've helped."

"Joy!" Luke tore into the living room, his heart pounding out of his chest.

"No!"

Anna and Nick Montgomery lay sprawled on the floor beside the sofa, their arms and feet bound with duct tape. His mother's skin was ghastly pale. Luke fell to his knees in front of them. "Please, no," he whispered. Trembling, he touched fingertips against his mother's carotid artery to check for a pulse. "She's alive," he called to Jasmine.

He quickly tore at his mother's bindings and freed her. He patted her face. "Mom, where's Joy?"

His mother's eyes didn't flutter.

Luke knelt beside Nick and unraveled the duct tape. "He's out too. His eyes are dilated. They've been drugged."

"What about Joy?" Jasmine asked.

A fear greater than any he'd ever known swept through him. He ran for the bedrooms, slamming doors open and tossing furniture out of his way. A tiny voice inside said he was destroying a crime scene, but he didn't care. "Joy? Joy!"

The bedrooms were empty. The bathroom. He tore closet doors open, praying she'd been hidden away from the terror of what had happened. Nothing.

"She's not here." Everything inside him shook. "Sweet Jesus, where is she?"

"Luke! Steve's alive."

He raced back to the kitchen. Jasmine knelt beside Steve. "Can you hear me?"

A weak moan escaped from Steve's mouth. He opened his eyes. "Sorry," he said. "Plan didn't work."

Luke crouched down and gripped Steve's shoulders while Jasmine dialed 911. "Where's Joy?"

Steve sucked in a pained breath. "Crazy bitch took her."

"Tell me where Joy is," Luke said. "She's only a baby."

Steve grabbed for Luke's shirt, but his hand slid away. "Crazy woman...wanted me to kill...family. Fooled her. Changed dose. Tried to keep this from happening. She screwed up everything. Gotta believe me. Missed shot on purpose. Tried to protect you, Jazz. Keep you alive."

"You're the plant? You're working for your family? Why take Joy?"

"Woman's not part of plan. Jazz's past." Steve sagged with a weak, sputtering cough. "Need help, Luke. Saved your family. Save Grace. Always loved…"

He passed out, and Luke grabbed his wrist. Still alive, but faint. "Damn it. Where's Joy?"

"Luke!" Jasmine pointed at the kitchen table.

Four pictures were propped up on the table, as if playing pieces for the board game underneath. He moved closer, afraid to see who was in the photos. His throat closed off.

Gabe in ICU, Anna unconscious, Nick sprawled beside her, and Joy, curled up on the couch. The now empty couch.

Under each picture had been scrawled a word.

Eenie. Meenie. Miney. Moe!

Moe! slashed across Joy's picture.

Luke's head snapped up. "What's she trying to say?"

"It's a message. To me." Jasmine's voice shook. "The game is called Truth or Consequences. It was popular when I was a child. Everyone in town had one."

Jasmine couldn't take her eyes off the game. "They were so proud of the connection to that old TV show since the town changed its name from Hot Springs in about 1950."

She lifted her gaze to Luke. "My mother died there. Gary Matthews died there. I stopped being Jane Sanford there. It all fits. I have to go home. Joy is in Truth or Consequences, New Mexico."

"What's this?" He picked up the note printed on one of the cards lying in the center of the board.

I'm waiting, Jane. No cops or she dies.

Jazz's body thrummed with frustrated energy as she and Luke watched from the cover of trees. She hated lurking from afar. She'd done enough of that to last her a lifetime. But she had no choice.

Jazz pushed aside a pine branch. Two sheriff's cars screeched to a halt in front of the cabin. Help had finally arrived for Nick and Anna. The controlled rage humming through Luke should have terrified her, except she could just as easily murder the woman who had taken Joy. She'd never been more terrified in her life—not for herself, but for that little girl. She might not be mother material, but she knew she'd sacrifice her life for Luke's child. She might have to.

"Do you think Steve will make it?" she asked.

"He didn't look good," Luke said. "He's lost a lot of blood."

"I can't believe he betrayed us both. How could we not have seen it?"

"I knew his family ties, and he still fooled me." Luke shoved his HK into its holster. "Grace didn't know. She would've told me."

"Do you think he and Tower were working together?"

"We may never know. If Paretti dies, the investigation dies. Hopefully I can convince Grace to go into witness protection. But for now, the trail to Joy leads south. That's the mission." His face had turned to stone, his eyes focused, readying himself for battle.

"To the redheaded woman in Truth or Consequences. To my past. She has a lot to answer for."

"Seth's on the Matthews search. Hopefully he'll find something so we can gain an advantage." Luke watched as an ambulance pulled up. "I don't want to leave Mom and Nick, but Caleb will be here soon, and Joy needs me more. We don't have time to answer questions, and we can't afford for you to be arrested. We've got to get to T or C." Luke took one last glance back, and the pine tree branch snapped into place. "I should have sent them farther away."

"It's not your fault. I'm the one to blame. Me and my past. I just refused to recognize it." This was the true reason they could never be together. She hurt everyone she cared about.

But that didn't matter now. Nothing mattered except getting Joy back safely to her father.

They trekked through the brush to their car, and Luke pounded his fist against the side of the SUV. "Steve was the man following you in the Pinto, not Tower. I should have clued in that day outside the sheriff's office when he pocketed the cigarette butt. I knew he had a closet smoking habit. I let my own expectations rule me. I was looking for the facts, not the truth."

Luke wrenched open the door of his SUV. "Come on, we've got to find a way to get to T or C fast, and driving is not the answer."

Jazz hopped in the vehicle and buckled up. "What are you thinking?"

"Regular airline won't get us to T or C, but we can still fly. There's a small airstrip not too far where Zach parks his plane when he visits here. Dad used to hang out and shoot the breeze with some of his retired army buddies. One of the pilots must have a plane we can charter."

Luke's SUV raced down the road through Kremmling toward McElroy Airfield. His hands gripped the steering wheel, and he held onto his control by a thread. Jazz checked Seth's weapon and pocketed the Beretta. They would be ready when they landed.

Minutes later, the SUV skidded to a halt in the dirt parking lot. They jumped out of the car and hurried toward the entrance to the small airport.

Luke yanked open the squeaky door. The counter in front of them stood deserted, but to the left four grizzled figures sat drinking coffee and studying a chessboard on the table between the sofas.

A man with a face that looked like it'd been carved by a bottle of Jim Beam limped toward them. "Can I help you folks?"

"My name is Luke Montgomery." He nodded toward Jazz and raised his voice so everyone in the place could hear it. "We need to get to Truth or Consequences, New Mexico, and we need to get there fast. It's an emergency. My three-year-old daughter has been kidnapped."

The men gasped, and one pointed toward his chess challenger. "Ace here has a Piper Lance."

A man in his late fifties with a Special Forces tattoo on one arm quickly rose. "It's the fastest bird here."

Not even looking at the board, Ace took a knight with his bishop. "Checkmate." He turned to Luke. "You say your girl's in trouble?"

"Yes."

Ace strode to the chart on the wall showing U.S. air space. He whipped a string weighted with a fishing line from the side of the board and pinned it at a large dot on Kremmling, Colorado, to south-central New Mexico. "About four hundred nautical miles." He turned to Luke. "Three hours give or take."

"Will you fly us? Now?"

The man nodded. "Give me a second to check the weather, and we'll go. Anything for Patrick Montgomery's son. He saved my life more than once when we were in the First Recon Marine Battalion."

Luke stared at the man. "Dad wasn't in the marines."

Ace ignored Luke, pointedly going about his business. Jazz's cop instincts kicked in. There was a story there.

After a few hurried clicks of the keyboard and mouse, the pilot raised his head. "Weather's 'severe clear' so we're in good shape. Flight time will be three hours, nine minutes. Let's go, Montgomery. You and your lady will be my first passengers in a while."

A few minutes later the plane roared to a start and sped down the runway.

"Kremmling Traffic. Lance 810 Hotel Lima. Taking the active runway 27 departing to the south."

The plane rose into the air, climbing straight up and over the mountains. They were off.

"Hang on, Joy," Jazz whispered into the clouds. "Your daddy's coming."

The past and the present were about to collide.

Three hours had never taken so long. By the time they reached the Truth or Consequences Municipal Airport, Luke was in full battle mode and ready to climb through the windshield of the plane. He pushed aside his worry and focused on his only task. To protect his daughter.

Ace had arranged for them to borrow the airport's loaner car so they hadn't wasted any time finding transportation. The Caravan's shocks were shot, but it drove, and Luke didn't give a damn about comfort at the moment.

The pilot saw them off, the concern in his expression a feeling Luke refused to acknowledge. Worry led to doubt, doubt led to mistakes, and they couldn't afford to make a single one. Not with Joy's life at stake.

A pothole catapulted Jasmine out of the seat and she gripped the armrest.

"You okay?" he asked, forcing the gruffness from his voice.

"We need backup," she said quietly. "We're going into this without knowing anything—we don't know who or why Joy's been kidnapped. We don't know if this woman's working alone. She's used accomplices before. We probably beat her if she's driving. If she flew, she could already be here."

"We can't call the police. The woman made it clear she'd kill Joy."

He could tell Jasmine was about to argue, but before she could open her mouth, his cell phone rang. His body tensed. He pressed the speakerphone. "Montgomery."

"I've been trying to reach you for an hour," Seth snapped.

"Good news?" Luke said.

"Mom and Nick are okay after a scare. Much more of the drug and Mom wouldn't have made it. I want a piece of this bitch, Luke." A short burst of static crackled then cleared. "Paretti didn't make it."

"Damn. We could've helped him."

"He didn't want it," Seth said. "Is Jazz there?"

She leaned toward the phone. "I can hear you."

"Gary Matthews." Some papers crinkled over the phone. "After he died—and by the way, he deserved everything he got—his wife and daughter went to Houston. The wife killed herself a few years later. The daughter, Lisa Matthews, vanished soon after, but not before she got herself into a lot of trouble. Including arson."

"Like your apartment," Luke said. "Does her name sound familiar?"

Jasmine bit her lip, her fingers clenching white. He could see she was trying. Well, she *had* to remember. For Joy.

"Lisa Matthews. She was a year younger than me," Jasmine whispered. "Popular, everything I wasn't. Maybe. Maybe."

Luke raised his voice. "Thanks, Seth. Lisa Matthews may be the hit. Find a driver's license picture to match with the police sketch."

"I'm on it, and I'm on my way to T or C."

"I can't wait for you." Resolve timbered Luke's voice.

"Understood."

With a hard punch, Luke turned off the speaker phone. He slammed on the gas, propelling them through the New Mexico desert and away from the airport, toward the town where his daughter waited. "Lisa Matthews. What do you remember?"

"I don't even recall what she looked like, except everyone liked her." Jasmine leaned forward, her body taut with tension. "It's all a blur. The last time I saw Lisa was that morning. I think." She closed her eyes. "Gary Matthews was dead; I was covered in blood. That's what made the front page. Me, splattered in blood, being carried out in the sheriff's arms. She was there, watching in the front yard. She had dark hair, I think, not red. That's all I know. Why can't I remember?"

The hilly landscape leading from the airport flattened out as Truth or Consequences came into view, its edge wrapping against a large lake.

"Oh God, we're here," Jasmine murmured.

The small New Mexico town looked dingier than she remembered. Elephant Butte Lake had been a victim of the drought, its low water level obviously rough on tourism. Like so many other rural towns, a string of failed businesses greeted them as they entered the city limits.

Luke glanced at her. "Which way?"

She fought down the rising suffocation. "Keep following Main and cross the tracks."

They turned down several streets where quaint, well-kept houses lined the pristine sidewalks, the lawns green, the fences white. "I always wanted to live in one of these," she said, her voice wistful. "*Families* lived in these houses. Mothers and fathers who loved their kids. Who sat down to dinner together and put up Christmas trees—"

"Jasmine."

"It doesn't matter. It's in the past."

He came to a dead end street. "Right or left?"

"Right. Then a few more turns. Straight into my hell."

Luke's tension ratcheted higher. When they reached a stretch of rundown and condemned houses, she asked him to pull over.

Luke stared around him. "My God, she's got my baby in this dump."

"We're two blocks away. It's worse where we're going."

"I'll kill her." He turned his cold gaze toward Jazz. "No one should live like this."

Jazz fought the fear and shame his words wrought. A swirl of dark memories threatened to pull her into a vortex. Nausea rose in her throat as she remembered the closet, her mother's bedroom, the pain she'd endured at the hands of Gary Matthews.

Jazz shuddered. Not anymore. That was the past. "We'll get Joy back, Luke. I swear—"

Luke's cell phone rang. The number was blocked. It wasn't Seth. Luke activated the speaker phone. "Montgomery."

"Your car's been in Kremmling for hours," rasped a mechanically altered voice. "Which means you flew."

Jazz saw the realization flash through Luke's eyes. Somehow the woman had tracked the vehicles in Colorado. She knew they were here. "I want my daughter. Let her go."

"Order me again, Montgomery, and your daughter goes home in a body bag." The sound of fury reverberated through the car. "I like killing. I like it a lot. Got it?"

Luke's jaw spasmed. "Yes."

"Good. Jane? You and I have unfinished business. Have you guessed who I am?"

Jazz closed her eyes at the tinny, mechanical voice. She wasn't one hundred percent sure, but it had to be...

"Answer me, bitch. Do you know who I am?"

Jazz stared at Luke and he nodded. They had to take a chance. For Joy.

With a silent prayer, Jazz whispered, "Lisa Matthews, Gary's daughter."

A bark of laughter sounded through the phone. "You were so busy hiding who you were, you didn't see what was right in front of you. Did you think you were so brilliant no one would ever find you? What a joke. I had to lead you by the nose."

"You've proved you're smarter than we are. Where's Joy?" Jazz demanded.

"Your lover's daughter. Cute little thing. I could make a pretty penny selling her. We're not that far from the border."

Jazz's insides went cold, but she forced her mind back to her training. She needed to know Joy was alive. "Can I speak with her?"

"Say please."

Jazz bit back vile curse. "Please."

"Pretty please?"

She swallowed down the nausea. "Pretty please."

"I can't wait to see you grovel in person, Jane. You do it so well over the phone." A moment passed, followed by the sound of a door being unlocked. "Wake up, brat. Someone wants to talk to you."

"Munchkin? Are you okay?" Luke's knuckles whitened on the phone. He obviously used every ounce of discipline to keep control.

A sharp static hit the phone and a normal-sounding whimper and a sniffle came over the phone. "Daddy? Can

I come home? Hero and me are scared, and Hero has a boo-boo."

Blood pounded through Jazz, stealing her breath, her vision. Images of being locked up, frightened, slammed into her like physical blows. She was tough. Joy was...Joy was...innocent. A raging fury swept through Jazz that Lisa had done this to Joy and to Luke.

"I'll get you real soon, honey."

"Hurry, Daddy. The witch got me."

"You're done. Get in there." A door slammed and Joy's muffled screams for her father could be heard over the sound of it being relocked.

"Joy!"

The fury in Luke's voice and the fear he didn't try to hide tore Jazz's heart out. Lisa Matthews was doing all of this because she hated Jazz.

Lisa came back on the line. "Are you ready to deal with me now? Since I can reach you on this phone and you're no longer flying, I know you must be close by."

"We're near," Luke acknowledged.

"Good. Do exactly as I say. You're going to come to me. No cops. No tricks. Or your daughter is dead. Understand?"

Luke gripped the wheel. "I understand."

"Good. Tell Jane to go to the house where her whore of a mother sold herself to the highest bidder. You have fifteen minutes. Park your car on the street opposite the house and get out with your hands in the air. Don't be late."

Luke slammed down the phone. "Damn her to hell. I'd hoped we'd have an element of surprise since we got here so fast."

"She must have learned that Kremmling had an airport and figured out the rest," she said.

"It docsn't matter now."

Jazz picked up his phone. "We can't call the cops, but maybe we can call an ex-cop."

"Clarkson?"

Jazz nodded, unable to believe she was reaching out to the man who'd rescued her from the streets so long ago. The same streets where another little girl's life now hung in the balance. Maybe he could help work another miracle. "Lisa's using my past to attack us. Let's use it to defeat her. Clarkson can't help us now, but he can call the cavalry. Keep the police from shooting us if they see us with a gun."

"Call him, Jasmine. We have to save Joy," he said. "She's my life."

Jazz's heart shattered into a million splintered shards. *I'll save her, Luke. No matter what the cost.*

Chapter Fourteen

Jazz punched the end button on Luke's cell phone, her heart full of conflicting emotions. "Sheriff Clarkson's a good man. I didn't realize how good at the time. He'll call for backup the moment you let him know Joy's safe."

"Good." Luke checked his HK.

She twisted in the seat of the stopped van. "If anything bad happens..."

"Nothing bad will happen. I won't let it. That means we work together. As a team. Stick to the plan."

Her hands shook as she pulled out the Beretta and stuffed it in her jeans behind her back. Where was the calm, cool sniper? What had happened to her? Jazz struggled to pull her usually icy demeanor around her, but the image of Joy in that woman's hands—Jazz fought to regain control. Did love do this?

"How can you be so calm?" Jazz had never faced a situation like this as a cop. She'd never had to worry about someone she loved in trouble.

"Because that's the only way I can save Joy," Luke said, his voice steady and solid.

He reached over and clasped Jazz's shoulders, his gaze intense and focused. "You can do this. You're not the girl who lived here. You're a cop. A sniper. A warrior. I have no doubts."

Jazz nodded, pulling strength from his faith. She took in a deep breath and let her imagination dip her into that lake of tranquility. For Joy. She could do this.

She raised her hand to Luke's cheek and memorized his features, wondering if she'd see him again. In her heart she knew Lisa Matthews would have a plan. She hadn't dragged them here to have a chat. She wanted Jazz dead. The fire, Tower's murder, and Steve Paretti's death spoke volumes about this woman's total disregard for collateral damage.

"Lisa's obsessed with you," Luke said. "So distract her. Say anything. Do whatever it takes to convince her to release Joy. As soon as she's safe, we'll take her."

"Just get Joy away from her, Luke. I'll take care of myself."

"Don't do anything crazy, Jasmine."

A bittersweet smile escaped her. "I'm trained for the crazy." She hesitated as a realization hit home, giving her a strange sense of peace amidst the turmoil. "Being a cop is who I am, even without a badge." She kissed him and closed her eyes, letting herself remember this moment, when she felt truly one with Luke. "I'm ready."

He nodded, his expression grave as he put the car into gear. They drove past the next few houses, each looking shabbier than the last even in the soft light of a crimson New Mexico sunset. On the left, a particularly worn-down shack came into view, some of the windows broken and its rusty roof sliding off. "That's it," Jazz said, pointing.

"Joy's in there?" Luke cursed. "It's ready to collapse."

The car screeched to a halt. Jazz jumped out, and Luke did the same. She placed herself in front of him, hands held high.

He grasped her arm, ready to pull her aside, but she whispered. "Lisa wants me. Let me do this. For Joy."

A torn curtain at the window rustled, and Jazz tensed as if preparing to take a shot. Her fingers itched for her sniper rifle. Being without her team on a mission made her feel vulnerable, jumpy. But she had Luke. He was the best backup she could have.

"We need to draw her out," he said. "Jasmine, call her. Now."

"Lisa?" Jazz's voice rang out, strong and certain. "We're here."

The face from the police sketch, her features cold and hard, stared at them from behind the tattered window covering, but her hair was no longer red. Blond curls framed her face, not softening it, just emphasizing the anger there. Jazz searched long-ago thoughts and images. Why couldn't she remember the girl this woman had been?

Lisa smashed the window and pulled a screaming Joy forward, a gun pressed to her temple. "About time you got here. I'm sick of waiting." She shook Joy. "Shut up or I'll shut you up."

"I won't forget that," Luke whispered, his voice deadly cold. The corded muscles on Luke's neck popped, and Jazz knew he fought every instinct to stick to the plan, but he held firm. They had to wait for the right time.

The door opened. Lisa held Joy, wrapped in a pink blanket, in front of her as a shield, the gun still pressed to the terrified girl's head. Tears streaked her cheeks.

Jazz and Luke advanced slowly toward the house. She could feel the fury radiating off Luke in waves. The moment Joy got a look at her father's face she started straining against the woman's hold.

Jazz's heart stopped, but Luke called out, "Be still, Joy. I'll come get you in a minute. I love you, baby. Just be still for now."

The little girl whimpered and hugged Hero, but quit struggling.

Lisa laughed, her face twisted in disgust. "You don't know what love is, Montgomery. Not if you think you're getting it from that whore. She walked the streets. She sold herself. But maybe you don't care about her any more than the other men who've had her—and there've been plenty around here who have."

The taunt rattled Jazz's resolve to stay calm, but all she had to do was glance at Luke. If he could keep from rushing forward, so could she. Emotions were useless now. Follow the plan. "This is between you and me, Lisa. Let the girl go."

"Why? You barely remember who I am." The woman tightened her hold on Joy, who kept crying out for her father. "You should. Everybody knew me and loved me and you took it all away."

Jazz eased forward a few steps, trying to think of a way to free Joy. "The past doesn't matter. I didn't know, but I do now. Please—"

"The past is *everything!* You should know that," Lisa yelled. "You were jealous of me. You stayed in the corner during recess watching me, watching everyone, and hiding in dirty rags. I was the prettiest girl at school. Everyone wanted to be my friend until you murdered my father. We lost our friends, our home, everything. My mother killed herself. You destroyed my life then. Now I'm going to finish destroying yours."

"Lisa, I'm sorry. Blame me, but please don't take it out on an innocent child."

The woman's face went red. "It's too late for sorry!" she screamed.

"Lisa, dear God," Jazz pleaded. "I'm the one you want. Don't do this. Don't play with Joy's life." The words came from a place of fear deep inside Jazz—fear on behalf of the innocent, fear born out of love. It was a place that held more power than Jazz had ever known. The nightmare would be embedded on her psyche forever.

"This isn't a game." Lisa smiled. "But we could make it a game. What's my favorite color? Get it right, she lives. Get it wrong, I blow a hole through her head."

Lisa turned the gun on Luke, who'd been inching to the side, closer to Joy. "One more step and you both die."

Glancing back at Jazz, Lisa said, "Go on. You always stared at me when I wore my daddy's favorite dress. What was the color? You have five seconds. *Five.*"

"You can remember, Jasmine. I know you can," Luke whispered.

"*Four.*"

She stared into Luke's eyes and the confidence displayed in them. He couldn't reach his daughter in time, and he still believed in her. Fighting panic, Jazz focused, dredging up the pictures in her mind that she'd tried so hard to eradicate. Painful and degrading, she let the flood slash through her, until...

A pretty little girl, a popular girl on the playground. Herself standing in the corner alone. Jane hadn't had friends. She couldn't have invited them over. Her mother might have been with a customer—one of their fathers.

"*Three.*"

Please God, help me. Help me remember what I need to know.

Like the flash from a rifle, a terrifying memory shot through her. That last horrific night. The night Gary Matthews had stolen what was left of her childhood. She'd been in her closet, her mother passed out. Gary had yanked her from her hiding place. Touched her hair. Her face.

"Pretty girl," he'd murmured. "Not black hair like my Lisa, no, you're blond and sweet like honey. If you're good like her and let me do what I want, next time I'll bring you a pink dress with a pretty pink ribbon—"

"*Two.*"

"—just like the one I bought her. Pretty as sunshine in that yellow dress. Now come here, little girl, and give me—"

"Yellow," Jazz gasped, nausea roiling at the flashback and at the realization that Gary had abused Lisa too. "Yellow was your favorite."

Lisa stepped back. "He told you. Didn't he! One of those nights when he left my mama and me."

Jazz cut Lisa off. "You said you'd let Joy go if I answered correctly."

Insanity lit Lisa's eyes. "Fine. At least *I'm* not a liar."

237

Lisa pushed Joy forward and the little girl fell. Luke scooped her up and pulled back level with Jazz. Lisa aimed the gun at Joy's heart, but her gaze stayed focused on Jazz. "I belonged to him. He loved *me*."

"He told me he loved you," Jazz lied quietly. She was acutely conscious of Joy sobbing in Luke's arms. "I want Luke to take his daughter and go now."

Lisa smiled. "I bet you do. First, put your weapon on the ground and kick it to me. Carefully, Jane."

Jazz hesitated. Without the Beretta, Lisa would have the upper hand.

"Don't play with me, Jane. Give me the weapon I know you have on you, or the girl is dead." Lisa's fierce grip on the gun tightened. "I promised to give her back. Nothing more. I won't hesitate to splatter the ground with her blood."

With a soft curse, Jazz set the pistol down and booted it toward Lisa.

Satisfied, Lisa raised the weapon and pointed it at Luke. "Take your brat and go."

He held Joy, still wrapped in her pink blanket and clutching her stuffed fish, Hero, with a desperation Jazz knew would take a long time to go away. If ever.

"Jasmine—"

"Go, Luke. I'll be fine. Protect Joy." Jazz gave them one last look. She didn't know what would happen, but it wouldn't matter if she died as long as they were safe.

"I'll be back," Luke whispered in her ear. "Believe me."

Jazz nodded and turned back to Lisa, who still had the weapon pointed at Luke's back.

Joy's sobs filtered through the air as Luke quietly opened the Caravan. Within seconds the engine revved, but Jazz didn't take her gaze off Lisa, a sudden disquiet filling her. The woman had killed every loose end, and that's what Joy and Luke were. Why had Lisa let them go?

Jazz glanced down the street, the rough sound of the engine growing more and more distant as the taillights faded away. The van turned a corner, and she could breathe again. She paused. All she had to do was keep Lisa occupied a bit longer. Luke would be calling Clarkson any minute, but the eager look in Lisa's eyes scared her. She tried to remain calm and steady. Tried to be SWAT, a sniper, even though they'd stripped her badge. "I thought we could talk now. There are things you wanted me to understand."

Lisa smiled and pulled out a small device from her pocket. "It's a really simple lesson. Do you know what this is?"

Jazz's throat went dry. It looked like a remote of some kind. Dread rushed through her.

"He loves you," Lisa said. "I can see it in his eyes. Like I saw it in my father's eyes. I was his special girl, his princess, and you killed him."

"Lisa, they're innocent." She took a step forward.

"I was too." Still holding the gun in one hand, Lisa raised the detonator.

Jazz tackled her to the pavement. The gun went off. Searing fire burned across Jazz's bicep, but she knocked the gun aside, fighting for the remote that was just out of reach.

"Too bad the kid's so attached to that fish." Panting, Lisa pressed the button.

An explosion rocked the ground.

"Oh, God, no." Jazz twisted and looked to the east. Smoke curled into the crimson and lavender sky, forming a charcoal plume marring the heavens. No one could have survived the explosion. Pain as she'd never known ripped at her heart.

"I win, Jane. You didn't even think to check the stupid fish." Lisa had rolled to the side and was now kneeling, holding the gun on Jazz. "You're not a real cop. You're nothing but a fraud. The daughter of a whore. A whore yourself."

A lifetime of control turned to dust as rage exploded within Jazz. She didn't think, didn't plan, she let the fury consume her. She launched herself at Lisa.

The woman tried to side-step her, but Jazz hooked her arm around Lisa's waist and spun her down. They landed with a thud, and agony pierced through Jazz's injured arm, but nothing could touch the pain in her heart. She slammed her elbow into Lisa's ribs. A choked sob escaped, and the crazy woman spun to her back, but Jazz was waiting for the move.

She twisted around, ripped the gun from Lisa's hands, and knocked it to the ground. Lisa, screaming and cursing, crawled toward the Beretta that lay in the dirt. As her fingers closed around the gun, Jazz kneed her hand and grabbed the weapon. "You're finished."

Madness filled Lisa's eyes. "I'll kill you, Jane. Just like I killed them. You'll never see them again. They're dead. They're burning, Jane, because they loved you. *I* did that to you." She laughed.

Everything inside Jazz clamored for revenge. Hands shaking against the Beretta's grip, she pushed herself away from her enemy and stood.

"Shoot me, Jane. You know you want to. Do it!"

Jazz primed the .357 and eased back even more. "Get up."

With an expression of disbelief, Lisa staggered to her feet and faced Jazz. "What are you? A wimp? I killed them."

Jazz fought back a sob, her grief and anger almost crippling her. Oh, God, how would she ever survive this? She aimed the weapon at Lisa's heart. The near point-blank target was tempting, the easiest shot she'd ever make. Who would care? Luke was gone. Joy was gone. She had nothing left to live for. An empty hole burned where her heart had been.

"Go ahead, Jane. Pull the trigger."

"Don't tempt me."

Lisa glared. "Oh, you still think you're better than me. We're the same, you and I, the same. Our souls were sucked out of us a long time ago. Everyone knows the truth. You're nothing. You've *always* been nothing."

"I made something of myself."

"You lived a lie. You're not real. You're invisible, just like me. A murderer, just like me. Go on, pull the trigger. If you don't, I promise I'll kill the rest of the Montgomerys. Luke and Joy were just the beginning of my toying with that big, happy family."

Jazz pressed a shaking finger against the trigger then something made her ease up. Could she shoot a human being in cold blood, not for a mission, but for revenge?

No matter how much Lisa deserved it? Would that mean she *was* no better than Lisa? Maybe Lisa was right—maybe they were the same.

Only one second of hesitation and Lisa sprang at Jazz, the momentum toppling them both to the ground, slamming her gun hand into the dirt, loosening her grip. Lisa dove for the weapon. Jazz kicked out, but Lisa accepted the stunning blow with a smile. She snagged the gun and rolled to her feet.

She pointed the .357 at Jazz. "Mama wanted you dead. Now you are."

Tires screeching loudly jerked Lisa's attention.

Jazz didn't blink. She dove to the ground at the diversion. A van barreled in a beeline through several lawns toward Lisa with a furious Luke behind the wheel.

"Luke!" Jazz screamed. But where was Joy?

Lisa waved the gun toward the vehicle, her face twisted in disbelief. "No. No. No. You're dead. I killed you. I know I killed you."

Luke leapt out the door of the moving car and tackled Lisa. The van smashed the porch and plunged through the front door and window with a violent crash. Timbers cracked. The roof collapsed.

Luke shoved Lisa into the dirt. She fought like a woman possessed, snapping her teeth, trying to scratch his face. Her kicks struck at his knees, his groin, anywhere he was vulnerable. Jazz bounded toward them and trapped the woman's legs while Luke pinned her arms and hands above her head. His grip white-knuckled, he straddled her hips. "It's over. You lose."

Lisa shrieked in fury, her head shaking back and forth in denial. "You can't win. I won't let you. I'll kill you all. Jane. You. Your daughter. What's left of your family. Everyone. You have to pay. I promised. It's not over. I'll win. I have to win."

"Shut up," Luke said, his voice deadly controlled. "You're not going anywhere."

Lisa's eyes widened. Her mouth went slack. She blinked, and her forehead furrowed. Suddenly her head tossed from side to side. She arched, trying to break Luke's hold, but he didn't budge.

"No, Daddy. No. I'll do whatever you want. I love you the best. I promise. I'm your princess. I'll be good." Lisa's smile grew wide, but tears streamed down her cheeks. "See. You don't have to leave tonight. I won't tell Mama. I'll be very quiet. Just don't leave."

Lisa began to sob, the cries of a child who had never known childhood, who had let anger and hatred eat away at her soul.

Luke didn't break his hold, but his face paled.

Jazz took a shaking breath. "Joy?"

"She's safe. With Clarkson."

Sirens blaring, several police cars screeched up and came to a halt. Doors flew open and a bevy of men jumped out with weapons drawn. Within moments Luke climbed off of Lisa and they helped the broken woman to her feet and toward the vehicles where a deputy began reading rights to her.

"I could've been her," Jazz said quietly as they watched the pitiful picture of the woman. Jazz had no doubt she would eventually be charged with Paretti's and Towers' murders.

Luke pulled her into his arms and held her against him. "No. You're stronger than she is. Stronger than you know."

Jazz stilled, reveling in his strength and the comfort for one last time. Before she could argue the point, an old man hobbled out of the back of one of the vehicles holding a tiny girl in dusty jeans and a pink shirt in his arms. Joy.

She wriggled down and ran to her father, holding up her arms. "Daddy!"

Luke shook his head and rolled his neck. He breathed in deeply and knelt down. With an expression laced with pure love he hugged the little girl to him, pulling back and brushing away his daughter's tears. "What's wrong, munchkin?"

Joy put both of her hands on his cheeks. "Hero blowed up."

"I know, but he saved you. He did a good job."

Joy hiccupped. "Cuz he's a real hero?"

"He sure is, baby."

Jazz touched Luke's arm. "How did you escape the blast?"

"No way would I leave you. I stopped right after I turned out of sight of the house and got out. Joy wanted to bring her blanket and Hero, but they were too bulky. Then Joy told me Hero had been hurt. I noticed the ripped seam and saw the explosives. I tossed it into the field just before it exploded. A few seconds later, and, well, things would have been different."

Jazz hugged them both. "Thank God you're both safe."
A gruff voice intruded on her relief. "Jasmine?"

Slowly Jazz turned. The man before her smiled, sparkling eyes crinkled at the corners. His hair was white now, his face cracked with age, but she would never forget those eyes. They still twinkled. Gratitude swelled in her heart.

"Sheriff Clarkson?" She embraced him. "I'm so glad to see you. Thank you."

He patted her back with a weak hand. "I didn't think I'd ever hear from you again, but I always hoped you'd call me. I understood why you didn't…"

Jazz couldn't breathe. This man had saved her life. "I don't know what I would've become without you. You took a big chance and broke a lot of rules when you believed in me. I didn't understand what that really meant then. I do now."

The old man pulled out a roll of butter rum Life Savers from his pocket. He offered her one, and she grinned, popping a candy in her mouth. "Why did you do it?" she asked.

"I liked your spunk when I arrested you." He laughed, his belly shaking a bit. "I liked that you kicked the Johns in…" He glanced at Joy, who listened wide-eyed from her perch in Luke's arms, "…in their personals. They deserved it. You deserved a chance."

"You didn't just give me a chance. You gave me a whole new life."

~∾~

Ace landed the Piper Lance at McElroy Airfield and taxied toward the terminal. After coming to a stop, he turned in his seat and smiled down at Joy, who lay asleep in the chair next to Luke. "She gonna be okay?"

It took Jazz a moment to regain her bearings. She turned in her seat and saw the love on Luke's face as he gazed at his daughter. She nodded, yawning. She'd passed out the moment the plane took off from T or C, not waking until they touched down. "It'll take some time, but she'll be home soon with people who love her. That'll help."

"Give me a few minutes to go through my landing checklist and we'll get you out of the plane and home," Ace said as he pulled off his headset. "Luke, if you ever want to know more about your father, come see me. I'll tell you about him."

Luke unbuckled his safety belt and stood up. "I intend to."

Ace jumped down from the plane and gave them a secretive grin. "You folks stay here. I'll let you know when I'm done."

"You and Joy are two of a kind. I've been waiting for you to wake up." Luke knelt next to Jazz's seat and cupped her face with his hand.

She closed her eyes and leaned into his touch, soaking up the warmth of his skin and the tenderness of his caress.

He gently kissed her and clasped her hands with his. "I thought I'd lost you."

"I know," she breathed. "When I thought you were gone, I almost lost myself. I realized I'd never..."

He tugged her toward him and brought her lips to his, the kiss oh so sweet, oh so tender. When they parted, he smiled and his heart lay open in front of her.

"We've never dared say it, have we? Both of us too cautious to trust. But it's always been true." His chocolate eyes held her gaze. "I love you, Jane Sanford, Jasmine Parker. Whatever you call yourself doesn't matter to me. It's *you* I love."

They were words no one had ever spoken to her, and her last defenses crumbled. "How can you still love me after everything that's happened, after everything I put you through? After what I almost cost you?"

"You saved Joy. You put your life in jeopardy for us."

She shook her head. "I put you and your daughter in danger in the first place."

He clasped her shoulders and held tight. "Listen to me. You didn't do anything. A crazy woman did this. You, on the other hand, are everything I've ever wanted in a woman. You're brave and honorable—and too tenacious for your own good, but it doesn't matter. I want you. I want a mother for my daughter who she can be proud of and from whom she can learn how to be a strong woman. I want a partner. A lover. A best friend. Someone I can always believe in." He paused and stroked her cheek with a gentle hand. "Jasmine, I want you…in my life…from now on. As my wife…and Joy's mother."

The words stunned her. Terrified her. No. She couldn't be a mother. She didn't know how. She didn't fit in their family. "You're just saying that now because Joy is safe, but Luke, this proves I don't belong. I don't know anything about being part of a family, being a wife. Or, God, being a mother."

"Do you love me?"

"You deserve better." She tried to pull away from him, felt her heart shrinking, trying to protect itself from a hurt she didn't know if she could bear.

He wouldn't let her go. "Oh no you don't. I'm not giving up on you, because I know once you commit, you do it all the way. I want that from you, Jasmine. Your heart and soul. I want it all."

"Luke—"

He cut off her protest. "Good-bye won't work. I'm fighting for you this time—all the way. I love you." He stared her down. "Do you love me enough to take a chance?"

She shivered at the words. She felt like she was bursting through the door without a Kevlar vest. Leaving herself wide open and vulnerable. "No one ever loved me like you do. No one ever came back for me. No one ever protected me, even from myself."

He'd gone tense and stiff, unwilling to look away.

"Just you. You keep me safe," she whispered. "Yes."

"What?" Shock and wonder crossed his face.

The last of her resistance collapsed and she laughed. "I. Love. You."

He clutched her to him. "Thank God."

She leaned in close, breathed in his essence, secure within the comfort of his arms, lulled by the strong, steady beating of his heart. Something shifted deep inside her and warmth filled her, like sunlight reaching her darkest recesses. For the first time in her life, she was free—of the past and of the fears that had kept her from giving this man all that was good and powerful and loving within her.

She raised her gaze to his and smiled, her emotions breaking out and overflowing. "I love you, Luke Montgomery. And I want to be part of your family. Forever."

Immeasurable happiness transformed his face.

Yes. This was right, and real. "I can live without being a sniper. I can even live without my badge. But my life would be truly empty without you."

He lowered his mouth to hers and kissed her softly, his lips promising a vow she knew would last for a lifetime.

A round of applause from outside the plane broke through her haze of happiness.

Luke raised his head a fraction and saw a large group of familiar faces. "I think it's fair to say the arrest warrant is behind us."

"Jazz, stop the mushy stuff and get your butt out here," Carl Redmond shouted, amidst a bevy of whoops.

"What in the world?" She climbed toward the door as Luke unbuckled a sleepy Joy from her seat.

"Daddy? Are we home?"

Ace wrenched open the door. "Time to go," he said with a wink. "People are waiting."

Jazz, Luke, and Joy climbed out of the plane to cheers and whistles. Jazz couldn't believe it. The entire SWAT team stood there, along with Seth and Caleb. They circled around them, questions flying back and forth about what had happened in Truth or Consequences.

Finally Sarge stepped forward, his movement stopping all conversation. He walked over to Luke and stuck out his hand. "You were right."

"And wrong," Luke said. "I thought Paretti was one of the good guys."

"Me too," Sarge said. "But you helped us clean house. I, for one, am grateful."

Jazz knew Luke wasn't finished yet, of course. He would find a way to help Grace somehow. She slipped her hand in his and squeezed tight. He smiled at her, his gaze knowing and determined. No, he wasn't through. He would always search for the truth. For justice. Because he was a hero. Her hero.

"Cops are like everybody else. Most good, some bad." Sarge faced Jazz. "And some, damned amazing," he said, holding out his hand, her badge lying in his palm. "Wouldn't want anyone to think my lead sniper wasn't the best. Position's yours, if you're still willing."

Jazz scanned the crowd. She'd pushed them away at every turn and never let them really get to know her, never let herself truly be a part of them, and here they were. Again. She'd stayed alone, watching, just like she had on the playground all those years before. How different might life have been if she'd reached out?

"There need to be some changes," she said.

Sarge quirked a brow.

"I'd like to be part of the SWAT family this time, Sarge. I won't just watch from the outside. I'll do my part to make it happen. I hope you guys are willing to reciprocate."

Sarge grinned and held out his hand. "It's a deal."

The team clapped her on the back and congratulated her and Luke on taking down Lisa Matthews. After a few more apologies about Tower and Paretti, they drifted away. Dirty cops were hard for all of them to deal with, and Paretti had been one of their own.

"I'm so proud of you." Luke pulled Jazz into his arms and kissed her softly.

She sighed as Luke's warmth and confidence enveloped her.

"Princess?" Joy tugged on Jazz's shirt. "My daddy's kissing you. Are you going home with us?"

With a soft stroke of her hand and a promise for later, Jazz eased from Luke's embrace and smiled at the girl who looked at her with such faith and trust. She would protect and love Luke's daughter with all her heart. This little girl would never doubt that she was cherished.

Jazz knelt down. "Would you let me, Joy?"

The blond curls bounced as she nodded, her face serious. "Yeah. If the bad witch comes back, you'll make her go away."

"Oh, honey, the bad witch won't be back anymore." Jazz kissed the girl on the cheek and picked her up in her arms, cradling her close. "You're safe now. I'll help your daddy take good care of you."

Joy hugged her blanket and nestled closer to Jazz. "My daddy always chooses the bestest people to take care of me."

Luke kissed his daughter's cheek and enfolded Jazz in his arms. "Yes, I do. Ready to go home?"

Jazz nodded, but Joy looked worried.

"Daddies live with mommies." Joy bit her lip and looked at Jazz from beneath her lashes. "You're a princess."

Jazz's heart raced. "What are you trying to say, sweetheart?"

"My friends have mommies, but I don't," Joy said softly.

Jazz froze. The pain of not having a father, of being different, of being teased washed through her. She knew how Joy felt, but she didn't know how to heal the little girl's heart.

"Could you be my mommy instead of being a princess?"

Tears burned Jazz's eyes as she reached out to touch Joy's earnest face. "Oh, honey, I would love to be your mommy. That would be the best name I could ever have."

Luke pulled them all close and, for Jazz, the warm embrace cradled her heart, protected and safe. She could depend on him, without hesitation, without fear. He would always be there for her, no matter how tough things got. She had no doubts.

"Daddy, you're squishing me."

"Sorry," Luke said, his voice rough with emotion. "I guess we all know where we belong now."

Jazz clasped Luke's hand, squeezed tight, and smiled as she met his loving gaze over Joy's head. Dreams were real. They came true. She'd never be alone again.

Jasmine had her family.

THE END

Acknowledgments

This book is the destination in a long journey of a dream fulfilled, and the beginning of a new and exciting excursion, but I never walked alone. So many held my hand and propped me up in guidance and support along the way. I wouldn't be here without them. I could never name them all, but in particular I have to thank—

Jill Marsal, literary agent extraordinaire—her belief in me and this book, her editing skill, and her savvy brought me to this wonderful place.

Ann Steinmetz—for asking me if the heroine could be the sniper. One simple question, and a book was born.

Laura Baker and Kelley Pounds—friends and critique partners who were there from the beginning. Our magical triad created the heart of Jazz's story.

Tammy Baumann, Louise Bergin, and Sherri Buerkle— my amazing critique group who won't let me get away with anything—thank goodness!

Claire Cavanaugh, my dearest friend—by my side through more than anyone will ever know. You are the sister of my heart, and the soul of this book is yours.

Charlotte Herscher, editor extraordinaire—your insights and skill astound me. I couldn't have been luckier.

To Alex Carr and everyone on the Montlake Romance team—you took a chance on me, and I will be forever grateful.

Sharon Sala, an amazing writer and even better person—your faith drew me from the darkness into the light of hope. My grandmothers would have loved you!

Finally, Dale Perini, my father, teacher, advisor and coach for all things guns—this one's for you! Who knew holding a rifle steady could be so hard.

About the Author

Award-winning author Robin Perini's love of heart-stopping suspense and poignant romance, coupled with her adoration of high-tech weaponry and covert ops, encouraged her secret inner commando to take on the challenge of writing romantic suspense novels. Her mission's motto: "When danger and romance collide, no heart is safe."

Devoted to giving her readers fast-paced, high-stakes adventures with a love story sure to melt their hearts, Robin's strong characters and tightly woven plots have garnered her the prestigious Romance Writers of America® Golden Heart® Award. By day, she works for an advanced technology corporation, and in her spare time, you might find her giving one of her many nationally acclaimed writing workshops or training in competitive small-bore rifle silhouette shooting. Robin loves to interact with readers. You can catch her on her website (www.robinperini.com) and several major social networking sites.